A Curious
Incident

A Curious Incident

A SHERLOCK HOLMES BOOKSHOP MYSTERY

Vicki Delany

CROOKED
LANE

NEW YORK

Copyright © 2021 by Vicki Delany

All rights reserved.

Published in the United States by Crooked Lane Books, an imprint of The Quick Brown Fox & Company LLC.

Crooked Lane Books and its logo are trademarks of The Quick Brown Fox & Company LLC.

Library of Congress Catalog-in-Publication data available upon request.

ISBN (paperback): 978-1-64385-804-3
ISBN (hardcover): 978-1-64385-474-8
ISBN (ebook): 978-1-64385-475-5

Cover illustration by Joe Burleson

Printed in the United States.

www.crookedlanebooks.com

Crooked Lane Books
34 West 27th St., 10th Floor
New York, NY 10001

Trade Paperback Edition: December 2021
First Edition: January 2021

10 9 8 7 6 5 4 3 2 1

To my mom.
Always my inspiration

Chapter One

"I am not a consulting detective."

"Can't you at least say you'll try and help her?"

"That would be unfair to her, Jayne. I can't give the girl false hopes."

"I suppose you're right. Poor thing. I wish there was something we could do."

I glanced across the room. The little girl was perched on the stool behind the sales counter, watching us, all wide eyes, knees and elbows, long sun-kissed golden hair, and hope.

Hope that I was about to crush.

I sighed, pasted on a smile that no doubt looked as fake as it felt, and walked across the shop floor toward her, feeling perfectly terrible.

She blinked rapidly, fighting back tears.

"All I can do, Lauren," I said, "is keep my eyes open. You'll do that too, won't you, Jayne?"

"Absolutely," Jayne said.

"We'll tell all our friends to be on the lookout. Maybe you and your mum can put more posters up around town?" I'd seen plenty of those signs over the last two days. One hung in my own shop window, another in the window of Mrs. Hudson's, the tearoom next door.

"But," Lauren said, her lower lip trembling, "she's been gone for two whole days! Aunt Irene said you make it your business to know what others do not. She said you can find out things no one else can. She said you're better than the police. She said . . ."

Mentally, I cursed Irene Talbot. I might have once or twice attempted to help the West London police in the performance of their duties—okay, I solved their cases for them—but they would have arrived at it eventually. I think.

Locating a missing house cat is far out of my area of expertise.

I'm Gemma Doyle, and I'm part-owner, manager, and general dogsbody of the Sherlock Holmes Bookshop and Emporium, located at 222 Baker Street in West London, Massachusetts, and all I want is to be a shop owner. Not a consulting detective.

My assistant, Ashleigh, stood behind the girl, making frantic gestures at me. I ignored her. I would not promise to find the blasted cat, because I couldn't. Jayne, still dressed in a hairnet and apron, touched Lauren lightly on the arm in a gesture of support. When Lauren had asked if she could meet me, Jayne Wilson had come out of the kitchen of the tearoom next door to bring her to my shop.

My own cat, Moriarty, was curled up in Lauren's arms. He glared at me, no doubt also telling me to get out there and solve the case. I briefly considered offering Moriarty to Lauren as a replacement for her missing pet.

Moriarty and I weren't exactly the best of friends. He was a good shop cat and generally got on well with our patrons, many of whom adored him. But, for some unknown reason, he disliked me intensely, and he never missed an opportunity to let me know precisely what he thought of me.

If I sent Moriarty to a new home, he'd find his way back here, just to spite me.

And the poor child would have lost another cat.

"I can pay you," Lauren said. "Out of my allowance. What do you charge?"

"It's not that," I said. "I'm sorry, but I need to be completely honest with you. I can't do anything to help you."

Moriarty, Ashleigh, Jayne, and Lauren all looked at me as though I'd promised them a visit from Benedict Cumberbatch and instead sent Great-Uncle Arthur wearing a curly wig.

"That's okay." Lauren put Moriarty on the counter and gave him a sad pat. She hopped off the stool. "I understand," she said bravely. "I'll go now. Mom will be finished with her lunch soon."

"Why don't you give Gemma your phone number and address," Ashleigh said. "She can call you if she has any ideas."

I threw Ashleigh a poisonous look, which she pretended not to see.

Lauren rattled off a number and an address not far from my own house.

"I'll take you back to your mom," Jayne said. "Come on." She put her arm around Lauren's thin shoulders, and together they walked through the sliding door into the tearoom. Jayne turned her head and gave me a glare of disapproval.

"I am not a consulting detective!" I called after them.

Moriarty turned his back on me, lifted his tail high, and leapt off the counter. He stalked across the room, as disapproving as Jayne.

"Why I am feeling guilty?" I said to Ashleigh. "Why does everyone think I can find the cat? The next time I see Irene Talbot, I'm going to kill her."

"Poor little thing," Ashleigh said. "She really is upset."

I sighed. "Yeah, I know."

"I don't think Irene actually told her to ask you to help find Snowball . . ."

"Is that the cat's name? Not very original."

"The girl's eleven years old, Gemma. Originality isn't a strength at that age."

"I suppose not. Is the cat white?"

"Didn't you look at the poster in the window?"

"I might have glanced at it. As I have no interest in lost cats"—I threw a look at Moriarty, who was pretending to ignore me—"I didn't pay much attention."

The missing-cat poster was stuck to the window next to one we'd put up yesterday when a couple of women from the West London Garden Club asked if we'd help spread the word about their annual garden tour.

"I thought you noticed everything." Ashleigh always dressed to suit whatever mood she was in that morning or what was currently on her mind. Today, no doubt inspired by the garden club visit, she wore a floppy straw hat with a wide ribbon around the brim, a pair of baggy trousers tucked into yellow-and-purple rubber boots, and a T-shirt that proclaimed "Gardening is Life!" among a plethora of flowers.

"Not everything," I said. "And never info about missing cats. Or about garden clubs either, as I have no interest in gardening."

"Sounds like Irene's been spinning stories about how her good friend Gemma Doyle is smarter than the police, and when Lauren and her mom came in for lunch and Lauren found out that you work right next door, she decided to talk to you. Smart kid, I'd say."

"I liked her," I said. "I'd help her if I could, Ashleigh, but I never make promises I can't keep."

The chimes over the door tinkled. Two women came into the store, and Ashleigh and I went back to work. Moriarty did not. His job is to greet customers, but apparently he'd gone on strike today. He stayed in his bed under the big center table all afternoon, bristling with disapproval.

It was late June and the start of the summer tourist season on Cape Cod. We were busy most of the day as a steady stream of customers came into the shop. Whenever I glanced next door at 220 Baker Street, I could see a lineup at the counter for takeout, as well as people waiting patiently for tables for afternoon tea, Mrs. Hudson's specialty.

Every day at precisely 3:40, Jayne and I have our daily business partners' meeting in the tearoom. We sip tea, eat whatever remains of the day's baking, and chat. Occasionally we might even talk about the businesses. Great-Uncle Arthur and I own the Emporium, and we're half partners with Jayne in the tearoom. I run the bookshop, and Jayne's the manager and head baker at Mrs. Hudson's. The tearoom, of course, is named in honor of Sherlock Holmes's long-suffering landlady.

Our shop is dedicated, as the name indicates, to all things Sherlock: the original stories, contemporary pastiche and short-story collections, other books by Sir Arthur Conan Doyle, nonfiction relating to the author's life and times, and works of fiction set in Holmes's time frame, sometimes called the Gaslight Era. We also stock merchandise related to the Great Detective, of which there is a substantial amount. Earlier this year, Great-Uncle Arthur received an award from an English Holmes society for helping to spread word of the Great Detective in North America. The award, an ugly glass statue, currently stands on a top shelf above the sales counter, next to the framed reproduction cover of *Beeton's Christmas Annual*, dated December 1887, in which "A Scandal in Scarlet," the first Holmes story, appeared.

Today at three thirty, the shop was comfortably busy. "I'm going to skip the partners' meeting with Jayne," I told Ashleigh.

"Alert the press," she said.

"If I did that, Irene would assume I was embarking on a case." Irene is a reporter at the *West London Star*. "I have to get home and pay some attention to Violet," I said, referring to my cocker spaniel. She's technically Great-Uncle Arthur's dog, but he travels a great deal, and most of the dog-ownership responsibility has fallen to me. I don't mind. I love Violet, and—unlike my cat— she loves me in return. Our neighbor Mrs. Ramsbatten, who pops in to give Violet a walk when Uncle Arthur's away, had gone out of town for a few days, and it wasn't fair to Violet to leave her locked up in the house all day.

"Why don't you bring her to work with you?" Ashleigh said. "She's a well-behaved dog."

Moriarty had finally emerged from his bed and was making his way across the shop floor. He leapt straight into the air, hissing and spitting.

"That's why," I said. "Back soon."

I went into the tearoom and asked Fiona, one of the waitresses, to tell Jayne that something had come up and I was going out.

"You should have said you'd help that little girl find her cat," Fiona said.

"Does everyone in West London know my business?"

"Pretty much," she replied.

I walked briskly down Baker Street toward the harbor. The town of West London is situated in the Lower Cape area of Cape Cod, nestled between the Atlantic Ocean and Nantucket Sound. It was a perfect summer's day and the tourists were out in force, popping in and out of stores, lining up for lattes at coffee shops, or enjoying cool drinks on restaurant patios. On Harbor Road they shopped for or munched on fresh fish, watched seals play in the cool waters under the pier, or explored the grounds of the historic lighthouse. The ocean was calm today, and brilliant white sails and powerful motorboats dotted the water. On the horizon, a cruise ship drifted past. I looked northeast out to sea in the general direction of dear old England and wondered how my friend Grant Thompson was getting on now that he'd taken up housekeeping with my brilliant, mercurial, single-minded sister, Pippa. My mother had reported that Pippa was happier than she'd ever known her eldest daughter to be and that Pippa wasn't working quite the long hours she always had. That pleased me very much. The cheerful tone of my parents' emails also pleased me: clearly, they'd recovered from the upsetting events of January during my last visit.

I walked down Harbor Road for a few minutes, simply enjoying the break from the shop and the beauty of the day, and then turned inland at Blue Water Place, my street. The 1756 saltbox house where I live with Great-Uncle Arthur soon came into view. Arthur is one of the world's great travelers, and at the moment he was in Thailand with friends from his Royal Navy days. Or was it Trinidad? I can never get his whereabouts straight.

Our garden was a riot of color and beautifully maintained foliage. No thanks to me; I have a pure-black thumb when it comes to gardening. Mrs. Ramsbatten and some of her garden club friends who'd recently moved into apartments but missed their gardens maintained it for us. For the heavy work, cutting the grass and such, we shared the services of a lawn maintenance company.

Butterflies flitted about, drifting from one fragrant plant to another; a bee buzzed past my ear, and a large black crow eyed me from the branch of an ancient oak as I walked up the driveway and let myself into the house through the mudroom entrance. The scent of basil rose from the herb bed Mrs. Ramsbatten and her friends had planted by the door. Violet greeted me with her usual excess of enthusiasm, and I proclaimed my joy at seeing her with a hearty thumping of her rump and sides. Mutual greetings over, she ran in excited circles while I got the leash off the hook, and we set off on our walk.

I didn't want to take too much time away from the shop, so rather than getting the car and taking Violet for a good run on a deserted stretch of the coast or along a meandering woodland trail, we stayed on our street.

Summer hours at the Emporium are long, and I like to be on hand from opening until closing, seven days a week. It's a long day alone for Violet, but fortunately Mrs. Ramsbatten is happy to pop in and give the dog some attention and a bathroom break. Mrs. Ramsbatten is in her eighties and walks with the aid of a cane, so Violet doesn't get a proper walk, but I'm happy knowing she at least gets a romp in the yard, some company, and a refreshed water bowl.

This week, my neighbor was visiting her sister in Sandwich for three days, so I was trying to make a point of getting home to Violet at least once during the day.

A Curious Incident

We trotted down the sidewalk, cool in the shade of the green canopy and dappled sunlight formed by the huge trees, some of which were as old as my house. When we reached Mrs. Ramsbatten's yard, Violet jerked at the leash and tried to veer into the garden. I pulled her back. "Your friend's not there, Violet. You'll see her soon." She'd done the same thing yesterday, and I assumed Violet was wondering where Mrs. Ramsbatten was. It was nice to think that Violet was fond of the woman.

An aging Ford sedan was parked in her driveway. My neighbor didn't use her car very much these days, if at all, and it was covered by a light layer of dust.

Fifteen minutes later, we retraced our steps, heading home. As we passed in front of Mrs. Ramsbatten's neat white picket fence, intertwined with bushes bursting with red flowers, Violet whined and once again yanked at her leash. I was about to pull her back when I had a thought.

I dropped my end of the leash.

The dog scratched at the gate, and I opened it. Violet hurled herself through it and ran across the immaculate lawn and around to the back of Mrs. Ramsbatten's house. I hurried after her. By the time I reached the backyard, Violet was scratching at the door of the small black-and-white garden shed, with its cheerful red door and flower boxes overflowing with tumbling ivy and colorful annuals. When I called to her, she turned her head and looked at me. She barked once, then returned her attention to the red door.

"What have you got there?" I asked her. I put my ear to the door and listened. Inside, something rustled. Mice, probably, startled by the sound of the dog, or garden implements settling.

But perhaps not.

I keep a small flashlight attached to my set of keys. I took it out, switched it on, and turned the door handle. It wasn't locked. Slowly and carefully, I pushed open the door of the shed and shone my light in.

Two huge amber eyes stared at me from the far corner. Then the owner of the eyes, a pure-white kitten, arched its back and hissed.

I'd found Snowball.

Chapter Two

Murmuring soft words. I edged into the shed. I closed the door behind me, leaving Violet outside. I didn't want to scare the cat and chance it bolting and being lost again. Frightened eyes stared at me, and she offered no resistance as I scooped her up. The tiny body shivered, and I could feel the bones beneath the skin and fur. Today was Monday. Mrs. Ramsbatten had left on Saturday morning, and by Lauren's account, Snowball had gone missing two days ago. The little cat must have come into the shed, chasing mice perhaps, and then the door closed on her. Mrs. Ramsbatten's eyesight wasn't all that good, and she probably hadn't noticed the kitten hiding in a corner of the dark shed.

I cradled the cat to my chest and carried her to safety while Violet ran on ahead, making her way home. The first thing I did when we got to the house was pour some fresh water into a small bowl. The cat watched me warily from a corner of the kitchen. I scooped her up and put her on the counter next to the water. She gave me one dubious glance and then dove in headfirst. Next, I found a can of salmon in the pantry and dished up a small serving.

The fish disappeared in record time. The cat wouldn't have eaten for days, so I didn't want to give her too much.

When the water and salmon were gone, she sat down and began washing her whiskers. I put out one hand; she gave me a long look, then rubbed her face against my arm. She started to purr.

"You're welcome," I said. "Now it's time to get you home." I took a canvas tote bag down from a hook in the mudroom, scooped up the kitten, and dropped her into the bag. I didn't want her to escape, so I zipped the bag shut, leaving a sliver at the end open so air could get in.

"You," I said to Violet, "are the hero of the day, but I'm afraid you'll have to stay here."

The address Lauren had given me was only a couple of blocks from my house, so I walked quickly, cradling the tote bag in my arms while the little pink nose and twitching white whiskers tried to push their way out and plaintive cries broke the peace and quiet of the neighborhood.

The house I was after was a typical one for the street and the area. A late-model SUV was parked in the driveway beneath towering old oaks. The house was painted a cheerful yellow, with a dark-gray roof and matching shutters. Two stories, double garage. I estimated that it had at least four bedrooms, numerous bathrooms, and a den and TV room. The lot was large, and carefully trimmed shrubs and trees blocked the view of the neighbors. I walked along the brick pathway—not a weed pushing through the cracks—curving between shrubs of juniper and boxwood, to the wide front steps lined with terra-cotta urns overflowing with purple, yellow, and white flowers. Feeling rather pleased with myself, I walked up the steps and rang the bell.

The door opened and a woman peered out. She was in her mid-forties, nicely dressed in a typical summer-on-Cape-Cod way in white capris and a blue-and-white-striped T-shirt—Tommy

Hilfiger perhaps. She was about my height, five eight, but quite a bit heavier than she probably would have liked. Gold hoops adorned her ears, and a heavy gold chain hung around her neck. Her feet were bare, showing nails painted a bright red. Her glossy blonde hair, the color owing more to a bottle than to the sun, was pulled back into a high, sleek ponytail. Her lipstick was a fresh pale pink, and her recently applied manicure matched her pedicure.

Her clothes looked expensive, but they were too tight on her, particularly around the hips and stomach. She'd obviously put on weight since buying them, and the fact that she hadn't replaced them meant she'd been too busy to go shopping; she couldn't afford new clothes of the quality she liked; or she was in denial about having gained weight.

"Yes?" she said.

"Is Lauren at home?" My bundle squirmed, and I held it tight.

She narrowed her eyes. "Why do you want to know?"

"I'm Gemma Doyle from the Sherlock Holmes Bookshop on Baker Street. Lauren came to see me earlier today."

"If it was about that cat, I'm sorry. I wish I'd never bought the dratted thing. I told Lauren to keep it inside, but she forgot—she can be such a scatterbrain —and it got out the day before yesterday. Lauren's been in tears ever since. Nothing but high drama. As if I don't have more important things to worry about."

"Uh, okay. But I would like to talk to her. May I come in? Are you her mother?"

"I am. I'm Sheila Tierney." She spoke in a flat voice and made no attempt to crack a neighborly smile, to call Lauren, or to invite me in. *What*, I thought, *is this woman's problem?*

A tiny white paw emerged from my bag, and claws scratched at the air. Sheila Tierney blinked. "Oh," she said, "is that . . .?"

"Lauren?" I said.

The door opened, Sheila stepped back, and I came in. I closed the door behind me.

"Lauren!" Sheila called. "Lauren, get down here."

A tear-streaked face and tousled blonde hair appeared at the top of the steps.

"I brought you something." I opened the bag, and Snowball leapt out. She practically flew across the room. Lauren did fly down the stairs, screaming with joy as only an eleven-year-old girl can. She scooped the kitten up and held her so tightly I feared the little cat would be crushed.

"You found her!" Lauren squealed. "You found her. I knew you could do it!"

"Glad to be of help." I was feeling quite proud of myself. I hadn't done anything except follow my dog, but no one had to know that.

"Thank you, Ms. Doyle. I hate to be rude," Sheila said rudely, "but I'm on my way out." She opened the door.

"Wait! Wait!" Lauren called. "I said I'd pay you. I'll get your money."

"No need," I said. "This one's on me."

She gave me a radiant smile. I swear little Snowball smiled also. Sheila pointedly looked at her watch, telling me in no uncertain terms to be on my way.

"I'll never forget you," Lauren said in a low voice.

I touched my index finger to my forehead. "Gemma Doyle, Consulting Detective, at your service."

Chapter Three

"**I** am not a consulting detective."

"You might not want to be, but she thinks you are," Jayne said.

I put my elbows on the table and rubbed at my always-out-of-control, curly dark hair, making it even more out of control. I groaned. I had ten dollars I didn't want in my pocket, and I'd agreed to do something I knew I'd very much regret.

A week had passed since the Snowball incident. I'd proudly told Ashleigh, Jayne, Irene, Moriarty, and anyone else who happened to wander within hearing distance how I'd located the missing cat. "It's simply a matter of paying attention to your surroundings," I said modestly, "and picking up on the small clues."

The following day, Lauren had come into the store with a cup of tea and a blueberry muffin for me, along with her thanks. I was touched when Fiona later told me the girl had asked her what I liked for a snack, and then bought it for me. Lauren told me Snowball was fully recovered from her ordeal.

I thanked her for the treat, waved goodbye, and assumed that was the end of that.

It wasn't.

This afternoon, Lauren returned to the shop, once again wanting to retain my services.

This time, she wasn't asking me to locate a missing kitten, but to clear her mother of a murder charge. She'd offered me ten dollars as an advance on my fees.

"She said she can't pay any more than that now," I told Jayne, "but as soon as she's old enough, she'll get a job and pay me. With interest."

Jayne's face twisted in concern. "The poor thing. What are you going to do, Gemma?"

I pushed my plate to one side. We were in the tearoom, seated at the small table tucked into a window alcove overlooking the bustle of Baker Street. Mrs. Hudson's closes at four o'clock, and the last few customers were finishing their tea and settling their bills. This was a relaxing room, designed to be so: the walls above the white wainscoting were papered in soft shades of sage green and peach. The artwork consisted of paintings of castles and thatched-roof cottages nestled in verdant pastoral landscapes, and a portrait of Queen Elizabeth II was prominently hung on the back wall. Open shelves displayed rows of bone china teacups, teapots, and an assortment of locally sourced jams, jellies, and preserves, which we offered for sale. The delicious scents of warm baking being prepared for tomorrow wafted from the kitchen.

"I called Irene and asked her to join us," I said. "She'll be able to give us more details than I've read in the paper. I can't imagine Ryan'll be happy to hear that I've been hired to interfere."

Detective Ryan Ashburton is the man I love, and I know he loves me. But our relationship is difficult, and more than once my involvement in his cases has threatened the stability—what little of it there is—of our relationship.

"You told Lauren you'd help, then?"

"What could I say, Jayne?" I thought of Lauren's tear-streaked face, the fear in her eyes, the brave tilt of her chin, the adoring way the little girl had gazed up at me. "I told her I'd find out what I could, but I made absolutely no promises. What did you get up to last night?"

"Nothing much." Jayne's eyes slid to one side. Jayne was my best friend as well as my business partner. She was tiny and blonde and blue-eyed, with a heart-shaped face that turned men's heads wherever she went. She was one of the hardest-working people I knew, and probably the kindest. The Emporium closes at five on Sundays, and yesterday I'd suggested Jayne and I go for a drink down by the pier. She'd said she had plans and scurried away.

"What's 'nothing much' mean?" I asked. "You said you were going out."

"I was tired. That's all." The bells over the door tinkled, and Jayne said, "Oh good. Here's Irene now."

Irene Talbot dropped into a chair next to Jayne. "What a mess."

"Have a tart." I pushed my untouched plate in front of her.

"Don't mind if I do." She selected a tiny, perfect raspberry pastry.

"Coffee, Irene?" Fiona called across the room.

"Thanks. Okay, Gemma, I'm here—what do you want to know? I can't believe Lauren came to you for help."

"For which thank you very much. *Not*. It was bad enough getting me involved in the case of the missing cat, never mind this."

"I didn't intend—"

I waved a hand in the air. "No matter. It's done. Tell me everything you know. I read the account in the paper, but pretend I don't know anything."

Irene took a bite of her tart and thought. "Lauren's mother, Sheila, is my stepsister. Her father's my mom's second husband. My dad died when I was in fifth grade, and my mother married again two years later. Sheila's five years older than I am. We've never been at all close—natural enough considering the age difference and that she left home for college not long after our parents married—but living in the same town as we do, we get together at family events and such. Mom and Ralph—that's Sheila's dad—moved to Arizona a few years ago, but they visit regularly. I might not care for Sheila, but I adore Lauren. She's smart, funny, athletic, and very, very sweet. Sheila—none of the above. I've been spending more time with Lauren this summer than usual because things haven't been so good at home. Lauren doesn't gossip about her parents, but I can't help picking up on things. Her dad—his name's David Tierney—has been away from home a lot. He says he's traveling on business, but Sheila accused him of having an affair. Specifically with a woman by the name of Anna Wentworth. Anna and Sheila are—I guess I should say they *were*—both members of the West London Garden Club."

"Anna being the recently deceased," Jayne said.

"Right. Her supposed relationship with David is part of the reason Sheila's being questioned about the murder." Irene stopped talking when Fiona brought her coffee.

"My sister-in-law's a member of that club," Fiona said. "It's a hotbed of petty jealousy, bitter rivalry, and assignations under the rhododendrons, if you listen to her."

"And I might," I said.

"You can bet your bottom dollar, or the last clump of dirt at the bottom of your compost bin, they're talking about nothing other than Sheila Tierney today. More sandwiches? We have a few left."

"Thanks," Irene said. "I didn't have time for lunch."

The last of the customers left. Fiona went into the kitchen to get the sandwiches, and the other tearoom assistant, Jocelyn, began stacking chairs onto tables prior to doing the vacuuming.

"Were they?" Jayne sipped at her tea.

"Were who what?" Irene said.

"Were David Tierney and this garden club member having an affair?"

"At the time I didn't know, and I figured it was none of my business. But from what everyone's saying since Anna's murder, it doesn't seem so."

"Anna Wentworth might have been a diversion," I said, "if his affair was with someone else. Or perhaps there was never any affair. Or they might have been discreet about it, but Sheila knew. The wife usually does. Let's start at the beginning. What did you tell Lauren that made her think I could help her?"

"You did help her," Jayne said. "And now she's hoping you can help her again."

"Lauren was at my house one night a couple of weeks ago," Irene said, "and I found a Sherlock Holmes movie on Netflix."

"Which one?" I asked.

"Does it matter?"

"'It has long been an axiom of mine that the little things are infinitely the most important.'"

"Huh?"

"'A Case of Identity.' Meaning I won't know if something matters until it does. What was the movie?"

"*A Game of Shadows*, with Robert Downey and Jude Law."

"Dreadful parody of Holmes," I said.

"I thought Jude Law made a good Watson," Jayne said.

"I didn't. Sorry," I said to Irene. "Please continue."

Vicki Delany

"After the movie was over, Lauren said that Holmes was so clever, and I . . . uh . . . might have mentioned that I have a friend who thinks like Sherlock Holmes."

"You do?" I said. "Who's that?"

Jayne choked on the mouthful of tea she'd just swallowed. Irene stared at me. "Don't you know?"

"If I knew to whom you were referring, I wouldn't have asked."

"It doesn't matter," she said.

Fiona arrived with a plate of tea sandwiches. I was pleased to see one cucumber had survived, and grabbed it before anyone else could. Jayne had recently changed her recipe, and instead of cream cheese she added mayonnaise with lovely chopped green herbs and the slightest splash of lemon, making the sandwiches better than ever. "I assume it was then you told Lauren about my store."

"I did. She knew about it because her mom's a regular in here, the tearoom. She'd never been into the Emporium, though."

I filed that thought away. Every child should be exposed to books—the greater the variety, the better. Even if they don't intend to buy, people are welcome to browse my shop and see what we have to offer. "I met her mother when I returned the cat. Can't say I liked her much, but that was only one quick impression. Can you describe her father to me?"

"I can do even better." Irene dug in her cavernous bag. "I found a picture that was in the paper last summer when Sheila made some announcement about the garden club."

She placed a clipping from a newspaper on the table. The picture showed Sheila, standing amid a plethora of blooms. A man stood next to her, his head turned to one side, clearly insignificant in the grand scheme of things. Irene tapped his face with her index finger. "That's him, David."

20

I studied the picture. It was grainy, and he was out of focus. "This isn't good. Describe him as you see him."

"Kinda handsome in a snobby sort of way. Medium height, short dark hair. Uh . . . uh . . . Not overweight."

"That narrows it down to less than half the population of West London," I said. "The larger half being either female or not slightly 'snobbishly handsome.' Whatever that means."

Irene opened her mouth. She closed it again.

"What?" I said.

"I was about to ask if you could do better—then I remembered who I'm talking to."

I was about to ask her what that meant, but decided I had more important questions. "Did you ever meet the late Anna Wentworth?"

"No. Not exactly the social circles in which I mix. Sheila mentioned her once or twice, but just in passing, and nothing stands out as being of any importance. Anyway, things were tense at Lauren's house; her parents were fighting all the time, and Lauren was clearly unhappy, so I've had her over for pizza and a movie or a sleepover a couple of times since school ended for the summer. She doesn't have any brothers or sisters. Her mother's aloof at the best of times, and her father's not a lot better."

"You don't like him either," I said.

"Loathe him, to be honest. He and Sheila are a perfect match."

"Gee," Jayne said, "tell us what you *really* think."

"To be fair, if I must, they know I don't approve of their parenting style, and neither of them likes me much either." Irene shrugged. "Families. What can you do?"

"Tell me what happened last night. Assume, once again, I don't know anything."

"Sunday was the garden club's annual early summer garden tour."

"It's the centerpiece of their year," Fiona cut in. After delivering the sandwiches, she was spending an inordinate amount of time and attention wiping down the table next to the window alcove. She spoke over the roar of the vacuum cleaner. "Eight gardens are chosen to be featured on the tour each year, and it's enormously prestigious to be part of it. Competition is ruthless just to get your house on the tour, never mind winning the trophy for the best garden."

"Anna and Sheila's gardens were part of the tour this year," Irene said. "Lauren told me she was forbidden from playing in their yard in case she trampled a patch of grass or stepped on a petunia or something."

"No wonder the poor girl needed her cat," Jayne said.

"Sunday's weather was perfect," Irene continued. "All the tickets had been sold, and the great and the good of West London and environs gathered. Keen gardeners came from all across New England. Garden gates were thrown open, the tour began, and . . ." Irene paused, drawing our attention.

I knew the story. It had been in the papers, on the radio, and everywhere on Twitter, even before news of the murder of Anna Wentworth broke.

". . . someone snuck into Sheila Tierney's garden in the middle of the night Saturday and cut every one of her roses down to bare branches. They wrecked the rhododendrons, beheaded the begonia, decimated the daisies, slashed the snapdragons, pillaged the pansies. And tore up part of the lawn and knocked over the statues for good measure."

"Who did it?" Jayne asked.

"No one knows. No one confessed. Sheila had a purple fit."

"Understandably," Jayne said.

"Almost as purple as your prose," I said.

"She stormed over to Anna's house, and in front of dozens of ticket buyers as well as the doyens from the garden club, she accused Anna of destroying her garden out of jealousy. She also accused Anna of stealing her husband and various other indiscretions."

"I heard it was quite the knock-down, drag-out fight," Fiona said. "They actually came to blows and had to be forcibly separated."

"What did Anna have to say about these accusations?" I asked.

"That Sheila was off her rocker, and the idea of her being jealous of Sheila was preposterous, because Sheila, poor Sheila, had absolutely nothing Anna could possibly want. Including her husband."

"Ouch," Jayne said.

"Ouch, indeed. Sheila was dragged off home, screaming vows of revenge, and the garden tour continued. The patrons, I'm sure, were thrilled to have gotten far more for their money than they expected. Later that night, Anna was out walking her dog, no doubt basking in the glory of having been awarded the best-in-tour trophy, when someone bashed her over the head. She was found dead in a town park."

I leaned back in my chair. I hadn't learned anything new. It had been in the news and was all anyone was talking about today, but it was good to have the story repeated. "Sheila was arrested for the murder of Anna?"

"Taken in for questioning, but not actually arrested. As far as I know, the police found no evidence pointing to Sheila as the killer, but she had been heard to threaten Anna earlier in the day by a substantial number of people. She maintains her innocence."

"What's Sheila's alibi?"

"She doesn't have one. Lauren spent the night at my house, which had been prearranged in expectation of Sheila celebrating winning the trophy, and David was out of town. She—"

I lifted one hand. "He was out of town? Do you know where or why?"

"No, I don't. He travels quite a bit on business, or so he says. 'Out of town' can mean a lot of things."

"Interesting that Sheila planned on doing this celebrating without the company of her husband."

"As I said, the marriage isn't doing so well. Anyway, the police dragged Sheila downtown in the middle of the night, but they had to release her because they don't have any evidence of her being at the scene of Anna's death. You can be sure they're looking hard for it and building their case. They have no other suspects—again, as far as I know. I got a call from Sheila at five this morning, asking me to come and get her at the police station. I probably should have left Lauren in bed, but I didn't know how long I'd be, so I woke her up and took her with me. That was a mistake. Sheila was ranting and raving about going to prison for something she didn't do, calling the West London police incompetent, and threatening to sue them."

"And so Lauren decided to call on outside help," Jayne said.

"Yeah," Irene said.

We started at a rapping on the tearoom door. A man's face peered in, smiling and waving as he mimed drinking coffee. Fiona broke off from scrubbing the spotless table and unlocked the door for him.

"I was passing and saw you all still here." Detective Ryan Ashburton leaned over and gave me a light kiss on the top of my head. "Any chance of a cup of coffee for a hard-working cop?"

"I haven't emptied the pot yet," Fiona said.

"Thanks," he said. "I'll have to take it to go. I have an appointment at the bank across the street to look at a suspect's accounts."

"How's the case going, Detective?" Irene asked. "Are you going to formally arrest Sheila Tierney?"

He gave her a tight smile. "No comment." He looked tired, I thought, the tender skin under his ocean-blue eyes drawn, and the stubble on his jaw thick. But he managed to still look mighty good, as he always did, with his six-foot-three frame, wide shoulders, powerful arms, strong jaw, and high cheekbones. He was dressed in jeans and a black T-shirt under a short leather jacket.

"One day you'll slip up and tell me all," Irene said.

"One day. But not today. I'm sorry," he said to me, "but dinner's off tonight."

"I assumed that," I said.

"Strange case, this one. I'm thankful that for once it has absolutely nothing to do with you, Gemma."

"Will you look at the time," Jayne said. "Gotta run. Those dishes won't wash themselves."

Irene leapt to her feet. "I'm off. Call me if you need anything more, Gemma."

The vacuum cleaner roared to life. Fiona ran for the kitchen.

"What did I say?" Ryan asked.

"About that . . ." I said.

Chapter Four

Sherlock Holmes didn't have a business to run. He could devote all his time to being a consulting detective without having to deal with pesky things such as handling employees and business partners, ordering stock, serving customers, paying and collecting bills, or dealing with irate authors who didn't know why I wasn't featuring their book prominently in the shop window.

He didn't have a cat who hated him or a dog who loved him and needed regular attention.

He didn't have to cook for himself or even clean the rooms at 221B Baker Street, as the faithful Mrs. Hudson took care of those pesky details for him. Although, honesty forces me to admit, I've been known to let those tasks slide myself.

But most importantly, Sherlock Holmes didn't have a significant other who blew a gasket on being informed that he'd been asked to 'informally' look into a police investigation.

"What could I do, Ryan?" I said after Jayne and the others had fled. "The little girl asked me to help."

"What could you have done? You could have said no, Gemma."

"I did that the first time." Over dinner one evening last week, I'd entertained Ryan with all the details of the Adventure of the Missing Cat. "But then I ended up solving the mystery anyway. Lauren Tierney's faith in me is, unfortunately, now boundless." I gave him what I intended to be a wistful smile.

He did not return it.

He dropped into a chair. "Aside from anything else, Gemma, I'm afraid you're going to break the little girl's heart."

"You think her mother did it?"

"I haven't got an opinion yet one way or the other. I don't know much more than what's been in the papers. Not that I'd tell you if I did. Sheila Tierney and Anna Wentworth didn't get on, to put it mildly. Someone destroyed Sheila's garden, and Sheila believed Anna did it, and confronted her over it. Whether she later murdered the woman is what we're trying to determine. She denies it."

"Here you go, Detective." Fiona put a take-out cup on the table.

"Thanks," he said. "Right now, we've got nothing we can take to court, which is why Mrs. Tierney hasn't been charged, but we're going over the area where the body was found, with a fine-toothed comb. If there is something, I intend to find it. Without your help, Gemma." He stood up.

"Can I ask one quick question?"

"Might as well. What?"

"Who found Anna? The paper didn't say."

"Her husband. The dog came home without her, dragging his leash behind him, so he assumed something had happened, and he went out looking for her. It didn't take long: the dog led him straight to her. She hadn't left the house more than half an hour earlier, according to her husband. We're talking to anyone who was on that street around that time or might have glanced out their window."

"I don't intend to get involved, Ryan. Really. I told Lauren I'd do what I could because I didn't know how to say no. I'll give her my advice, tell her that I have full trust in the West London police, which is true, and she has to put her trust in you also. I'll give her back her ten-dollar retainer on my services."

"You took ten dollars from an eleven-year-old girl?"

"I refused, but she left it on the counter. I only saw it later."

Ryan left, shaking his head. I watched him cross the street and run nimbly up the steps of the bank. Almost certainly he was checking into the finances of the Tierney family.

I sipped my tea and thought about all—precious little though it was—I'd learned about this case from Irene.

I'd been totally honest with Ryan. I'd go to the Tierney house and speak to Lauren. I'd tell her to put her faith in the police.

But I'm a curious sort, and my curiously had been roused. This case appeared to have its origins in a ruined garden, so I might see what I could find out about the inner workings of the West London Garden Club.

Common, or garden, gossip, I have found, is often the best way to get at the underlying kernels of truth in people's relationships. I've also found that a surprisingly large number of people who delight in spreading the gossip in their private circles are reluctant to share such details with the police. Particularly if the gossip concerns the deceased.

All that "don't speak ill of the dead" rubbish.

The dregs of tea were cold in my cup and the sandwiches nothing but crumbs when I finally got up and unlocked the sliding door leading to the Emporium. Several people were browsing, and Ashleigh was at the nonfiction shelf, helping a customer make a selection among the biographies of Sir Arthur Conan Doyle and the nonfiction books about his era. The customer eventually chose *The Wicked Boy* by Kate Summerscale and brought it to the counter. Ashleigh rang it up, popped the book in a paper bag, and waved the customer on her way.

"What did you think of *Out of Africa*?" I asked after the customer was gone.

"Loved it," Ashleigh said. "Then again, I love anything with Meryl Streep. Hey! How'd you know I watched it last night?"

I winked at her. My shop assistant did more than dress according to her mood; she changed her entire persona on a daily basis. A couple of weeks ago, I'd overheard her and Fiona discussing the movie. Ashleigh said she'd never seen it, and Fiona said it was one of her all-time favorites. Today's outfit was one in Ashleigh's regular rotation—African safari: beige pith helmet, khaki-colored belted jacket, and sturdy brown hiking boots. It was elementary to conclude that she finally got around to watching Streep and Robert Redford romancing their way around Kenya.

"I have to go out for a bit," I said.

"Okay, but don't forget I asked to leave early today."

"You did?"

"Yes, Gemma, I did. I have a doctor's appointment at five fifteen."

"Are you sick? You don't look sick."

"No, I'm not sick. I told you, although I don't have to inform my boss about my medical problems, you know, it's for a renewal of my asthma prescription."

I vaguely remembered something about that. I glanced at the clock behind the sales counter. It was ten to five. I'd been sitting and thinking in the tearoom longer than I'd realized.

29

I didn't have time to do what I needed to do and be back in ten minutes. The consulting detective business would have to wait for closing time.

"Okay," I said. "My errand can wait. See you tomorrow."

* * *

Even in the summer we have early closing on Mondays. I locked the door of the Emporium precisely at five to seven and headed home.

Ryan had not called to tell me he'd solved the case and our dinner date was back on. I hadn't expected him to, but it would have saved me a lot of trouble.

* * *

I walked past my house without stopping to get Violet. I'd never been inside Mrs. Ramsbatten's home and didn't know if my dog would be welcome. It shouldn't matter: I didn't intend to stay long.

I opened the gate in the white picket fence and walked up the moss-lined flagstone path between two rows of lush, perfectly trimmed bushes bursting with red blooms. Not an overblown flower or dying bud could be seen. Mrs. Ramsbatten opened the door to my knock.

"Gemma! This is a surprise, but a nice one. Please come in. What can I do for you?" She was just shy of five feet and almost as round as she was tall, with silky white hair forming a halo around her head, plump red cheeks, warm hazel eyes, and rimless glasses. She wore a colorful housedress and had fluffy slippers on her feet. If she ever disappeared in December, I'd assume she'd gone to stay with her husband, Mr. Claus, at the North Pole.

I stepped over the threshold into the small, neat foyer. A pie-crust table, dark with age and layers of polish, held a silver platter containing the day's mail: one letter and three flyers from fast-food restaurants.

"I wonder if I could have a few minutes of your time," I said. On the way over, I'd debated how to approach the topic I was interested in. As I'd never called on Mrs. Ramsbatten in the five years we'd been neighbors, I couldn't pretend to be dropping in for a casual chat.

"Of course," she said. "Is everything all right? Arthur?"

"Uncle Arthur's well. As far as I know."

"He sent me a lovely postcard from Tunisia."

That was it: he'd gone to Tunisia.

She led the way into the living room and asked me to take a seat. "Would you like a cup of coffee? Or perhaps you'd prefer tea." She chuckled. "You English and your tea."

"No, thank you." I settled into an armchair covered in faded red and gold chintz. The last of the day's sunlight streamed through the large bay window and shone on the row of potted plants lining the window ledge. The room was immaculately clean, and that was no small feat considering there was enough furniture in here to stock a warehouse. Two couches, a love seat, several armchairs, a coffee table that looked like it had been carved out of an entire tree, several side tables. Every inch of available space was covered with collectables: china figurines of shepherds and shepherdesses; small sculptures; souvenir plates, including several celebrating the marriage of Prince Charles and Lady Diana Spencer; teacups and matching saucers; family photographs in silver frames; blue Wedgewood bowls and candlesticks; more candlesticks; several clocks, all showing exactly the same time; a collection of miniature porcelain and painted wood houses. One table appeared to be dedicated to tiny hedgehogs. The walls were hung with a plethora of art, paintings ranging from what looked to my untrained eye to be original works from noted Cape Cod artists to mass-produced prints of old masters.

Not a single speck of dust rested on anything. *She must,* I thought, *spend her entire day—when not working in her garden or ours—dusting.*

I didn't know where to look first. If anyone was ever murdered in this room, it would take the police months to sort through it all.

A gas fireplace, unlit in early summer, filled the far wall. Mrs. Ramsbatten plucked a postcard off the mantle and waved it at me. "See? Here it is. Arthur's always so thoughtful." The mantle was lined with postcards. Everything from tropical beaches to roaring lions, dancing Hawaiians, majestic snow-topped mountains, the Blue Mosque, Buckingham Palace, soaring cathedrals, and rolling green hills. Some were new and crisp, many yellowing with age.

"Uh . . ." I said.

She settled herself in the chair opposite me, folded her hands in her lap, and smiled. "First, let me say I was totally devastated when I heard about that poor kitten."

"Not your fault," I said. "All's well that ends well."

"Yes, but it might not have. She must have run into the shed when I was putting away my basket of tools, hid when she heard me coming, and then I shut the door on the poor dear thing." Mrs. Ramsbatten patted her chest. "So lucky you found her in time. How clever you are, Gemma."

"Not me. Violet alerted me and I simply followed her lead. I took a soup bone out of the freezer that night as her reward."

"I'm glad to hear that. Now, what can I do for you, dear?"

"You're a member of the West London Garden Club."

"Oh yes. A founding member, as it happens. I was board chair for many years, but I've cut back my participation in recent years, although I'm part of the annual summer garden tour committee."

Brilliant! Just what I wanted to know. "I heard there was an incident yesterday."

The hazel eyes opened wide. "Incident! That's putting it mildly, Gemma. A garden was sabotaged. It was dreadful, simply dreadful. Unthinkable. In all our years, nothing like that has ever happened before. Those poor plants. The roses will never recover."

I'd meant the death of one of their members, but okay. The destruction was a good place to start. "Do you have any idea who'd do something like that?"

"I don't like to name names, dear, but some of our members have been known to let personal rivalry get the better of them." She shook her head. "Never to that extent, though."

"It was Sheila Tierney's garden that got hit, wasn't it?"

She nodded. "Come to think of it, Sheila's cat was the one locked in my shed, or so I heard."

"Sheila's daughter's cat, but yes."

"Sheila's a marvelous gardener, but I'm sorry to say she's disproved the point I've always made about gardeners and their gardens."

"What point's that?"

"I've long maintained that to be a truly first-class gardener, one has to be a good person. Anyone can nurture a plant"—I didn't interrupt to explain that any plant I brought home soon died—"pull weeds, and design a pleasing layout. But to have a truly excellent garden, the gardener must truly love the garden. The garden will then love the gardener in return. Only a gentle, loving, generous person can love a garden the way it deserves, and the garden will respond in kind."

"You don't think Sheila's a loving person?"

Mrs. Ramsbatten peered at me from beneath her bushy white eyebrows. "No. Thus disproving my theory. She did have a lovely garden."

Is it possible, I thought, *that Sheila realized at the last minute her garden wasn't going to be the winner, and she decided to save face by ripping it all up and accusing someone else?* She would get the sympathy factor, if not the trophy. "Do people think she might have sabotaged it herself?"

"Oh no, dear. No one thinks that. I was simply making a point about the woman's character. She was completely focused on winning the trophy this year. She received an honorable mention when she was last in the tour, three years ago, so she went all out to make sure she won this year."

"What about Anna Wentworth?"

"Poor Anna. Such a tragedy. I suspect that's why you're here, dear. Investigating, are you?"

"No. Not at all. Just curious."

She winked at me. "If you say so, dear. I didn't know Anna well. She moved to West London about four years ago, and it's taken her time to create her garden. You can't rush a garden, which, in my mind, is the most precious thing about gardening. A garden will be ready when it is ready, and not a moment before. No amount of yelling or badgering, or even begging, will get a plant to grow or a flower to bloom before its time. Anna wrote a couple of books on gardening, had what they call a blog—whatever that might be—and occasionally spoke at club meetings around the Cape and beyond. I haven't seen her garden myself, but I hear it's top notch. This was her first year on the tour, and everyone said she would be the one to beat for the trophy."

"You haven't seen her garden? You said you were on the committee."

"I wasn't part of the selection subcommittee; my role was selling tickets and helping with promotion. Yesterday morning, I was touring the first house when I got a call to tell me what had happened at Sheila's. I went there immediately to survey the damage and try to calm the woman down. I have to say, it was far worse than I'd been told. Perfectly shocking! Sheila was not inclined to be calmed."

"Did she say who she thought had done it?"

"Oh yes. She told everyone it was Anna and vowed to get her revenge. I'd only just arrived when she ran out of the garden, jumped in her car, and headed for Anna's. She looked, I must say, like a mad thing. Absolutely everyone is talking about what happened when she got to Anna's house."

"What precisely did happen?"

"Anna was in her garden, chatting to the tour groups, when Sheila arrived. She flew at Anna, yelling and screaming and throwing around accusations. I believe she even accused Anna of sleeping with her husband. Rather than simply turn and go into the house, as she should have, Anna foolishly responded in kind and hurled insults at Sheila. Accounts differ as to who threw the first punch, but onlookers had to physically separate them. It was like something out of a movie, one of my friends said. Someone threated to call the police if Sheila didn't leave, and several people forcibly walked Sheila to her car. She left, throwing threats behind her all the way. Anna was, needless to say, distraught and had a few choice words to say about Sheila after she'd left. The garden club doyennes had a heck of a time trying to get the tour back on track."

35

"Do you think Anna did it? Sabotaged Sheila's garden, I mean?"

Mrs. Ramsbatten leaned back in her chair and thought. "I can't say. I didn't know her well enough. She denied it, of course. Anna is—I should say she *was*—a member of our club, but she rarely if ever came to the meetings or the social activities. Not if she wasn't the featured speaker, at any rate."

"You said Sheila accused Anna of having an affair with her husband. Is that true?"

"That, my dear Gemma, I wouldn't know anything about. If they were carrying on, they didn't do it in full view of the West London Garden Club. Now, how about that cup of tea? I do an excellent G&T, if you'd prefer that."

Chapter Five

My phone rang as I was leaving Mrs. Ramsbatten's house, well-fortified with not one but two gin and tonics. She did, I thought as I staggered down the sidewalk, have a heavy hand on the gin bottle.

As we sipped our drinks, Mrs. Ramsbatten told me about her life. She'd earned several degrees in mathematics, and early in her career she'd worked alongside Admiral Grace Hopper in the development of COBOL, one of the earliest computer languages. She'd later gone to work at IBM where she met Mr. Ramsbatten, and together they'd been part of the development team coordinating with Microsoft on MS-DOC, the operating system for the first IBM PC.

"I suspect," I said as I accepted the second drink, "you know what a blog is."

She winked at me. "I try to keep up, yes. But I've done my bit, and I'm content to work on my garden and let the world of technology carry on without me. As it has had to do without Mr. Ramsbatten." Her voice had turned wistful and she'd stared into space. "He truly was a genius."

I shook off the effect of the G&Ts and answered the ringing of my phone. "Hello?"

"Hey, Gemma. I've been talking to my mom . . ."

"Good evening, Jayne."

"Yeah, good evening. I've been talking to my mom. She's a member of the West London Garden Club."

"Your mother's a member of everything. If she moves, half the cultural institutions of West London will fall"—I hiccupped—"into chaos."

"Your voice sounds strange. Have you been drinking?"

"I had a small tipple with my next-door neighbor." Home again, I put my key in the lock, twisted it, and the door opened. I was quite proud of myself for getting it on the first try. Violet ran in excited circles around my legs.

"Mom knew Anna Wentworth moderately well," Jayne said.

"Did she now?"

"I told Mom you're investigating her death—"

"I'm not investigating."

"Whatever. And she said to tell you the garden club has called an emergency meeting for tomorrow evening. You're welcome to come as her guest."

"I might just do that, but right now I want to have a look at the scene of the crime. Scenes of the crimes, I should say. It's eight thirty, so I have some daylight left if I go now."

"Go where?"

"The place where Anna was found. I'm sure the police have it cordoned off, but I can try to get a peek. And then Sheila Tierney's garden."

"Good thing you're not investigating," Jayne said. "You're not driving anywhere, I hope."

"Not necessary. I can walk."

"Do you want me to come with you?"

"Yes."

"Be there in ten."

* * *

True to her word, Jayne pulled up eight minutes later, giving me enough time to feed Violet and freshen myself up. By which I mean brush my teeth and gargle with mouthwash. If I was going to have a chat with the police, I didn't want anyone thinking I'd been drinking.

Not that I'd been *drinking*. It was only two G&Ts with a friendly neighbor.

I studied myself in the mirror and hiccupped. I splashed more water on my face. Come to think of it, I'd had my back turned and had been studying a particularly fine painting on her wall as Mrs. Ramsbatten prepared my second drink, and I might have heard her say, "Oops" as the gin splashed into my glass.

Jayne's car pulled into the driveway, and Violet and I let ourselves out of the house. Jayne and Violet exchanged greetings, and we all set off as the streetlights flickered to life.

The sun had dipped below the horizon, wrapping everything in deep purple dusk, but at this hour in late June, it would be light enough for a while yet not to need artificial light.

The spot where Anna Wentworth had died was not far from my house. A quiet residential street near a large and grassy town park with a nice children's play area, a scattering of picnic tables and benches, and a thicket of large old oaks and maples. I often came here to let Violet romp off leash.

We saw the red and blue lights as soon as we turned the corner. The park was cordoned off with yellow police tape, and a cruiser and a white panel van blocked the road in front of the treed section. Officer Stella Johnson stood on the sidewalk, presumably to keep the curious away.

I assumed she'd count me among the curious.

Almost twenty-two hours had passed since Anna's body had been found. Most of the initial forensic work would have been done long ago and all the potential clues removed, leaving me precious little to work with.

Not that the police were likely to let me work with anything at all.

"Engage Stella in conversation," I whispered to Jayne as we crossed the road. I slipped the leash into Jayne's hand.

"Why don't you?" she whispered back.

"Because my conversational skills are limited, and I prefer to divert my attention elsewhere."

"Hi, Stella," Jayne called. "You have a nice night to stand out here. How's it going?"

"Boring," she said. "What are you two doing here?"

Violet sniffed at Stella's uniform pants. She bent over and gave the dog a hearty pat. Violet wagged her tail.

"Just taking the dog for a walk," Jayne said.

I edged away from them and stepped ever so casually off the sidewalk into the park. The line of trees came close to the road, and underneath the heavy, leaf-filled branches and between the solid trunks, darkness came early. A thin beam of light flashed from inside the copse, and a woman said something I didn't quite catch.

I checked the position of the streetlights. This particular spot was exactly halfway between two on this side of the road. The light on the other side was burned out. It would be very dark when the daylight completely faded, and darker still among the trees.

"Do you like being a police officer?" Jayne asked Stella Johnson.

"Not when I have to stand around for hours chasing away nosy citizens," she replied. "Gemma, what are you doing?"

"Do you have a dog?" Jayne asked. "Violet senses something on your pants."

"Yes," she said, "we do. Gemma, you can't go there."

I pretended not to hear her and lifted my leg to swing it over the crime-scene tape.

I put it down again very swiftly when a dark figure stepped out of the night, a bright light shone in my face, and a familiar voice said, "Not you again."

"Good evening, Detective," I said.

"Enjoying a pleasant chat, Officer Johnson?" Detective Louise Estrada asked.

"Uh . . ." Stella Johnson said.

"Never mind. I know what it's like to try to get Gemma not to do something she wants to do." Estrada looked at me. "Take one step closer and I'll arrest you for interfering with a crime scene."

I knew better than to think she was joking. "I assumed you'd be here, Detective, and I thought you might appreciate some help."

"Oh, for heaven's sake. I do not want or need help from any passerby. But if I did, rest assured you'd be the last person I'd call."

I decided to ignore that comment. "Have you found the murder weapon?"

More voices and two people dressed in white coveralls emerged from the copse. "That's it for now, Detective," one of them said. "We've got everything we need. Oh, what a nice dog. Can I pat him?"

"Sure," I said.

"No," Estrada said. "This person has been ordered to leave."

Jayne straightened her shoulders. "I don't think you can order us to leave the public sidewalk."

Estrada crossed her arms over her chest. She was tall and lean, olive-skinned and dark-haired, dressed in a brown leather jacket, black trousers, and ankle boots. She managed to look formidable even when she wasn't trying. Right now, she was trying. "I don't think it would be a good idea for you to attempt to imitate your friend here, Jayne."

Jayne deflated. "Sorry."

The forensic officers opened the back door of their van and began stripping off their white coveralls. Like magic, as though they'd heard a secret signal, people began gathering on the sidewalk or standing on their front porches to watch.

"Good night, Gemma." Notably, Detective Estrada had not answered my question.

"Good night," I said.

"'Night," Jayne said.

Violet paused to sniff at Estrada's legs. Estrada looked down at her and let out a short, sharp growl. Violet yipped and hurried to catch up to me. I took out my phone, pressed a few buttons, and put it back in my pocket.

"Learn anything?" Jayne asked when we were out of earshot.

"I doubt it would have mattered if I'd been able to get into the park, but I'll come back after they've gone. The police have had more than enough time to trample over everything with their big feet and pick up anything they suspect might be a clue."

"This isn't a Sherlock Holmes story, Gemma. The police today don't mindlessly trample all over clues."

"I am, of course, speaking theoretically. They don't always realize what's significant. However, in this case, I suspect anything to be found would have been apparent. Imagine the scene: a woman with her dog; a person stepping out of the darkness; a blow to the head. Any evidence left by the killer would be obvious—a cigarette butt, a dropped driver's license. The spot was carefully chosen."

"In what way?"

"It's darker at that precise location than any place else on that street, darker in fact than almost any place else in this neighborhood. I need to find out if that was Anna's regular dog-walking route and her regular time. Quite possibly it was, which means her attacker could have known she'd be passing and planned accordingly."

"Any chance this was a random attack on a woman alone at night with only her dog? As much as I hate thinking about something like that happening in West London."

"Highly unlikely. Particularly not after the incident earlier."

"You mean the vandalism to Sheila Tierney's garden? You think Sheila killed Anna in revenge for destroying her garden?"

"I haven't dismissed that possibility, but it's entirely plausible someone else took advantage of the day's drama to do what they intended to do anyway."

Jayne shivered. "I feel very cold all of a sudden."

"Murder is a cold-blooded business."

"Why are we walking so quickly? I've already been to the gym today, thanks. I went after work."

"I'm conducting an experiment. It might have been more effective without the dog," I said as Violet veered off the path in pursuit of something only she could detect. I tugged at the leash to get her back on track, and she came, although reluctantly.

We turned several corners, and soon the Tierney house came in sight. Every light, inside and outside the house, was on. I took out my phone and stopped the timer app. "Four and a half minutes. It's taken us four and a half minutes to walk here from the scene of Anna's death. Say four minutes if we didn't have Violet."

"Still less if we'd run."

"Yes, but a running woman attracts attention." This was an affluent neighborhood of comfortable family homes, close to the ocean and to town. A neighborhood where people walked, particularly in the warm evenings when daylight lingered for hours. Exercising their dogs, taking their kids to the park before bed or heading home from a soccer game, going for an evening stroll, returning from dinner at the pier or a movie in town.

Anna Wentworth had died at approximately quarter past ten. Not long after full dark. Late for people with kids to be out, but still early enough that a person out for a walk wouldn't be commented on or remembered.

"This time," I said to Jayne, "leave the talking to me."

"Thank heavens for that. I have absolutely no idea what to say to a murder suspect, other than 'did you do it?'"

The front garden of the Tierney home had not been vandalized, and no sign of the damage done was apparent from the street. The SUV was in the driveway and the garage doors were closed. I pressed the bell and heard it pealing inside the house. The front door was inset with a pane of frosted glass, and I could see into the lit foyer. The shape of a man's head popped around the corner. I smiled and waved. He blinked, appeared to recognize me, and then the door creaked open.

"You're the woman from the bookstore, right?" he said. "You helped Lauren with her cat. Sorry, I've had reporters poking around all day. Come in—quickly, before a photographer tries to take a picture and imply you're my mysterious lover."

Jayne, Violet, and I stepped into the house, and the door shut behind us.

David Tierney was a moderately attractive man in his forties, and he didn't seem partially snooty to me, as Irene had said. Deep purple shadows lay under his eyes, he'd missed several spots when shaving and had also nicked his chin, and a coffee stain marked the front of his T-shirt. As he was supposedly a businessman, I assumed he didn't regularly go around ill-groomed. The stress of the past two days was apparently getting to him.

"I'm sorry for your troubles," I said.

"Yeah." He rubbed the patch of stubble on his chin. "Thanks. First, I have to thank you for helping Lauren and finding Snow-ball. You were a lifesaver."

"My pleasure," I said.

"What can I do for you? I'm afraid this isn't a good time for a visit."

"I understand. Are you aware Lauren came to see me this afternoon?"

He shook his head. "No, I wasn't. I thought she was visiting a friend. Why did she do that?"

I lowered my voice. "Is your wife at home?"

"Yes, but Sheila's not receiving visitors. She's upstairs, locked in the bedroom, not talking to me, and refusing to see anyone. Even Lauren. This has all been very . . . upsetting to her."

Upsetting to Lauren as well, I thought. At eleven years old, the girl would need her parents to help her deal with all that was happening.

I'd met Sheila Tierney exactly once, but that had been enough time for me to suspect she didn't place her daughter's needs high on her list of priorities.

Lauren slipped quietly into the foyer, Snowball nestled in her arms. The girl's eyes were huge dark pools in her lightly tanned face. She nuzzled herself against her father, and he rested his hand on her shoulder. Violet barked at the sight of the cat, and Snowball hissed in return.

"One day," I said, "we'll introduce these two properly and they can be friends. But perhaps not right now."

"Have you found out who killed Mrs. Wentworth?" Lauren asked.

"Lauren!" David said. "That's hardly Ms. Doyle's responsibility."

"It's okay. Lauren asked for my help." I fixed my eyes on hers. "The West London police are very good at their jobs, Lauren. You have to believe that. They won't charge your mother if she didn't do it."

"I wouldn't be so—" David started to say.

"Not now," I interrupted. "You asked for my help, Lauren, but I have to tell you that real life isn't like TV. It's highly unlikely an amateur can solve a case the police cannot."

"Aunt Irene said you do it all the time."

"Not exactly all the time."

"You found Snowball." The way the girl looked at me broke my heart. She really believed in me.

Jayne must have thought the same. "Gemma isn't saying she won't do what she can, Lauren, but she's trying to be realistic."

"I don't understand," David said. "What has any of this got to do with the cat?"

"Nothing, really," I said. "I'd like to speak to Sheila if she's willing to talk to me about what happened."

"I suppose I can ask her," David said slowly. "Don't know that she'll want to, though. She can be . . . um . . . stubborn sometimes."

"Thank you. I'd like to see your garden, if that would be okay. Where the vandalism happened."

"I'll take you," Lauren said. "It's a mess."

David hesitated. I gave him a smile. He shrugged. "Okay. Lauren, will you show Ms. Doyle to the backyard. I'll tell Sheila you're here. No guarantee she'll talk to you."

"Which," I said to myself as much as to Lauren, "is why I can't do what the police can."

Still carrying her cat, the girl led us through the house. I kept hold of Violet's leash and she trotted along beside me. A wide oak stairway curved upstairs, and the foyer opened onto a hallway leading deeper into the house. I glanced into rooms as we passed. The house was new, everything beautifully decorated and spotlessly tidy. The art was good, but chosen, I thought, more to complement the decorating scheme than because the buyer liked it. The whole house—the downstairs anyway—had a soulless quality, as though the decor had been plucked directly out of a designer's catalogue, with no attempt to customize it for taste or comfort. The kitchen was enormous, tall windows trimmed with yellow and blue valances, glass-fronted cream cabinets, blue glass backsplash, a granite-topped island, and polished hardwood floors. French doors opened onto a spacious wooden deck, placed to give the most optimal view of the garden. Snowball squirmed in Lauren's arms, but she held onto the cat tightly.

Jayne sucked in a breath. It was fully dark now, but the outside lights were strong, and more light streamed out of the kitchen.

The devastation was immediately obvious. Naked branches and bare earth. Torn flowers scattered across the ground, shredded leaves, holes scratched into the golf-course-quality lawn here and there, apparently at random. Some large white and gray

47

stones, which had probably been arranged in a deliberate design, were piled in a shapeless clump on the grass, and pottery was either smashed or the vessels tipped over.

"Did your parents do anything to tidy up? After this happened?" I asked.

"No. Mom was too upset all day, and then the police came."

"Were you here Sunday morning? Did you see the damage?"

"Oh yeah. I heard Mom screaming, and I thought she was being murdered or something." She ducked her head. "Sorry— that wasn't funny."

"I understand."

"I came running down the stairs and found her having a total fit."

"Had you been outside yourself that morning?"

"No. I was told I had to stay in the house when the garden visitors were here. I was still in bed when I heard Mom screaming. I was supposed to go to Aunt Irene's for a sleepover later anyway, so I called her and told her what was happening, and she came to pick me up."

"Where was your father?"

"He got home this morning. After Aunt Irene and I went to the police station to get Mom."

"Do you know where he was on Sunday?" I had to ask the question, and I hoped Lauren wouldn't realize I was checking on his alibi.

She was a smart girl—she shot me a look, but she answered. "Something to do with work. He travels a lot." She ducked her head again and stroked Snowball.

"I see," I said. "I'm going to have a look around. You and Snowball stay here with Jayne."

I handed Violet's leash to Jayne, opened the French doors, and stepped onto the wooden deck that ran the width of the house. The deck held a table and eight chairs, a gleaming steel barbecue, and a white wicker couch with matching chairs covered with bright blue and yellow cushions. Iron urns and terra-cotta pots overflowed with lush flowers, tall grasses, and trailing vines. The deck area appeared to be untouched, no doubt because the vandal didn't want to get too close to the house.

The yard was about a fifth of an acre in size, and the garden appeared to have been formally laid out in a series of perennial beds interspersed with bushes and trees. I walked across the lawn, taking care where I put my feet.

Ryan would have had this area searched, particularly as the vandalism might relate to the murder, but the police didn't have unlimited resources, and the scene of Anna's death would have taken most of their attention.

Other than the deck, which had been left alone, the damage was widespread. I studied the garden carefully, but I could see nothing I thought might be significant. The vandal or vandals had brought scissors or shears of some sort—branches of bushes and stems of flowers were cleanly cut—but they hadn't taken down anything more substantial, such as large tree branches. That would suggest they'd carried nothing bigger than would fit in a pocket or tote bag. The dug-up patches of lawn were no larger than a couple of inches across, doable with a small trowel. I could see no noticeable pattern to the destruction or figure out why some patches of plants had been left alone while others appeared to have been completely destroyed.

I examined the earth in the disturbed flowerbeds, looking for footprints. It hadn't rained for several days, but Sheila kept her garden watered, and a few imprints of small feet were pressed into the earth. Lauren or her friends, I assumed. A light, round depression about twice the size of a quarter marked the ground next to some of the prints. I studied the marks carefully, but couldn't guess what had made them unless it had been a toy of some sort. I searched for threads or scraps of cloth that might have become snagged on broken branches, but came up empty-handed.

I rubbed my fingers lightly across my right cheek and studied the ruins of the garden for a long time. When I was satisfied I could learn no more, I headed back to the house.

There was a savageness to this destruction, shocking in its depth of feeling. Not that I'd thought the mob had put out a contract on Sheila Tierney's garden, but it was clear that whoever had done this had truly hated Sheila.

Sheila or her husband, David. I mustn't forget that David lived here too.

Jayne and Lauren stood at the kitchen windows watching me. David had joined them, but not Sheila.

"I noticed some firm patches of bare earth between the flower beds," I asked when I was back in the kitchen. "Did the garden have statues?"

"Yes," David said. "Sheila likes Greek- and Roman-style figures, and we had a few dotted around. Nothing very big, though. The police took them. Looking for fingerprints maybe?"

"Probably. Is Sheila coming down?"

He shook his head. "She's asleep. I left her. It's been a hard day. I'll tell her you were here and suggest she give you a call in the morning."

"Do you do any of the gardening yourself?"

"Some. I mow the lawn, lug plants around, dig up new beds, trim dead branches, take things to the dump." He smiled but his smile was strained. "I'm not allowed to do much more."

Allowed was an interesting choice of words. I let it pass. "You and Sheila do the maintenance yourself? Must be a lot of work."

His face twisted and he rubbed at his chin. "We used to have a landscaping company that came twice a week, but . . . we let them go." His eyes turned from me and darted around the room, settling on nothing. "They . . . uh . . . didn't get along with Sheila."

He was lying. I filed that thought away and thanked him for his time.

"You were outside for a long time," Lauren said eagerly. "I bet you discovered all sorts of things the police missed, didn't you? Like Sherlock Holmes does." Snowball had disappeared. Bored, no doubt, as no one was paying her any attention.

"I'll have to think it all over," I said. "It's quite a mess out there."

"I like it." Lauren lifted her chin and spoke firmly. "I'm glad they did it."

"Lauren!" David said. "You don't mean that."

"I do. Maybe now I can play in my own backyard without Mom yelling at me to stay away from the stupid flowers." She looked down at Violet, sitting politely at her feet. "My friend Alice has a dog. When I go over there, we can play with the dog in the yard. Throw the ball and everything. No one yells at us if the ball goes into the flowerbeds and we have to go after it. I hate our garden! I'm glad it's ruined. So there!" She burst into tears and ran out of the room.

"I'm sorry," David said. "She's upset. She didn't mean that."

"Sure she did," I said. "No child wants to live in a museum. Thanks again for your time."

And with that, Jayne and I left.

Chapter Six

"For someone who insists she's not investigating," Jayne said, "you spent a lot of time poking around that garden."

"What can I say? It presents an interesting puzzle."

On the way back to my house, we took a detour to the town park. Officer Johnson and the crime scene tape were gone, and I ducked into the woods after asking Jayne to stay on the sidewalk with Violet.

I switched on the flashlight app on my phone and used it to illuminate the trail laid down by countless feet wearing big heavy boots. I soon came to a patch of disturbed earth beneath an ancient oak tree. This, I assumed, was the spot where the body had been lying when it was found. I was only a few steps from the street, close enough that I could hear Jayne telling Violet I'd be right back, but the only light came from my phone. I didn't see anything significant, but I hadn't expected to. The police had been thorough.

I switched off the flashlight app and stood still, enveloped in the near-complete darkness. A car passed on the street, a small animal moved in the undergrowth, and Jayne continued chatting to Violet. The sound of the incoming tide crashing to shore was faint and distant. My eyes slowly became adjusted to the ambient light leaking through the trees, and I retraced my steps.

When I emerged onto the sidewalk, Violet swung toward me and Jayne started to speak. I held up my hand. It was ten o'clock. Twenty-four hours ago, Anna Wentworth and her dog had walked down this sidewalk and gone into the woods. Only the dog had come out again.

Almost certainly, Anna would have been on the sidewalk when she approached this spot. Did she go into the woods voluntarily? If so, why?

She didn't have to have been lured there. She might have simply allowed the dog to lead her into the woods, perhaps so it could visit a favorite spot under a tree. I thought it unlikely her attacker would strike when she was standing in plain view on the sidewalk. It might have been dark, but this was an open space. Cars and people passed, windows overlooked the street. This wasn't a neighborhood where people pretended not to notice what was going on.

As if to prove my point, Jayne whispered, "Incoming."

A car pulled up beside us. The driver's door opened and a man got out. Violet wagged her tail and dashed forward to greet him. He ignored her and she scratched at his right leg. Violet doesn't like to be ignored.

"Good evening," I said. "Nice night for a walk."

"Nine-one-one got a call that two women were nosing around the murder scene," Ryan Ashburton said. "As I was on my way here anyway, I said I'd take it. I'm not at all surprised to find that it's you two."

"I'm not nosing around anything," Jayne said. "I'm out for a walk with my friend."

"Gemma?"

"I wanted to see the scene for myself. I stopped by earlier, but Louise didn't want my assistance."

"No kidding. She called me and said she's wondering if there's any way to get your work visa revoked and send you back to England."

"Very funny."

"She wasn't joking, Gemma. Even Louise might, if pressed, agree that in previous cases you had reason to be interested in what we were up to. Those cases involved people you know and care for."

"Except for Maureen," Jayne said, not at all helpfully. "Gemma doesn't like Maureen. She helped her because Maureen said she couldn't."

"That makes me feel so much better," Ryan said.

"We've just come from the Tierney house. Where, by the way, I have a right to be because Lauren's my friend." I sighed. "Ryan, if you could see her. The girl's confused and terrified. Her mother's locked herself in her room, and I get the feeling her father's away so often, Lauren and he don't have much of a relationship. She wants to do whatever she can to help, and in her mind that means asking me for my help."

"Gemma . . ."

"I told her I trust the police and she needs to do so too. Believe me, Ryan, I don't want anything to do with this, but if I can help, I will. I have on occasion been able to figure out things before the police did."

"You have to admit she's right," Jayne said. "Gemma's mind works in a way no one else can understand. You were prepared to close the Sir Nigel Bellingham murder as a suicide, but Gemma put the separate pieces together. Never mind what happened over the winter when we were in London for the conference."

"It's only because of those occasions that I'm not arresting you—both of you—for interference," he said. "You have helped us, and even Louise and my chief admit it." He coughed and leaned over to pat Violet. "Have you . . . uh . . . seen anything here we might have missed?"

I hid a grin. "No. It's possible, likely even, that Anna's killer knew her routine. Did she take this route every night?"

"Not every night, but often enough, according to the neighbors. Anna walked the dog most evenings, always on her own, usually around this time. Her husband didn't ever take the dog out or come with them. If she wasn't home, her husband let it out in the yard."

"Did the neighbors notice if she regularly went into these woods?"

His eyes flicked in the light from the headlights of his car. "I don't think our officers asked that."

"They should. It's the perfect spot for an ambush, particularly if she did step off the sidewalk. An ambush implies malice afore-thought. How long has that streetlamp across the street been out?"

"I don't know. I'll check."

"What do you know about the murder weapon?"

"Almost certainly she was felled by a blow to her head from a rock. We found one nearby that was likely what was used. No fingerprints on it."

"Which also means aforethought," I said.

Ryan nodded.

"Why do you say that?" Jayne asked.

"It would be extremely difficult to wipe prints completely off a rock because the surface is so textured. Therefore, the person likely wore gloves to handle it. At this time of year, no one has gloves in their pocket unless they're up to no good."

"They could have used something else," Jayne said. "A scarf, a plastic bag that just happened to be in their pocket."

"We're not ruling anything out," Ryan said.

"You said you were on your way here anyway," Jayne continued. "Why?"

"She was killed at this time last night. I wanted to check out conditions around here." He spread his hands. "Not much happening."

"There's enough," I said. "Lights are still on in these houses. People are watching TV." A car drove by, the driver paying us no attention. "Traffic on the streets."

"Yup," Ryan said. "It's quiet, but not deserted."

We stood in silence for a few minutes. Violet sniffed at the ground and headed for the trees. Jayne pulled her back.

"Did you see the body?" I asked at last.

"I did," Ryan said. "I was on call last night, probably got here no more than fifteen minutes after nine-one-one got the call."

"Did Anna look like she'd confronted her attacker? Fought with him or her before being overcome?"

"At first, I thought so. She had a couple of scratches on her face. But I soon realized they weren't completely fresh, and I've since been told she was in a fight earlier in the day, witnessed by a good number of people. I saw no marks on her hands. Her fingernails were cut very short, but they were clean. All that's just a visual impression. The autopsy might tell us more."

"When is the autopsy?"

"Tomorrow."

A light over the front door of the house directly across the street came on, and the door opened. A man stepped out and stared at us. Ryan lifted a hand, and the man went back inside. The door shut behind him, but the light remained on.

"I wonder," I said, "if the neighbors were that attentive to their surroundings prior to a murder happening almost on their doorsteps."

"Quite possibly not," Ryan said. "This is a peaceful neighborhood in a low-crime town. People aren't on alert."

"What are you going to do now?" I asked.

"I'm heading back to the office to read through the witness statements about the argument between Anna and Sheila earlier on Sunday, and after that I hope to get home for some sleep. The autopsy's scheduled for first thing tomorrow."

"Will you tell me what, if anything, you learn?"

"No. I'm off. Jayne, see that Gemma goes straight home, will you?"

"Ha! As if she ever does anything I tell her," Jayne said.

* * *

When we got to my house, Jayne said her good nights and left.

I realized I hadn't had dinner and pulled a container out of the freezer. Uncle Arthur's the cook in our house, and he likes to make gigantic servings of stews and curries in the slow cooker and freeze the extras. This one was labeled "Squash and lentil curry" in his large, clear handwriting. I dug further into the back and found a container of cooked rice. Putting the two dishes into the microwave was the sum total of meal preparation I felt like doing tonight.

The effect of the two gin and tonics had worn off long ago, so I took out a bottle of sauvignon blanc and poured myself a glass.

While the food warmed, I took my drink into the den, found my iPad in the reproduction antique secretary, and curled up in my favorite wingback chair. Violet ran in ever-decreasing circles on the hearth rug, finally finding the perfect spot on which to take a pre-bedtime nap.

This house is far too big for two people, but Uncle Arthur and I like to have our own space, so it suits us. His suite is on the upper floor (which, being in a saltbox, is only half the width of the house); my bedroom and home office are down the main floor hall. We share the kitchen, living room, and den.

I glanced at the portrait of a dark-haired opera diva hanging over the fireplace. She'd died before I was born, but I've studied her portrait so often that I sometimes feel as though I know her. She was Great-Uncle Arthur's one true love, dead far too young. I don't even know her name, and I know nothing about her other than that she had been on the cusp of fame when she died. Arthur never spoke of her, and I'd never asked, but occasionally when we were sitting comfortably in this room after dinner, reading in companionable silence, I caught him staring wistfully at the portrait. The shadow of sorrow would pass over his eyes as though he was thinking of what might have been. Then he would give his head a shake and turn his attention back to his book.

I opened my iPad and set about finding out what I could about Sheila Tierney and Anna Wentworth.

The timer on the microwave tinged, and I put my glass and iPad down and struggled to my feet. I served up my dinner, carried it into the den, and returned my attention to the wonderful world of the internet.

Anna had kept a blog on seaside gardening that, judging by the number of comments, was quite popular. Over the past three years, she'd written two books on the subject, which had been published by a major press. I checked her books' rankings on Amazon and saw that they were both still very popular. Both books showed the little number-one icon, indicating that at one time they'd been bestsellers in the gardening category.

Her web page contained links to gardening clubs all over New England, including the West London one. Most of the pictures were of gardens and plants, but one showed a laughing Anna holding an enormous bouquet of pale pink peonies.

I studied Anna's face carefully, but I was sure I'd never run into her, even though she'd lived only a couple of blocks from me. West London might be a small town, but it wasn't that small. If she hadn't been a reader or a lover of Sherlock Holmes, she might never have come into the Emporium, and I wasn't exactly a keen gardener. I'd neglected to ask anyone what Anna's husband's name was, and I kicked myself for the oversight. Her bio said she was married but didn't give his name.

The website hadn't been updated with news of her death.

I went on to find out what else I could that might provide a possible clue as to who killed her and why. My reading turned up a man by the name of William Wentworth, who was a member of the West London Yacht Club and had placed second in a regatta last year. Not a particularly uncommon name, so this might not be Anna's husband, but chances were good it was. Apart from this one mention, the man had no internet presence. At a quick look, I couldn't find out what he did for a living. If necessary, I'd do a deeper search another time.

Sheila Tierney didn't have her own web page, and I had to go back in time to find out anything about her. She'd been a history teacher at West London High School until about four years ago. She wasn't old enough to have retired, and she'd worked until Lauren was seven, so I wondered why she'd left. I found no evidence of her moving to another school. Perhaps the family financial situation had changed for the better, so she could give up her job.

I next looked up David Tierney and soon found mention of his company, D&S Restaurant Consulting Services. The business, I read, had developed a software program allowing fast-food restaurants to accept online orders and then leverage those orders directly into social media promotion. David's company provided consulting advice for his clients, not only on installation and training for his product but also on how to best use the social media results generated.

The concept, according to the business and computer industry press, was "original" and "groundbreaking," and David and his "vision" were lauded extensively.

That might explain, I thought, why he traveled a great deal and why his wife had been able to quit being a teacher and devote her time to gardening.

Last of all, I went to the page for the West London Garden Club. It had not been updated and was still advertising tickets for the early summer garden tour. The pictures were mostly of members' gardens, each one looking more spectacular than the last. Mrs. Ramsbatten's name was on the list of board members, and Sheila was mentioned as the fundraising chair.

I shut the iPad and leaned back in my chair. My wine glass was empty, and the curry and rice had gone cold and looked thoroughly unappealing.

I'd learned nothing of any apparent significance, but that, I knew, didn't matter. If an investigation—not that I was investigating—was all about fitting the pieces together, it was first necessary to gather the pieces. Unlike in a jigsaw puzzle, many—most—of the pieces would prove to have no significance and would not be needed. But one never knew which pieces were important, not until the picture was complete.

Chapter Seven

True to his word, Ryan did not call me with an update after the autopsy on Anna Wentworth.

Sheila Tierney did not call me to suggest we meet for a chat.

My investigation—not that it was an investigation—was, in fact, stymied.

Tuesday morning, I opened the shop at the regular time of ten o'clock. Ashleigh arrived at eleven. Business was steady throughout the day, but not overwhelming, and I took a break at two to head upstairs and get some work done on the store accounts. I'd been doing that for no more than ten minutes when I heard someone ascending the seventeen steps from the ground floor, and soon Irene Talbot knocked lightly on the open door.

"Hey," she said. "Got a few minutes?"

I pushed myself away from the computer. "Come on in. What's up?"

"I wanted to stop by and thank you for agreeing to help Lauren. She told me you went around to her house last night."

Moriarty slipped into the office behind her and leapt gracefully through the air, to land on top of the filing cabinet, where he perched, glaring at me.

"I'm going to have to disappoint her, Irene. I told her to trust the police."

"She mentioned that. She also said you spent a lot of time in the garden, just looking at everything. She wondered why you didn't have a magnifying glass."

I groaned. "There's nothing I can do. I simply don't have any resources in this case. I don't know the people involved, and the police aren't sharing information with me."

"Can't you use your feminine wiles on Ryan and get him to let something slip?"

"Ha!" I said. I wouldn't risk my delicate relationship with Ryan by doing something like that. And even if I tried, he was on to my tricks.

He was, I feared, beginning to know my methods.

"Besides," I said, "the point is probably moot."

Irene lifted a stack of *Villains, Victims, and Violets*, edited by Resa Haile and Tamara R. Bower, off a chair and dropped onto it. "Why do you say that?"

"It's entirely possible, likely even, that Sheila did kill Anna. She was enraged at what she thought Anna had done to her, and had to be forcibly restrained from attacking the woman earlier in the day."

"That's what I was afraid you'd say."

"Sheila's your stepsister. Is that sort of behavior typical of her, would you say?"

Irene rested her chin in her hands and thought. "Honestly, Gemma, I'd have to say no. She's a good bit older than me, so we were never close, but I know her well enough not to like her, as a teenager and as an adult. I'd call her selfish, self-absorbed, thoughtless. She always wants—*needs*—to be the center of attention, and she's quick to anger. And yes, she'll lash out on occasion, verbally if not physically. I wasn't at all surprised to hear that she'd driven over to Anna's to confront her.

"But the Sheila I know isn't one for methodical planning. To stalk Anna, lie in wait, attack her in the dark? Not her style, Gemma."

"They lived not far from each other. Is it possible Sheila was out for a walk, saw Anna, and got mad all over again?"

"Sheila out for a walk? She's as likely to sprout wings and fly. But even if she was—say, someone told her to get out of the house and walk off her anger—I can't see it. From what little I've learned, the neighbors heard nothing and saw nothing, and there were no marks on Anna indicating that she'd been in a fight. Since the earlier altercation with Sheila, anyway. If Sheila had confronted her again, it would have been up close and personal, and everyone for miles around would have heard the yelling. Plus I can't see Sheila keeping quiet if she had killed Anna. She'd be far more likely to want to tell the police, and everyone else, that she was completely justified and then go on to provide an extensive list of Anna's faults."

"You make a strong case," I said, "but the police aren't going to take any of that into account. If you want Sheila not to be charged, you'd better hope she's never been in that patch of woods."

"As I said, that's unlikely. She isn't one for walking. Whoa there!" Moriarty had leapt off the shelf, sailed across the room, and landed in Irene's lap. "Scared me half to death." Irene patted the general vicinity of her heart.

"Which was probably his intent."

She looked at the cat fondly and stroked his back. He purred.

"As you know, I went to the Tierney house last night," I said, "but Sheila was asleep. Or pretending to be. I didn't see her. I had a look at the garden, though. Someone really went at it. I was expecting it, but even so, I was shocked at the extent of the damage."

"Yeah. Someone hates Sheila, all right. That garden's the most important thing in her life."

"Except for David and Lauren, surely."

"Including David and Lauren."

"You told me Sheila accused her husband of having an affair with Anna, but most people didn't think that likely. Maybe it was another woman, and David broke it off, and this woman took her anger out on the garden. Sheila mistakenly thought it was Anna who'd done it."

"Which means more complications."

"So it does."

"If David was having an affair with Anna or anyone else, it was news to me, Gemma. I'd have said he was too involved in his business to be up to anything. Including with his wife."

"What does that mean?"

She shrugged. "I keep in touch with Sheila. For Lauren's sake, not Sheila's. David's almost never around. Always away on business, Sheila says, and I believe her. He's made a lot of money over the last few years. Enough that they could put Lauren in a fancy private school and Sheila could quit her job at the high school. They joined the West London Country Club, which isn't cheap, and renovated the kitchen last summer, and they were talking about putting in a swimming pool. Lauren would love a pool. Sheila was okay with that because swimming pools provide excellent background in photographs and offer a myriad of opportunities for imaginative landscaping. Her words, not mine."

"Lots of busy and successful businessmen still manage to have affairs. Or so I've seen on TV."

"So they say. But as for successful, I've the feeling things aren't going so well regarding the business. Sheila hasn't said anything, of course, but I can see signs of cutting corners, and she's put on about twenty pounds in the last few months. Stress, I'd say."

I thought of her ill-fitting clothes.

"Time I was on my way. Up you get, big boy." Irene poked Moriarty in the ribs. He didn't move. She poked harder. He still didn't move. She picked him up and put him on the floor. He gave her a poisonous look. I laughed and he turned the look on me.

"The police chief's giving a press conference in half an hour," Irene said, "and I want to be there."

"Let me know if you find out anything."

"As soon as that's over, I have to leave for Boston. Bad timing, but I'm scheduled to attend a conference, and it's important that I go. I'll be away until Friday morning. I hope my editor-in-chief remembers to assign someone to cover the story."

She waved and left. Moriarty stalked out after her, and I returned my attention to my accounts.

* * *

The accounts didn't get done. Almost as soon as Irene's footsteps faded away, I heard another set climbing the stairs.

"Knock, knock," Donald Morris called out.

"No one at home," I said.

For some reason, he didn't believe me and came into the office anyway. Donald is one of my most avid customers and a close friend of Great-Uncle Arthur. To say Sherlock Holmes is important in Donald's life would be an understatement. When he inherited a small amount of money from his father, Donald quit his family law practice to take up the life of a Holmes scholar. He soon discovered that being a Holmes scholar doesn't pay all that well, but he's content to pursue a life of genteel poverty while he studies the life and times of the Great Detective and his creator.

Donald could be annoying, exasperating, irritating, and fussy, but he was kind and meant well toward everyone. Whenever I found myself peeved and bored at his constant chatter about Sherlock Holmes, I reminded myself that Donald had saved Jayne's life and mine when we were in England over the winter.

As today was a hot summer day, he was not dressed in imitation of his idol in an Inverness cape or ulster coat, but in jeans ironed to a knife edge and a T-shirt printed with a silhouette of Holmes as he's best known—hawk nose, high forehead, deerstalker cap on his head, pipe clenched between his teeth.

Without being asked, Donald sat in the chair recently vacated by Irene and gave me a wide smile.

"I'm sorry, Donald," I said, "but I'm very busy. I'm dreadfully behind on paying some of these bills. I don't want to have the bailiff after me."

"I don't think they have debtors' prisons in Massachusetts these days."

"Figure of speech. But I *am* busy." I picked up a pen and chewed busily on the end.

"I won't be long then." He settled comfortably into the chair and crossed his legs at the ankles.

Who, I wondered, *irons their jeans?*

"I thought you might need some help with the Anna Wentworth murder investigation."

I sighed. "I'm not investigating that."

"You're not? I assumed you'd be interested."

"Yes, I'm interested. Everyone is interested. It's a shocking case."

"Unlike most people, Gemma, when you're interested in things, you take it one step further and try and find the answers."

"I don't know if that's true, but it's not this time."

He started to get to his feet. "I'll be off then. I thought you might like to come with me to pay a call on Anna's husband."

I put down my pen. "You know him?"

"Oh yes. Fairly well, as it happens. Lovely man. He had a marvelous party at his house two years ago in honor of January sixth."

The sixth of January is celebrated as Sherlock Holmes's birthday. No birth date was ever mentioned by Sir Arthur Conan Doyle, so I don't know why Sherlockians have settled on that day, but they have. People gather in New York City from all around the world for a weekend celebration, and many individuals host and attend parties and dinners. I once went with Uncle Arthur to a birthday party at Donald's house on January sixth.

It just so happens that Jayne's birthday is also January sixth, so I always remember and buy her a small gift. I never remember anyone else's birthday. My mother writes to me the week before my father's birthday to remind me to mail a card, and he does the same for her.

"You mean he's a Sherlockian?" I said.

"Oh yes," Donald said. "I assumed you'd know him. Don't you?"

"I don't believe so. William Wentworth? He belongs to the yacht club. I looked him up last night, but I didn't recognize him or his name." And I would have if he'd ever given it to me or used a credit card in my store.

"That's not his surname. He and his wife had different last names. Michael Nixon. Mike."

I mentally slapped my forehead. What an incredibly stupid assumption on my part that had been. "Mike Nixon. I do know him. He comes in once a month to check out what's new in the store." An image flashed in my mind of a man excitedly browsing the new-arrivals shelf. Mid-forties, mildly attractive with short black-and-gray hair, heavy eyebrows over dark eyes, a silver mustache and goatee, broad-shouldered and barrel-chested, dressed in some variation of khaki trousers and golf shirt. "Where possible, he tries to buy in paperback, not hardcover. He has no interest in Sherlock pastiches or historical fiction, but he's an avid reader of nonfiction about Sir Arthur and scholarly works on Holmes."

Donald pointed to the stack of *Villains, Victims, and Violets* on the floor. "Books like that one."

"He also likes modern thrillers of the sort I don't stock." I put down my pen, closed the spreadsheet on my computer, and got to my feet. "I'll take him a gift. Pass me one of those books, will you?"

Donald did so, and we went downstairs. Ashleigh was ringing up two "I Am Sherlocked" mugs for a man while his wife watched with disapproval. "Not exactly," she sniffed, "the souvenir from Cape Cod your mother is expecting."

"I'll take a picture of you beside that cutout from the TV show," he said. "That'll make it a souvenir from Cape Cod."

She didn't look as though she bought his logic, but he paid for the mugs with a smile for Ashleigh, and the woman arranged herself in a pose next to Benedict Cumberbatch.

This was no ordinary life-sized cardboard cutout. Benedict himself had signed it a few weeks ago when he visited the Emporium, as arranged by Uncle Arthur. Every piece of merchandise I had in stock relating to the TV show *Sherlock* had been snatched up; the police had done crowd and traffic control on our section of Baker Street; the visit made the front page of most of the Cape Cod newspapers; and we were on the TV news that night. Sherlockians and Cumberbatch fans were still talking about it, and I had trouble keeping anything in stock with his picture on it.

I have to admit, if only to myself, my cheek still tingled where he'd given me a kiss of farewell.

"I'm going out for a while," I said to Ashleigh. "Won't be long."

She glanced at Donald. "That's what you always say, Gemma."

"Sorry. I have my phone if you need me."

"I never do," she said. "Isn't that right, big boy?"

Moriarty jumped up onto the sales counter for a scratch. Ashleigh obliged.

We left the store in the nick of time. Donald had parked in the loading space, and the parking enforcement officer was heading our way, ticket pad out and a determined look on her face.

"Better step on it," I said.

I threw fast-food wrappings, paper cups, magazines, and a copy of *Teller of Tales: The Life of Arthur Conan Doyle*, by Daniel Stashower, into the back seat, and jumped in.

Donald waved cheerfully to the parking enforcement officer as he pulled into traffic.

When I say "into traffic," I do mean *into* traffic, as Donald never worries whether or not another vehicle is coming. Today a delivery van screeched to a halt inches from the rear bumper of Donald's rust-chewed 2001 Toyota Corolla, and in front of us a bicycle swerved wildly.

I would have clutched the door handle, but I feared it would snap off in my hand.

We lurched up the street and took the first right turn. A woman snatched her child out of the crosswalk.

Fortunately, we weren't going far, and only moments later we pulled up in front of Anna and Mike's house in a burst of exhaust fumes. I leapt gratefully out of the car.

Built in the mid-seventies, the house itself was a small, neat brick bungalow with a carport instead of a garage, although it sat on a large lot. The front garden, as I'd expected, was lush and immaculate. We walked up the stone path, and Donald rang the bell. The sound echoed throughout the house. We waited.

"Did you tell him you were coming?" I asked.

"Yes." Donald pressed the bell again. At last, the door opened and a face peered out. "Oh, Donald, it's you. Hello. I was afraid the vultures of the press were calling again. Come in. Come in. Gemma, nice to see you."

I smiled at Mike Nixon as we stepped into the house. "I am so sorry about your loss."

"Thank you." The smile he gave me was wide, but sadness filled his eyes. Those eyes were red and swollen, but dry now. *All cried out*, I thought with a pang of sympathy.

A Bichon Frisé ran down the hall, nails clicking on the hardwood floor, barking furiously. He ran around me in an excited ball of white fluff and tried to leap onto my legs. As I was wearing a knee-length skirt with bare legs, I danced out of the way.

"Down, Peony!" Mike said. "Down! I'm sorry about that. He simply won't learn not to jump on people."

"That's okay." I leaned over and held out my hand for the little dog to sniff. "He senses my dog, Violet, and wants to find out more about her. Is he named after the flower?"

"Peony is . . . I mean he was Anna's dog. Peonies were Anna's favorite flower. I'm sorry the season for them has passed. She would have loved an abundance of peonies on her grave." He turned his face away from me, and I continued to fuss over the dog.

Once Peony and I had made our acquaintance, I straightened up and handed Mike the book I'd brought. "A small gift. I don't think you've read this one yet. It's rather fun and makes some original points."

"Thank you, Gemma. It's a nice day. Would you like to join me for a drink in the garden?"

"If you're not busy," Donald said.

I'd like nothing better, I didn't say. I was interested in having a look at this garden.

Mike dropped the book onto the bench in the foyer and led the way through the house, to the back, while Peony scrambled on ahead. I peeked into rooms as we passed. The furniture was mass produced and cheap, the art on the walls the same. The beige leather couch in the living room almost disappeared against the beige walls and the beige drapes. Several magazines, their covers featuring flowers or gardens, lay on the coffee table. The bookshelves were sparsely filled. I wasn't able to read the titles on the spines at a distance, but I recognized many of them as coming from my shop. It was possible Anna kept her own reading selections elsewhere, but judging from this room, she wasn't much of a book reader. The carpet beneath the dining room table was faded and worn, not because it was an antique, but because it didn't often get cleaned. A quick peek into the kitchen showed me it hadn't been renovated for several decades; I believe that color of fridge and stove is called harvest gold and was once hugely popular, although I can't imagine why.

At the end of the hallway, we walked down two narrow steps. Mike opened a door and we stepped outside.

I'd been looking forward to seeing this garden, and it didn't disappoint. The property was about a quarter of an acre, every inch filled with lush perennials, perfectly trimmed bushes, emerald-green grass, and magnificent old trees. More flowers, annuals mostly, filled iron urns, and various stone statues peeked around corners and out from under branches. Birds hopped about under feeders or drank from the artificial pond in the center of the yard.

A gray jay flew overhead and landed beneath a feeder. *Snip snip snip* came from my left, and I turned to see a man in brown overalls, trimming a boxwood hedge.

Mike gestured to the stone-floored patio to our left, and Donald and I took seats around the glass-topped table beneath an open red umbrella.

"Can I offer you something to drink?" Mike asked. "The sun's over the yardarm somewhere."

"Water, please," I said. "We don't want to keep you."

"I have no place better to be." He swallowed heavily and turned his face away from me.

"A glass of water would be nice," Donald said.

Mike went to get the drinks. Peony took a seat under the table.

Donald and I sat in companionable silence for a long time. Snipping and trimming, the gardener came closer. He was a young man, dark eyed and dark haired, his thin face and heavily muscled arms browned by the sun. Peony leapt off the deck and ran over to him. The gardener momentary stopped his work to give the dog a pat.

"Beautiful garden," Donald said at last.

"It certainly is," I said.

"Anna's pride and joy." Mike had returned. He put the glasses on the table, water for us, a beer for himself. "She won the best-in-show trophy this year. For all the good it did her." He lifted his glass. "To Anna."

"Anna," Donald and I said.

"Is the garden an interest of yours as well?" I asked. "Will you keep it up?"

"No. It was Anna's passion. All I did was admire it. Early days yet, but I'll probably sell the house."

"Oh," I said.

"I'm sure you'll have no trouble getting a good price," Donald said. "Not from a keen gardener."

"I hope so. To be honest, I'd have preferred a nicer, more modern house. If not that, then I wanted to build an extension and update this one, but Anna wouldn't dream of losing an inch of garden space. The size of the property was, to her, the entire point of living here."

I didn't know what Mike did for a living. Whenever he came into the shop, all we talked about was what books were new and might be of interest to him.

"Are you a doctor?" I asked. I'd noticed a couple of medical journals on the coffee table in the living room, next to a library copy of *Elevator Pitch* by Linwood Barclay.

"No. I work for a medical supplies company. We sell heart monitors and pacemakers. I travel to medical conferences all over the country. My hobby's tennis. I'd love to play at the West London Country Club, but membership there's well out of my price range, so I play at the community courts. Do you play, Gemma?"

"Never had the time, I'm afraid."

"I suppose that store keeps you on the hop all summer. I was always glad Anna had the garden to keep her busy when I was away."

More than busy, I'd have said. But I didn't. "She was also an author, wasn't she?"

He shrugged. "She wrote a couple of books on gardening. They did okay. And she had her blog. It was very popular, I've been told. Anna tried to interest me, but the gardening bug never bit me. Just as well; I wouldn't have had the time." He sipped his beer.

Snip snip snip. The gardener came closer, Peony trotting along behind.

"Do you have any idea who killed her?" I asked.

Startled, Mike looked up. "Sheila Tierney, of course. Everyone knows that."

"Because they were gardening rivals?"

"That sounds silly, I know. But you have to understand the depth of passion, the love, Anna had for this garden." He lifted his arm and swept it from side to side. "It was as though every flower, every plant, every bush was her child. We never had children ourselves. No, maybe *love* isn't the right word. Gardening was a competitive sport to Anna. Winning the trophy was everything. I can only assume Sheila's the same. If someone had destroyed Anna's garden, she'd have gone after them with a vengeance."

"Did Anna destroy Sheila's garden?" It was a blunt question, but it had to be asked.

Mike didn't seem to mind. He took another sip of his beer and shook his head. "I don't know. I'd not have thought it was in Anna's nature to do something like that, but she could overreact sometimes. If something happened to upset her, I don't know what it might have been. I heard what happened on Sunday morning. They say Sheila physically attacked Anna."

"You didn't see it?"

"Wasn't home. I was in Vegas at a pediatrician's conference and got in late afternoon on Sunday."

"You weren't here for the tour then?" I asked.

"No need. I had nothing to do, and Anna wouldn't have wanted me underfoot at any rate. The tour was over when I got home. Anna was upset, to say the least. The day was supposed to be her triumph, and Sheila and her temper tantrum had spoiled it. Anna won the trophy, but that did nothing to mollify her. We had an uncomfortable dinner, and when it was over, Anna went to her office, saying she wanted to work on the blog, and then she took the dog out. She was still in a foul mood when they left." Tears formed in his eyes. He wiped angrily at them. "Sorry."

"Don't apologize," I said.

"It doesn't matter—not any more—if Anna vandalized Sheila's garden. Obviously, Sheila thought she did, and she got her revenge."

"Sheila hasn't been charged," I reminded him.

"Matter of time, I'm sure. It was Sheila all right. I never did like her. Cold as ice, that woman."

"Did you know her well?"

"Not well. She was Anna's friend, not mine."

"She and Anna were friends?" I finished my water. I was interested in what Mike had to say, and it was so very pleasant in this beautiful oasis. We were seated under the umbrella, but the heat of the sun filled the air around us. A yellow and black butterfly fluttered about, darting from one flower to the next. An airplane flew soundlessly overhead, and one bird called to another. A patch of lavender was planted somewhere close by, and its delicious scent drifted toward me. The gardener was working at the edges of the patio now, trimming a lovely full bush about five feet tall, covered with a mass of delicate pink flowers.

Donald sat silently, looking between Mike and me.

"Anna and Sheila were good friends for a while," Mike said. "Popping in and out of each other's houses for coffee and gossip, having us over for dinner, or Sheila and David coming here. The usual sort of thing. Anna was fond of their little girl. What's her name again?"

"Lauren."

"Right. Lauren. Good tennis player, for her age."

Mike had a deep, rolling voice, made more powerful by the emotion he was struggling to control.

"What happened to the friendship?" I asked

He studied my face. "This might sound like sour grapes, but I never liked Sheila. Sheila's a user. A taker. She uses people and then she throws them away. That's my impression of her anyway. She and Anna had a huge falling-out a few months ago. I never found out the whole story, but Anna said Sheila's jealousy was becoming too much for her to handle. Sheila liked to be the center of attention, and the success of Anna's books and blog was getting her the lion's share of attention in the Cape Cod gardening community. It came to a head, so Anna said, when Sheila contributed something to the blog and the information was incorrect. Anna caught the mistake in time and fixed it, but she believed Sheila deliberately tried to make a fool of her." He drained his glass.

"We should probably be going." Donald stood up.

I cursed under my breath. I had more questions. Such as did Mike think his wife had been having an affair with David Tierney.

Mike also stood. "Thanks for coming."

I had no choice but to get to my feet too.

Instead of taking us through the house, Mike stepped off the patio and took the flagstone path around it. The little dog didn't try to follow.

"I'm going to Boston week after next to have dinner with some of the members of The Speckled Band," Donald said, referring to that city's Sherlockian society. "Would you like to come?"

"I would," Mike said, "if I'm free. I've taken time off work, but you'll understand I have arrangements to make, and the police will need to speak to me as they build their case against Sheila."

I paused at the corner of the house and turned to take one last look at Anna's garden. The gardener had stopped work and was watching us with his large dark eyes. He made no move to look away. Peony, the Bichon Frisé, sat in a patch of shade at his feet.

I hurried to follow the men.

Chapter Eight

The emergency meeting of the West London Garden Club would be held at the Harbor Inn at seven o'clock. Ashleigh agreed to stay late and close up so I could go to the meeting. At quarter to seven, I was standing in front of the Emporium. Traffic was heavy on Baker Street as tourists headed for dinner or returned to their hotels after a day spent exploring the seaside. Across the street, a face appeared in the window of Beach Fine Arts. I smiled and waved, and the face retreated.

I might have saved Maureen Macgregor from being sent up the river for murder last summer, but you wouldn't know it by the way she treated me. Then again, Maureen was an equal-opportunity curmudgeon: She didn't like anyone.

I thought about "up the river," meaning to the big house—that is, prison. I liked that expression.

Leslie Wilson's car pulled up to the curb, with Jayne in the passenger seat. I jumped into the back.

"Step on it!" I said.

"Step on what? And why?" Jayne said. "We've plenty of time."

"I'm trying out my American expressions."

"Okay, but we don't say 'step on it' if we're not in a hurry."

"Whatever. Leslie." I spoke to Jayne's mother, "What's the word in the 'hood' 'bout the Wentworth dame bein' knocked up?"

"Was she?" Leslie replied in a shocked voice. "Did the autopsy reveal that?"

"That's usually a precondition for undergoing an autopsy, isn't it?" I said. "Being dead."

"If you're going to show off your Americanisms, Gemma," Jayne said, "you have to get them right. *Knocked up* means 'made pregnant.' You're thinking of *knocked off,* which means 'killed.'"

"Oh, right. In English, proper English as spoken by Her Majesty the Queen's loyal subjects, *knocked up* means 'woken up.' All highly confusing. Like what you call biscuits, which aren't biscuits at all."

"If I guess correctly," Leslie said, "you're asking me what people are saying about the death of Anna. The answer is that the general opinion is Sheila did it. Anna ruined her garden, they had a fight, and Sheila was dragged away. She then went home, spent the rest of the day nursing her grievances, and went out later and finished the job."

"Do people believe Anna destroyed the garden?"

"My friends don't know. They're all in some sort of shock. More shocked at that, I'd say, than at the killing. None of them can believe a gardener as expert as Anna would have deliberately destroyed one, no matter who it belonged to."

"People can do strange things when they're angry or consider themselves to be provoked," Jayne said.

"True enough," I said.

"Did you hear the chief's press conference?" Leslie asked. "I caught some of it on the news on the radio."

"Irene sent me a text," I said. "Nothing we didn't know. Killed by a blow to the back of the head by a blunt instrument. No signs of a struggle. People asked to come forward if they were in the vicinity of the attack at the time. No arrest has been made at this time, but they are confident that . . . blah, blah, blah. Which usually means they haven't got a clue, but in this case, I think it means they're focusing on Sheila Tierney. Who, according to her stepsister Irene Talbot, wouldn't have done something like that. At least, not in that manner."

We arrived at the Harbor Inn. The parking lot was filling up, and people were streaming inside. "Looks like they're going to have a good turnout," Leslie said as she hunted for a parking spot.

"Nothing like murder and gossip to bring everyone together," Jayne said.

We crossed the lobby quickly. The scents emanating from the outdoor restaurant reminded me I hadn't had lunch today. Come to think of it, I hadn't had dinner last night either.

"Want to go to the Café after the meeting?" I asked Jayne.

"Maybe for a quick drink if it's not too late. I had dinner before Mom picked me up."

The garden club meeting was being held in one of the conference rooms, and we could hear the excited buzz before we even reached the hallway. At five to seven, the room was almost completely full. Brian, the owner of the inn, was bringing in extra chairs.

"Standing room only," Jayne said.

"Not for me." Leslie dashed to snag a chair in the center of the middle row of seats.

"I'll stand," I said. The better to be able to see everyone and everything.

I wasn't the only one with that idea. I smiled at Ryan Ashburton standing on one side of the double doors and pretended not to see Louise Estrada on the other.

The room was a sea of gray and dyed-blonde hair, and three-quarters of the people here were women. Almost everyone was over sixty, although I did see a handful of people in their forties or fifties. People with full-time jobs and school-aged children didn't usually have the time to take up a hobby as demanding as serious gardening. Most of these people were well dressed and groomed, and I saw more than a few tennis bracelets, diamond earrings, expensive Italian loafers, and designer jackets.

I spotted Mrs. Ramsbatten in the front row, chatting to the woman next to her. Officer Stella Johnson's grandmother, a regular card partner of Uncle Arthur, was here, as were a number of customers of the Emporium or Mrs. Hudson's.

Four people, two women and two men, were at the front of the room, standing behind the long table, draped in a white cloth, that had been prepared with microphones, pads of paper and pens, glasses and water jugs. They talked in low voices and threw anxious glances at the restless crowd.

Finally, they pulled out their chairs and sat down, and an expectant hush fell over the onlookers. The older woman rapped the gavel on the table. "If the meeting can come to order. Thank you. I see some new faces in the crowd, so let me introduce myself. I am Patricia Markham, the chair of the board of the West London Garden Club. In a moment, Mr. Levy will present the preliminary report from the garden tour, but first I know you'll all want to join me in a moment of silence in the memory of our dear friend, long-standing member, master gardener, and inspiration to lovers of gardens everywhere, Ms. Anna Wentworth."

The room fell silent and heads bowed.

The silence didn't last. The door flew open to reveal Sheila Tierney standing in the entrance. She paused for a moment, giving every head time to lift and turn, and then she walked down the aisle, eyes fixed straight ahead, as slowly and graciously as though she were at church and this was her own wedding. Eyes widened and the whispering began.

Sheila wore a bright pink dress with a pink and green silk scarf tied loosely around her neck and high-heeled green sandals on her feet. The dress was new and expensive, and it fit properly, cut to accommodate the fresh poundage on her hips. Gold hoops were in her ears and a gold bracelet around her wrist. She looked to have come straight from the salon: her hair fell in a sleek golden cascade to her shoulders, her manicure was unchipped, and her makeup fresh.

She reached the front of the room, and the whispers died away. You could have heard the proverbial pin drop.

"It would appear," she said to the people at the front table, her voice pitched to carry, "you forgot to leave a seat for me."

"I . . . didn't know if you'd be able to make it," the woman with the gavel said.

One of the men leapt to his feet. "Here, take mine."

Sheila climbed the two steps to the podium. "Thank you, Norman." She sat down, feet together, back straight. She stared out over the audience. People shifted in their seats; some glanced away.

"Please," she said at last, "do continue."

"We were about to have a moment in memory of Anna," Mrs. Markham said.

"Is that so?" Sheila said. "I thought we were a garden club. Isn't our mandate to promote and nurture gardens in all their forms? Not to honor those who destroy them."

The room erupted. Some people sprang to their feet, yelling. Others turned to their neighbors and exchanged excited whispers. Mrs. Markham pounded her gavel on the table.

Louise Estrada and Ryan Ashburton threw each other glances.

"She's blunt enough," Jayne whispered to me.

"That's a preposterous accusation," a man yelled. He left his seat and hurried up the aisle. Ryan stepped away from the wall. "Everyone knows you wrecked your garden yourself."

"Why would I do that?" Sheila asked, her voice calm and steady.

"Because you're a bitter and jealous woman, that's why!"

"Point of order, Madam Chair," Sheila said. "Personal insults are not to be tolerated."

Mrs. Markham opened her mouth. She closed it again.

"Everyone in this room," Sheila said, "should be able to understand what my garden meant to me and how devastated I was at the damage inflicted on it. I worked hard on my garden and every plant in it, and I was extremely proud of it." She smiled. "I had picked out the place on my mantle where I planned to display the trophy. You all knew it was going to be mine."

People murmured.

The standing man shook his fist. "You deliberately destroyed it so you could accuse Anna."

Sheila shook her head slowly, as though remarking on the man's foolishness.

Mrs. Ramsbatten stood up. She waved her cane in the air, and the woman next to her ducked. "Do sit down, George. Sheila is on the board of this club, and she has a right to be here. Let's continue with the meeting."

George huffed but he slunk back to his seat.

"I, for one," Mrs. Ramsbatten said, "want to express my sorrow at the death of Anna Wentworth and offer my condolences to her husband, Michael."

"Hear, hear," a voice called. Mrs. Ramsbatten sat down.

Ryan made his way toward me. "Isn't that your neighbor?" he whispered.

"Yes, it is. She and some of her friends take care of our garden for us. Why do you ask?"

"No reason. Does she always use a cane?"

"Most of the time."

"She's very short, isn't she?" he said.

I gave him a look, but he'd turned his attention away from me.

The room fell silent. Once again, heads bowed.

Not every head. Ryan, Estrada, and I watched the crowd. Sheila Tierney watched us.

"That's enough," she declared after about fifteen seconds had passed. "Now, on to business. Mrs. Ramsbatten, how many tickets were sold for the day?"

Heads popped back up.

Mrs. Ramsbatten stood once again. At her full height, she was barely as tall as the people seated on either side of her. She spoke to Mrs. Markham. "Is this the order of business?"

"No, it is not. I don't expect you to have the final numbers for us yet, not after all that happened. We called this special meeting not only to remember Anna but to remind our members that if they know anything, anything at all that might help to find Anna's killer, the police would like to speak to them."

"Or find whoever destroyed Sheila's garden," a voice called.

People murmured in agreement.

"I recognize Detective Ashburton standing at the back," a woman yelled. "We all know what happened. Why don't you hand yourself over to him right now, Sheila? Save him the trouble of having to come and find you."

Once again, the room filled with shouts. From what I could tell, about a third of the attendees protested Sheila being accused, another third were ready to march her to the gallows right now, and the rest thought she might have killed Anna, but if she did, she was right to do it: if anyone messed with their garden, they'd kill that person with their bare hands.

Ryan whispered into Estrada's ear, and she nodded. They were on the point, I thought, of breaking up the meeting.

Before they could do that, Sheila Tierney rose to her feet. The crowd fell silent. "Anna Wentworth," she said, "was a thoroughly unlikeable person who cowardly snuck around to my home in the dead of night and destroyed my garden. She might have deserved what happened to her, but it wasn't me who killed her. I suggest the police, if they want to find the person responsible, focus their attentions elsewhere." She turned to face Mrs. Markham. "It is clear that I do not have the support of my fellow members. Therefore, I hereby quit this board and hand in my resignation to the West London Garden Club. I expect a full refund of my membership fees."

She stepped off the podium and stalked down the center of the room, followed by every eye.

She reached the closed doors and said, "Good evening, Detective," to Ryan; then opened the door and walked out. The door closed silently behind her.

A shocked silence lasted for about two seconds, and then pandemonium erupted. Estrada slipped out of the room.

"That was well worth the price of admission," Jayne said. "What do you think she was playing at?"

"Irene said Sheila loves to be the center of attention," I said. "Maybe that's all it was. Maybe she did think she'd find some support here. Or maybe she hoped to set the cat among the pigeons and confuse everything."

"She certainly did that."

Mrs. Markham pounded the table with her gavel. No one paid her the slightest bit of attention.

Ryan walked to the front of the room, then turned and faced the crowd. He didn't have to say a word. All conversation halted mid-sentence.

"Thank you," he said. "I'm Detective Ashburton of the WLPD. I'm investigating the murder of Anna Wentworth. If any of you have any information, anything at all you think pertinent to our inquiry, I'd like to talk to you."

"Arrest Sheila Tierney," a voice called, "and be done with it."

"I'm afraid it doesn't work that way," Ryan said.

"As we are obviously not going to get any further work done," one of the men behind the table said, "I suggest we adjourn and table discussion of the tour to the regular meeting."

"I second that," someone called.

Hands shot into the air. Mrs. Markham gave the table one sharp rap and said, "Motion carried. Meeting adjourned."

People bounded to their feet. Some gathered in excited circles to talk while others headed for the doors. A good number made a rush for Ryan. Leslie Wilson remained in her seat, talking to her neighbor, and Louise Estrada slipped back into the room and made her way toward us.

"What brings you here tonight, Gemma?" she asked.

"We came with Leslie Wilson. She's a member of the club."

"Yeah," she said, "I'll totally buy that."

"It's true," Jayne protested. "Mom drove."

"She might have driven you, but I doubt your intense interest in gardening brought you out."

"I always enjoy a nice garden," I said.

"You have no reason to be interested in this case, Gemma. You have no connection with any of the parties involved. Stay out of it."

"What makes you think I don't know these people?"

"You think it wasn't one of the first things I checked?"

I wasn't sure what I thought about that. The first time we met, Louise Estrada had accused me of killing a woman. Our relationship had gone steadily downhill since then. She resisted what she considered my interference in police matters—what I call helping—and she didn't trust me not to have ulterior motives.

My on-again, off-again, on-again relationship with Ryan Ashburton didn't help things. Louise had complained to the chief of police that I had undue influence on Ryan. At first, I wondered if Estrada wanted Ryan's job and was out to undermine him any chance she got, but over the last few months, I'd thought she and I were starting to trust each other. Although she'd never come right out and say so, she'd seemed to appreciate my insights in the Lamb/Dumont cases last summer.

Apparently, I'd been wrong.

"If you start interfering in this investigation in order to show us up, Gemma," she said, "I will see that you're charged. Have a nice evening."

I watched her make her way toward Ryan and his crowd of eager-to-help citizens.

"She certainly told you," Jayne said.

"So she did."

"You still want to stop for a drink?"

"I could use something to eat," I said. "I doubt Ryan will be able to join us. Talking to those people is going to be a waste of time, but I understand it needs to be done. In this sort of a law-abiding, tax-paying, respectable crowd, anyone who had anything to say would have contacted the police already. I notice most of the people around Ryan are women. Fancy that."

"Why don't we have something in the bar here," Jayne said, "rather than go to the Café?"

"I like the Blue Water Café," I said.

"And I like it too, but you always have an ulterior motive for wanting to go there. Just so you know, Andy's gone to his parents' place for a couple of days. His brother and his family are visiting from California."

"How do you know that?" I asked.

She winked at me. "Because, Gemma, when I was out with him on Saturday night, he told me."

I gaped at her. "You were out with Andy? Like on a date?" My wildest dreams were coming true. "And you didn't tell me?"

"Yes, Gemma, we had a date. Your dreams for me might be coming true, and I'm telling you now. We've had a couple of casual dates, so early days yet. We went to a bar to listen to live music and out for a coffee after, and we both enjoyed the evening so much we want to do it again as soon as he's back. We've known each other for years—it seems like forever—but now I'm seeing him in a totally different light." She blushed prettily.

I was thrilled. Our friend Andy Whitehall was the owner and head chef at the Blue Water Café, a restaurant by the harbor. He adored Jayne and always had, and I figured he was perfect for her, but she'd always been oblivious to his intentions as she dated one unsuitable—in my opinion—man after another.

"Ready to go?" Leslie tucked her arm into her daughter's.

"We thought we'd stop for drink and maybe something to eat first," Jayne said. "Is that okay with you?"

"Sure."

In the summer months, the restaurant at the Harbor Inn expands onto the veranda, giving a fabulous view down the hill and out to sea. I hesitated at the French doors leading outside. It was a beautiful night, warm and clear, and almost every table was taken. "You two don't want dinner, and I don't mind having something light, so why don't we go into the bar instead? Easier to get a table."

A good number of club members had the same idea as us, and the bar was filling up. I snagged a small round table and comfortable leather chairs in the far corner of the room, and we settled ourselves. I wanted to quiz Jayne on every detail of her date with Andy, but I didn't know if she'd told her mother about that yet. Even I can be circumspect sometimes.

Not that Jayne wouldn't have done the same to me. She'd initially been more keen on Ryan and me getting back together than I had.

About that, I had to admit, she'd been right.

The waiter arrived and we placed our drink orders. I accepted a bar snacks menu.

"That was interesting, to say the least," Leslie said. "I've never seen many of those people before."

"They're not club members?" I asked.

"Most of them probably are. Not everyone attends every meeting. Some members don't go to any, but they pay their dues to get the newsletter and be on the roster for garden visits. No one checked memberships at the door, so I suspect we also attracted a fair share of the nosy and the ghoulish."

"I didn't see anyone from the paper," Jayne said.

"Irene's gone out of town for a few days," I said. "Some conference or other. The paper probably didn't have anyone else to send, or they didn't think it worthwhile."

The waiter brought our drinks—a soft drink for Leslie, who was driving, and wine for Jayne and me. We clinked glasses and I opened the menu. "Calamari looks good. I'll get that plus the bruschetta. Jayne? Leslie?"

Leslie shook her head and Jayne said, "Nothing for me, thanks."

I handed the waiter the menu. "Better make that two bruschetta." I knew from past experience that when Jayne said, "Nothing for me," she meant she'd have half of mine.

"Is this chair taken?" A woman gestured to the spare seat at our table. A cluster of people gathered around the table next to us, finding seats, arranging chairs, putting down bags.

"Help yourself," Jayne said.

"I'm hoping to go to Tampa in January with Nora," Leslie said to Jayne.

"That would be nice," Jayne said.

"Her sister has a place they won't be using for a few weeks, so we can stay there rent-free."

The bar was open to the lobby, and I saw Ryan and Louise Estrada walk by. Ryan's eyes flicked toward me, and the edges of his mouth turned up ever so slightly. I smiled in return and they carried on their way.

"There goes that incredibly handsome Detective Ashburton," a woman said from the next table.

Another woman giggled. "I was tempted to confess all, just to have him clap me in handcuffs."

They burst out laughing. The youngest of them must have been in her seventies. The waiter arrived at their table and began handing out large glasses of wine. If one of them was driving, I thought, she might find herself clapped in irons sooner than she expected. And it wouldn't be so funny.

"Terrible about what happened to poor Anna," someone said.

"Yes. It doesn't bear thinking about. Do you think Sheila did it?"

"Of course, she did. If Anna had messed with my garden, never mind my husband, I'd have done the same."

Jayne and Leslie discussed family matters. The waiter brought my food, but I ignored it and cradled my glass in my hands, leaned back in my chair, and listened to the conversation at the next table.

"Do you know that for sure? That David Tierney was having an affair with Anna?"

"That's what I heard. I forget who told me."

"It's not true. David Tierney has enough worries on his plate without getting up to no good with Anna. Or anyone else."

"What does that mean?"

"Ron told me, in the strictest confidence . . ." All the women leaned in to hear this strict confidence. I have to confess, I shifted slightly toward them myself. ". . . David's about to go under. He came to the bank last month, asking for a loan so he could make his next payroll. *Another* loan. Ron had to turn him down. Unless things turn around, and fast, his company will be bankrupt by the end of the summer."

"I'm sorry to hear that."

"Well, I'm not. When he started making serious money, Sheila suddenly started acting like she was *soooo* much better than the rest of us. Serves her right if she has to go back to teaching at West London High."

"My grandson had her for American history one year. He hated her. Said she was a horrible teacher."

"I can't believe she had the nerve to show up tonight and expect us to carry on with the meeting as though nothing had happened."

"She thought nothing of the sort. She came to make her point. She made it and left after creating as much drama as possible."

"I know this is going to sound inappropriate considering the circumstances, but do any of you know if Manuel's looking for work?"

The table erupted into such a loud burst of laughter that Jayne and Leslie broke off their conversation to look at them.

"What's so funny?" the woman who'd asked the question said.

"I'm sure Manuel will be looking for *work*. I can't imagine Mike Nixon's going to keep him on."

"Why not? He's an excellent gardener, isn't he?"

"Oh, Betty, you dear innocent thing. Don't you know?"

"Know what? I am totally at a loss as to what's so funny. I use McHenry's Garden Maintenance but they're doing an increasingly poor job of it. I'm thinking of hiring a person rather than a company. You never know who's going to show up when you employ a company."

"Manuel, my dear, was providing *extra services* to Anna."

"What sort of extra services?"

More shouts of laughter. I also didn't know what was so funny, but I was beginning to guess.

"Services of a *personal* nature."

Slowly the light dawned. Betty, the woman who was looking for a new gardener, turned every shade of pink and red imaginable. It was like watching a spectacular sunset in rapid motion.

"Is that true?" another woman asked.

"Totally true. Rosemarie Evans caught them almost in the act."

"Good heavens."

"Right there on the lounge chairs in broad daylight. Rosemarie knocked at the front door. Anna didn't answer, so she went around to the back. Got the shock of her life."

"Perhaps I'll stick with McHenry's Garden Maintenance," Betty said. "Did anyone tell the police that?"

The women looked at each other. They shrugged and shook their heads.

"Not any of my business."

"I'm not one to repeat gossip."

"I don't want to be involved. I'm sure Rosemarie told them."

"Has anyone had a problem with grubs in the lawn this year? Mine have been terrible, and I don't know what to do."

"Did you check Anna's web page? I think she wrote a couple of articles on lawn pests."

"I'll do that. I'll miss her."

"So will I. She was a marvelous gardener."

"To Anna," someone said.

They lifted their glasses and drank. The conversation moved on to other topics.

A Curious Incident

I turned my attention back to Leslie and Jayne. One plate of bruschetta was empty, and half the calamari was gone. Jayne licked cocktail sauce off her fingers.

"Learn anything?" she said in a low voice.

"A good deal. Ready to go?"

"You haven't eaten," Leslie said.

"No longer hungry. Looks like it didn't go to waste, though."

Jayne ducked her head. "I guess I was hungrier than I thought. I paid the bill already. It's on me."

We left the bar and crossed the lobby. I pulled out my phone and sent Ryan a text: *Learned something perhaps vital in AW case. Call me.*

He hadn't called by the time we arrived at my house. I said my good nights and got out of the car, and Jayne and Leslie drove away.

It was barely nine o'clock, and I decided to wait up for Ryan's call. He might not have been told about Manuel the gardener. Running a police investigation was an exercise in sorting the wheat from the chaff. People who didn't know anything but wanted to appear helpful—or satisfy their own desire to be involved—inundated the police with unnecessary and excessive details, whereas those with genuinely pertinent information often kept it to themselves, either not wanting to gossip or speak ill of the dead, or because they assumed someone else would see to it. And that someone else would assume the first someone else would see to it.

It was entirely possible Anna had been up to nothing more scandalous with Manuel the gardener than discussing the placement of flowers or how much to trim back the bushes. Gossip had a way of taking on a life of its own.

Then again, there isn't a more powerful motive for murder than a secret, illicit affair.

Violet ran into the mudroom and then ran out again.

Then back to the mudroom, where this time she sat by the door and whined.

I got the message loud and clear. She wanted her walk. I got down the leash, snapped it on her collar, and we set out. Ryan would call me before coming over.

I checked my phone maybe fifteen times during our short walk. Neither Ryan nor anyone else seemed to have reason to call or text me tonight.

Restless, I cut the walk short, and Violet and I headed home. We turned into Blue Water Place in time to see a WLPD car pull up in front of my house. I called to Violet to hurry, and we sped up.

Ryan and Estrada got out of the car. They weren't parked in front of my house, I realized, but the house next door. They opened the gate and walked together up the path between the bushes. The white petals of the daisies glowed in the deepening dusk.

"What's going on?" I called to them.

Ryan rang the bell and Estrada turned to face me. "When I saw the address of the house we were interested in, I hoped we'd be able to get in and out without running into you. Do you make a habit of lurking around on the street?"

I lifted the end of the leash in evidence. "Not lurking. Just out walking my dog. Ryan, did you get my text?"

"I did," he said, "but something came up."

"What?"

"Go home, Gemma." Estrada said. "This doesn't concern you." She rapped on the door and called out, "West London police."

A Curious Incident

The curtain in the living room window twitched, and Mrs. Ramsbatten's curly white head and hazel eyes appeared. I waved to her and pointed toward the door. The curtain dropped, and a moment later the door slowly opened, and my neighbor peered out. "Yes?"

"Police." Ryan flashed his badge. "May we have a word?" His posture and voice were stiff and formal. I did not have a good feeling about this. Ryan had been particularly interested in Mrs. Ramsbatten's lack of height a few hours earlier. I'd noticed but dismissed that at the time as a minor observation on his part. I should have remembered—I was remembering now—that Ryan didn't do minor observations.

"What's this about?" Mrs. Ramsbatten was dressed for bed in fuzzy pink slippers and a long white cotton nightgown trimmed with pink lace.

"I'd prefer to discuss it inside," Ryan said.

She threw me a confused and frightened look.

"I'm sure it's nothing," I said. "Routine inquiries. Probably to do with the garden club meeting."

Mrs. Ramsbatten edged back. Ryan and Estrada entered her house. Violet and I stepped forward.

Estrada whipped around. "Thank you for your time, Ms. Doyle. Your assistance will not be needed."

"I'd like her to stay," Mrs. Ramsbatten said.

It wasn't easy, but I refrained from giving Estrada a smirk as I marched into the house. Violet followed me, and Mrs. Ramsbatten showed her guests to the living room. Ryan's eyes opened wide, and Estrada said, "Goodness. What a lot of . . . things you have."

"Would you like a cup of coffee, Officers?" Mrs. Ramsbatten asked. "Gemma, tea? Or maybe a nice G&T?"

"No, thank you," Estrada said. "This isn't a social call."

My neighbor slowly sat down. None of the rest of us did. Violet ran in excited circles, not knowing what to sniff first.

"You were at the meeting at the Harbor Inn earlier this evening," Ryan said.

"That's right," my neighbor said. "I'm a longtime member of the garden club."

"You had a cane with you. May I see it?"

Comprehension dawned behind her eyes. She understood why they were here. "What will happen if I say no?"

"I'll ask a judge to issue a warrant first thing in the morning," Estrada said, "allowing us to search this house for any cane or similar object as well as shoes or boots. I'm confident of getting it. Will it be necessary to secure the warrant, Mrs. Ramsbatten?"

My neighbor gave me a pleading look, as though asking me to intervene. Tears welled up in her eyes.

"What have you done?" I said.

"I . . . I didn't mean any harm. I couldn't sleep; I often don't these days. Old bones, you know. I was excited about the garden tour. I decided it wouldn't hurt to have a sneak peek at Sheila's garden. Everyone said it would be the one to beat this year. I was surprised at that." She threw me a look. "I didn't believe Sheila could be such an excellent gardener, so I wanted to see for myself."

"You're talking about Sheila Tierney?" Ryan asked.

Mrs. Ramsbatten nodded.

I sat down. Fortunately, a chair was right behind my legs. I'd noticed the tiny footprints and the small round indentations myself when I'd examined the garden, but I'd assumed the footprints were made by Lauren or her friends and that the print was something of theirs. I cursed myself: never assume. In the words of the Great Detective, "There is nothing more deceptive than an obvious fact."

That was bad enough, but I'd forgotten Lauren had told me she hadn't been allowed in the backyard, in case she disturbed anything before the start of the tour.

Had Ryan also found prints of a cane and small feet in the copse of trees in the town park?

"Just so we're clear here, ma'am," Ryan said, "can you tell me what night it was that you couldn't sleep and went to see the Tierney garden."

Mrs. Ramsbatten pulled a tissue out of the sleeve of her nightgown and sniffled into it. "Sunday morning, around two."

"The day of the garden tour?" Estrada asked.

"Yes. The house was in darkness when I arrived, except for a light over the front door. I parked on the street, let myself through the gate, and went around to the back. I particularly enjoy a garden at night. All the plants at rest, sleeping peacefully, waiting for the sun to peek over the horizon. Small nocturnal animals moving around, others rustling in their sleep. So delightfully peaceful."

"Spare me," Estrada said. "Why didn't you tell us this? You had to have known the police are asking for information in this case and that we believe the vandalism to the Tierney garden is related to the murder of Anna Wentworth."

Mrs. Ramsbatten threw me a glance. "I didn't think it mattered. I didn't want to waste your time. I saw no damage. The garden was, I have to admit, spectacular. I admired it and left. I saw no one else."

"We wasted valuable police time trying to identify the marks left by your cane," Estrada said. "Not to mention prints of your feet on patches of ground. We first thought the prints were made by Lauren Tierney, but they're smaller than hers. We've had officers visiting Lauren's friends' houses, comparing shoes."

Mrs. Ramsbatten hung her head. "I didn't think it mattered. I didn't see any damage when I was there."

"We'll decide what matters," Estrada said.

"Sorry," Mrs. Ramsbatten mumbled.

"Did you go to the park on Northland Street on Sunday evening?" Estrada asked.

Mrs. Ramsbatten's head popped up. "No! I mean, no. Why would I go there?"

"It was a nice evening on Sunday," Estrada said. "Nice night for a walk."

"No."

"We now have to go back to the park and search it again. If we're going to find evidence of your footprints and cane, it would be better if you tell us."

Estrada towered over her, but Mrs. Ramsbatten straightened her shoulders and lifted her chin: Mrs. Claus staring down an impudent but very tall elf. "I can promise you, Detective, I have not been to that park for several years."

"We'll see if that's true," Estrada said darkly. "If we find—"

I stood up. "It's all out in the open now. No harm done. I'm sure you'll want Mrs. Ramsbatten to think very carefully about what she saw, if anything, when she was at the Tierney home. Maybe someone lurking under a street lamp or something. Ryan, as long as you're here, I learned something earlier—"

Ryan ignored me. "You say you drove to the Tierney house," he said to Mrs. Ramsbatten.

Mrs. Ramsbatten folded herself into a tiny ball of pink, white, and gray. Her nod was almost imperceptible.

"What did you drive there in?"

Her voice was very low. "My car."

"You mean your 2005 Ford Fiesta?"

"Yes."

"The one with the vehicle permit that expired three months ago? Did you have with you the driver's license that was not renewed six months ago because you couldn't pass a vision test?"

"Yes."

Oh dear.

Chapter Nine

Ryan advised Mrs. Ramsbatten to sell her car as soon as possible. He also told her he'd have uniformed officers looking out for her driving it, and if they found her doing so . . . He didn't finish the sentence.

I was relieved that they didn't arrest her for driving without a license or for vandalism either, never mind murder.

"Batty old lady," Estrada grumbled as we walked down the sidewalk.

"She's not batty in the least," I said. "Just unable to sleep and interested in gardens and hoping no one would ask to see her driver's license at that time of night. You won't find any evidence of her being in the park. Even if she wanted to vandalize Sheila's garden, she had no reason to kill Anna, and she certainly wouldn't be capable of sneaking up on and overpowering a larger and much younger woman."

"Maybe she's not as frail as she seems," Estrada said.

"She's been living next door to us since we moved in. Gradually slowing down as the years passed. She's frail."

"You said 'even if she wanted to vandalize the garden,'" Ryan said. "What did you mean by that?"

"Nothing."

He studied my face. Estrada looked from one of us to the other. "What did you mean by that, Gemma?" Ryan repeated.

"Mrs. Ramsbatten isn't terribly fond of Sheila."

"By 'not terribly fond,' you mean . . ." Ryan said.

"Doesn't like her. It would seem not many people do. Even her students at the high school didn't. Or so I heard."

"You seem to be hearing a lot about this," Estrada said.

"Can't help it. A branch of the West London grapevine runs directly through the tearoom and from there into the Emporium. There's a lot of ground, though, between disliking someone and murdering them. Anyway, Anna was murdered, not Sheila."

"There was no moon that night," Ryan said. "It was dark, and the attack swift. We're not yet positive Anna was the intended victim."

"That complicates things. I never met Anna. Did she and Sheila look alike?"

"Sheila's a good deal taller and heavier," Estrada said. "Anna was slight, around the size of your friend Jayne."

"Easy to overpower in the dark then."

Estrada said nothing.

"Be all that as it may," Ryan said, "I don't like to have valuable police time wasted, and your neighbor wasted a heck of a lot of ours. What did you want to talk to me about?"

"Did I?"

"You called me. Said you had something to tell me."

I glanced at Estrada, whose head was cocked to one side as she listened to us. I'd dropped Violet's leash, and she trotted down the sidewalk and turned into our driveway.

"Garden club gossip says Anna was having an affair with her gardener. His name's Manuel something. Quite a handsome young chap."

"How do you know that?" Estrada asked. "What he looks like, I mean."

"I paid a condolence call on Mike Nixon. And before you ask why I did that, he's a regular customer at my shop, and Donald Morris, whom you know, is a friend of his. Donald invited me to come with him. We sat outside on the patio, and the gardener was at work."

"We've spoken to Manuel." For a police detective, Louise Estrada had a surprisingly open face. I could tell the news of this supposed affair had come as news to her. Then again, maybe she thought I could read her mind (people do sometimes) and tried so hard to cover up her reactions, she over-compensated.

"I don't know if it's true or not, about the affair," I said, "but I thought you might be interested."

"Dare I ask how you know about this alleged affair?" Estrada asked.

I told her what I'd learned in the bar of the Harbor Inn.

"Do you always make a habit of listening to other people's conversations?"

"Don't you?" I said.

"I am employed by the citizens of West London to do precisely that," she said. "You are not."

"I wasn't listening at keyholes or wiretapping phone conversations. I was in a public place, and the people next to me were freely talking."

"Thanks, Gemma," Ryan said. "We have interviewed the gardener. He said nothing about any affair or any sort of personal relationship between him and Ms. Wentworth, so we'll go back and talk to him again."

"If he also wasted our time," Estrada said, "he'll be very sorry."

Grumbling about civilians who interfere when they have nothing to contribute and those who don't come forward when they do, Estrada walked away.

"Good night, Gemma," Ryan said. "I can't be mad at you for coming to your neighbor's aid when you saw us arrive, or for telling us what you heard in a public conversation, but I will be if you keep interfering."

"I'll stay out of it. I told Lauren I'd see what I could do, and I have. I don't know what I can achieve that you can't. It's early still; any chance you can pop around later? I promise not to ask about the case."

He smiled at me. "I do love you, Gemma," he said in a low voice, conscious of Estrada sitting a few feet away in the driver's seat of the cruiser. "I expect to put in a night of it. We have to search the park one more time in case we missed any tiny footprints or cane imprints, and I want to talk to this gardener again."

Chapter Ten

I meant what I said—when I said it. I wanted nothing more to do with this case, but more to the point, I didn't know what else I could do.

Once again, my hand was forced, and I found myself getting more involved than ever.

At twenty past three on Wednesday, as I was beginning to look forward to my tea break/partners' meeting/gossip session with Jayne, Lauren came into the Emporium. Her eyes were red, and she sniffled into a tattered tissue. Her golden hair was dull and hung loosely around her shoulders, looking as though it hadn't been brushed this morning. Her T-shirt was rumpled, a stain marred her shorts, and the laces of her right trainer dragged on the floor.

I abandoned the customer I was attending to, in mid-sentence, and hurried across the room. "Lauren! Is something wrong? Have the police come for your mother?"

She shook her head. Her eyes were wide and frightened. "I don't know. I mean, I don't think so."

I shouldn't have spoken quite so loudly. The store was full, and all the customers stopped whatever they were doing to listen in. Moriarty vaulted off the lap of a woman seated in the chair in the reading nook, flipping through *Sherlock Chronicles*, a glimpse into the making of the Benedict Cumberbatch series.

"Why don't we go upstairs to my office," I said. "Ashleigh, will you take over here? First, please pop into the tearoom and ask them for a glass of milk and a sandwich. And tell Jayne I won't be at the partners' meeting today."

"I'll do that, Gemma," a customer said. "Lauren's in my daughter's class at school. How are you doing, dear?"

Lauren mumbled something polite yet noncommittal. I put my arm around her shoulder and led her upstairs as Moriarty ran on ahead.

I shoved a stack of books off the visitor's chair and told her to sit down. She did so. She looked very small and so vulnerable, crumpled in on herself, her hands twisting in her lap.

Small, vulnerable, and frightened.

"What's happened?" I asked.

"Mom's gone."

"Gone? What do you mean 'gone'? Did the police come for her?" I couldn't believe Ryan, or even Louise Estrada, would arrest Sheila and leave her daughter to wander the streets by herself.

Lauren's hair flew around her face. "I don't think so. I don't know. She's . . . gone. When I got up this morning, she wasn't in the house. I don't know where she went. I've . . . I've been waiting all day. I don't know what to do. So I came here." She lifted her head and looked into my eyes. "I hope that's okay."

"Of course it's okay. Where's your father?"

"Away on business."

"He went away while his wife's under suspicion of murder?" I shouldn't have said that out loud, but I did.

Lauren hurried to his defense. "Dad's super busy, Gemma. His job's really important. He owns his own company. He has employees. They need him."

"I'm sure they do." I didn't say that his wife and daughter needed him more.

"Besides, he can't handle drama. He and Mom don't get along so well anymore." Her voice broke. "They had a big fight last night. She went to the garden club meeting, and when she got home, she asked him not to go on his trip, but he said she got herself into this fix, so she could get herself out of it. He grabbed his bags and left for the airport. Snowball and I went to bed, and when I got up, Mom was gone too."

"She didn't leave you a note or anything?"

Another shake of the head. Moriarty jumped into her lap. He nudged her arm with his head, and she stroked him. He purred and curled into a contented ball. "This is a nice cat. What's his name?"

"Moriarty."

"Like the bad guy in Sherlock Holmes."

"Yes. You know that?"

"Everyone knows that. I wanted to come and see Benedict Cumberbatch when he was here, but Mom was . . . busy. Is he going to come back?"

"Probably not. I have a picture of him that he signed for me. Would you like it?"

She gave me a tight smile. "Yes."

Ashleigh slipped into the office, carrying a white paper bag. "Here you go." She put it on my desk. "Anything else?"

"No," I said. "Thanks."

"If you need anything . . ."

"Thanks."

She left and I ripped open the paper bag. "Here, have something to eat. Oh, look—you got roast beef on a baguette. That's my favorite."

Lauren held out a shaking hand. I put the food in it and placed the cup of milk on the desk.

"Would you like some?" she asked politely.

"I had a late lunch," I lied.

She took a small bite.

"Maybe your mum left you a note and it . . . blew away or something. Where might she have gone if she was upset? Her parents' place? A girlfriend's?"

"My grandparents live in Arizona. We don't see them much. I can't think of any girlfriends. The only real friend Mom had was Anna, but . . . well, they haven't been friends for a while."

"How about your aunt Irene? Why don't I call her now?"

"She's away. Some journalism conference in Boston. Doesn't matter, Mom wouldn't have gone there."

"Did she take her car?"

Lauren ate steadily as she talked. "I checked. It's in the garage."

At that moment, my phone rang. I glanced at it and was relieved to see Irene's number. I gave Lauren a thumbs-up and answered. "Irene, hi. I—"

"Gemma, thank heavens you're there. I need your help."

"What for?"

"Sheila sent me a text early this morning. I had my phone off, and the message somehow disappeared. I only saw it now, when I got a text from someone else. Sheila's left home and she needs me to go around and get Lauren. I called the house, but no one answered. Sheila's not picking up either. It's almost four o'clock, but she might be sleeping or not answering. I need you to go over there and—"

"It's okay," I said. "Calm down. Lauren's here. We're at the store."

An enormous sigh came down the line. "Oh, thank heavens. Is she all right?"

"Perfectly fine. Eating a roast beef sandwich as we speak." I smiled at Lauren and got a shy grin in return. She took a sip of the milk.

"I don't suppose you know where David is?" Irene asked.

"Out of town, according to Lauren."

"Sheila?"

"That remains unknown."

"I can't believe she'd do something like that. Run off in the middle of the night and expect someone to rush over and take care of her daughter. David's no better. Most spineless man I've ever known."

"In fairness, it doesn't sound like he knew she was going to do a runner."

"I'm sick and tired of being fair. To either of them. Thanks, Gemma. I know Lauren's in good hands with you."

"With me? Aren't you coming to get her?"

Lauren watched me with her dark intelligent eyes.

"I've a dinner meeting with some people I really want to meet, Gemma. People who might be influential in my career. Then tomorrow, a couple of prominent journalists will be speaking at the conference. You don't mind looking after Lauren, do you? I'll be home first thing Friday morning. Maybe even tomorrow night, if things wrap up in time."

"I—"

"Great! Thanks. I owe you one."

"That you do," I said, conscious of Lauren listening to every word. "Do you have any idea where Sheila might have gone?"

"We aren't close, as I told you. To be honest, Gemma, I don't know much about her life, outside of Lauren. Give my love to Lauren. Tell her I'm learning so much about what's happening in the changing media world, and I'm excited about it."

"Send me that text, will you? I want to see it."

"Okay. 'Bye." She hung up.

I put my phone away and smiled at Lauren. "Irene's . . . uh . . . caught up in her conference. She'll be home on Friday. In the meantime, if your mum doesn't come back, you can stay with me. Would you like that?"

She nodded. "Okay. I bet you have some good books."

"That I do. We need to go around to your house and collect a few of your things. Why don't you go downstairs and pick out a few books to take with you."

Lauren folded the remains of the sandwich in its paper wrapping, lifted Moriarty off her lap, and stood up. "Did Benedict Cumberbatch stay at your house when he was here?"

"No. He was only in West London for a few hours."

Lauren left, followed by Moriarty. I leaned back in my chair. Poor kid. I didn't know Lauren well, but what I did know, I liked. She deserved better than parents too self-absorbed to pay any attention to her.

As for Sheila, had she done a runner? Was she on the lam, as Americans would say? Sounded like it. Running away is a mighty strong indicator of guilt, but maybe she ran—guilty or not— because she thought the police were close to arresting her.

Was what Lauren told me even true? About David and Sheila fighting and David storming out? Not that I thought for a minute the girl was lying to me, but her parents might have set it up to look like they'd gone their separate ways. Meanwhile, maybe they were planning to meet up in Brazil or some such place that didn't have an extradition treaty with the United States.

Once again, footsteps on the stairs. This time, they were light and confident ones.

"What's going on?" Jayne said. "Ashleigh said you had an emergency."

"Of a sort." I told her quickly what had happened.

"That's terrible. The poor girl."

"I could have told her to call her friends and ask for a place to stay for a couple of days, but I didn't have the heart. How humiliating would that have been? I bet her mother's the topic of a lot of whispered conversations at her friends' houses."

"Probably a good thing school's out for summer vacation," Jayne said. "She doesn't need to walk the hallways while everyone's speculating as to whether or not her mother's a murderer."

"She can stay at my house until Irene or one of her parents gets back. I won't have to miss any time at work. She can sit in the reading nook with a book while I'm here."

"She's welcome to come next door for lunch or a snack," Jayne said.

"I might ask her to help out around the store. It would take her mind off things. What's the time now?"

"Almost four."

"We close at seven tonight. I'll take Lauren to her house, get what she'll need for a few days away, and then head to my place for dinner."

"Do you want some help? I have a gym class at five thirty, but I can come back."

"Thanks. I don't know much about looking after preteen girls."

"You think I do?"

"You're invited to have dinner with us. I'll find something in the freezer. In the meantime, I don't want to, but I fear I have to do my civic duty. The police are sure to have told Sheila not to leave town. Ryan needs to know she skipped out."

"I'll be back before you close the store, and we can walk over to Lauren's together." Jayne waved goodbye and left.

I opened my phone. The text from Irene popped up on the screen, and I read it quickly.

Sheila's message had been sent at five AM. *I HAVE to get out of here. Everyone's talking about me. Accusing me. Blaming me. Take care of Lauren for few days. Thx.*

No mention of where she planned to go—if she even had a plan—or if anyone was with her.

If Sheila doesn't want people talking about her, I thought, *she shouldn't have shown up at the garden club meeting last night and pretty much dared them to talk about nothing else.*

Was she deliberately that manipulative, or did she want to cause a fuss and was surprised when her attempt at taking over the center of attention backfired?

Right now, however, her thought process didn't matter one little bit as far as I was concerned.

I called Ryan and got voicemail. "Hi, it's me. You told me not to get any further involved in the Wentworth murder, but something happened that is totally out of my control. Really. Lauren Tierney showed up here a short while ago. Her mother appears to have skipped town. I figured you needed to know. I can't imagine that looks good. Lauren's father's away, presumably on business, and she has no place else to go, so I'm letting her stay at my place until things get sorted out. 'Bye. Oh, Lauren says her mom's car's still in the garage." I hung up.

Ryan would be furious—at me—but this time I was totally innocent. I had not interfered. Interference had found me.

He'd be furious at Sheila as well. Even if they didn't arrest her for the murder when they found her, they'd be mighty angry at her for leaving without telling them. They might even arrest her for the murder. As I'd said, skipping town doesn't look good.

Poor Lauren.

The police shouldn't have much trouble finding Sheila. If she didn't take her own car, someone had to have driven her. A taxi or a friend. The police would find out soon enough. It's mighty hard to disappear in the modern world. Not without a lot of shady contacts.

Did Sheila have shady contacts?

I had no reason to believe she was anything but what she appeared to be: an upper-middle-class West London garden enthusiast with a bad temper and an inflated sense of self-importance.

* * *

Lauren had curled up in the comfortable wingback chair in the reading alcove with Moriarty and *No Matter How Improbable* by Angela Misri. The cat didn't leave her side for the rest of the day.

As promised, Jayne arrived at quarter to seven. Ashleigh had left and a few customers browsed. Lauren read while Moriarty stood guard over her.

"Good book?" Jayne asked.

Lauren looked up with a smile. "Yeah! I want to be a doctor, but now I'm thinking I'd like to own a bookstore. Then I can read all day and meet famous authors and actors."

"While you sip champagne and nibble on bonbons," I said.

"What's a bonbon?"

"A small chocolate. You may notice I don't have any lying around for me to nibble on as I work. Speaking of work, tomorrow I'll put you to work stacking the shelves and packing up books to be returned because they didn't sell. That'll put you off owning your own shop." It would certainly put her off owning a store in which the storage rooms are on the upper floor and there's no lift. "Closing in ten minutes. We'll stop in at your house and then go to mine."

"Can I take this book? I'm almost finished, and I can't wait to find out what happens."

"Sure," I said.

The last customers of the day were two older women dressed in sensible shoes, black socks pulled up to their calves, and lurid Bermuda shorts, with T-shirts in clashing colors. Their hair was thin and their noses bright red, the result of too much time spent in the sun. One of them put a Sherlock Holmes finger puppet on the counter, and I went to the cash register to ring it up.

"*Such* a charming little town," the elder of the women said to me. "But sadly, nothing is as it seems these days." She tut-tutted in disapproval.

"We heard you had a gruesome murder recently." The other woman shivered with delight.

I gave them a sharp look. "I didn't have anything of the sort. That'll be seven dollars and fifteen cents."

One woman laboriously counted out the money in dollar bills and coins while her friend said, "I mean your town, of course. Not you *personally*. Did you know the dead woman? Bless her," she added quickly.

"I did not." I stuffed the puppet into a bag and shoved it at them.

Disappointment crossed her face. "I heard she was murdered by a garden club rival. Imagine caring so much about a garden! The woman must be insane. Is she going to plead diminished responsibility, do you think? Have you seen that garden?"

Lauren had stood up, ready to leave. Her lip trembled as she listened to the conversation, and tears welled up in her eyes.

"If you like that book," Jayne said quickly, "Gemma can recommend lots more."

Moriarty leapt onto the top of the shelf nearest the door.

"I don't know about any garden," I said, "and I don't pay attention to scurrilous gossip. If, however, you like tales of murder so much, maybe you should consider buying a book next time you're in a bookstore. Or can't you read?"

"What kind of a question is that? Of course, I can read!"

"How about you?" I said to the other woman.

She blinked.

"Brilliant," I said. "This is a bookstore after all. We sell books. But not today, and not to you. Goodbye. We're closed."

"You're mighty rude for a store clerk. I have half a mind to tell your boss."

"You do that," I said.

"Come on, Nancy, let's go. Never mind her; she's English. You know what they're like. She doesn't know any better."

"Cheerio!" I said.

They headed for the door at a rapid trot. Moriarty took one giant leap off the shelf and flew across the room, passing inches in front of their faces.

The women screamed and batted at the empty air, tripping over themselves in their haste to get out the door.

"We could have recaptured the colonies, you know," I called after them. "If we'd wanted to. We decided not to bother. We had an empire to build."

Moriarty looked at me. I looked at him. I lifted my right hand. He lifted his right paw. We gave each other a mental high five.

"Now, where were we?" I said. "Right—going to Lauren's and then home for supper. I'm starving. Come along, Jayne. Don't dawdle."

Chapter Eleven

As we walked, I asked Lauren if her mother ever went away for a few days, maybe for some "me" time.

"Nope."

"Does she have a favorite place on the Cape?"

Lauren thought. "She likes Hyannis Port. Last year, she wanted to move there, but Dad said we couldn't afford it."

"Any place in particular in Hyannis Port?"

"Nope. We went there for lunch once after shopping. It was super nice. I don't remember the name of the restaurant, though. Near the harbor."

"Your mum's on the board of the West London Garden Club. Does she belong to any other groups or organizations?"

"Nope."

"She used to be a high school teacher. Does she keep in touch with the people she worked with there?"

"No. She hated that school. Says it was the worst five years of her life."

Okay then.

"What school do you go to?" Jayne asked.

"West London Prep."

Jayne and I exchanged glances over Lauren's head. A private school. Very snooty, I'd heard, not to mention expensive.

"Do you like it?" Jayne asked.

"It's okay."

"You said your mum doesn't have any close friends," I said, "but she was active in the garden club. She must have had people around to talk about gardening or organizing the tour. Stuff like that."

"Sometimes," Lauren said. "She liked talking to people about gardening. Mostly 'cause they'd tell her that her garden was the best."

More glances between Jayne and me. Lauren was not presenting her mother in a particularly good light.

"Other than that, she didn't like the people at the club much. She was really mad over the winter when someone suggested having the annual meeting at the Beach Front Hotel 'cause it's cheaper than the Harbor Inn. Mom said she wouldn't step foot in the Beach Front." Lauren sighed. "Mom likes nice things. I hope she's someplace nice now."

"She'll be home soon." Jayne rested her hand lightly on Lauren's shoulder.

I wasn't so sure.

"I have tennis on Saturday. It's the tournament and it's really important I go 'cause it's a doubles game. I hope Mom—or Dad—is back in time to take me."

"They will be," Jayne said.

"If not, Irene or I will see that you make it," I said.

Lauren had a key and she let us into the house. Snowball ran to greet us the minute she heard the door opening, and Lauren bent down and scooped the kitten up. She peered at me over the ball of squirming white fur and pink ears. "I can bring Snowball, right, Gemma? She's never been alone overnight except when she was locked in that shed. She'll be extra super good, won't you, Snowball?"

The cat meowed in agreement.

What could I say? The only cat Violet had ever met was Moriarty. That meeting had not gone well, and I feared Violet had been traumatized for life. Even now, years later, she cowered against my legs, shivering with terror if a cat crossed our path on our walks.

"Do you have a carrying basket?" I asked.

"Yes." Lauren ran for the stairs. "I'll be right back."

"No hurry. Bring enough clothes for several days. Don't forget your toothbrush." I strolled down the hall and peeked into rooms.

"What are you doing?" Jayne asked.

"As I have been invited in, I intend to see what I can see."

"You mean you're searching for clues?"

"If you want to put it like that. The den's the best place to find papers and such."

"What did Ryan say when you called him?"

"I left a message, but he hasn't returned it. I would have thought he'd want to talk to Lauren to find out if her mother gave any indication of where she might have gone. Although I can tell him that she didn't."

"Did you call Lauren's dad?"

"No. I should, but I don't want to bother. By bother, I mean bother me, not him. I'd happily bother him. The fool."

"She's such a nice girl."

"She is," I said.

Whereas Anna had put all her time and energy into her garden, neglecting the interior of her house, Sheila's home was recently updated and well furnished. The couch and love seat in the living room were light-green leather, the coffee table made of wood and glass, the paintings bright and cheerful. A stack of gardening magazines sat on a side table next to a brown leather chair. Another side table held pictures in silver frames. No overlit school portraits of Lauren, no dated wedding pictures, no blurry photos of family gatherings. They all showed Sheila in her garden, shaking hands with town dignitaries—I recognized the mayor—or accepting some sort of award.

Self-obsessed was definitely the word of the day.

We went into the den, and I could immediately tell that this was David's room. Faded and worn furniture, big desk piled high with papers, many of which were covered in coffee stains, a half-empty mug. Framed photos of a smiling David shaking hands with variations of middle-aged men with expensive haircuts dressed in suits or golf shirts filled the walls. The computer was new and high end, and the office chair behind the desk probably cost in the several-thousand-dollar range. I switched the computer on, and while it booted up, I flicked through the papers on the desk. Spreadsheets and budget plans, mostly. I didn't have time to examine the pages in detail, but I cast my eyes over them. Plenty of brackets, meaning negative numbers. I found an envelope with the return address of a law firm, but it was empty.

Conveniently, the computer was not password protected. I pulled up the expensive chair and took a seat. My body just about melted into the leather comfort. "I might get a chair like this for my own office. I assume it would be tax deductible."

"What are you doing?" Jayne asked. "You can't search their computer."

"I can, and I intend to. Any expectation of privacy the Tierneys might have had disappeared when they abandoned their daughter into my care. Besides, if David wanted to secure his information, he should have password-protected it."

"Would that have kept you out?"

"For a minute or two. Go upstairs and check how Lauren's getting on, please. If you can stay in her room with her, that would be good. I want to have a look around the house."

I opened computer files at random and scanned them quickly. They confirmed what I'd learned earlier in my search of the internet. David Tierney's company sold software he'd developed himself that took online orders for fast-food restaurants. The program then used the orders to somehow assist with using social media to generate more sales. I wasn't entirely sure how that would work; if I put my customers' data on the internet, I'd hear about it soon enough, but that didn't matter now. David had two full-time permanent employees, and he used contractors and other consultants as required. His computer files were neat and well organized, which made it easy to snoop. His office was in the nearby town of Chatham, but it appeared as though he did a lot of work on this computer. It didn't take me long to realize David was in financial trouble—severe financial trouble. Going back month by month, I could see the negative numbers on his balance sheets growing steadily. Six months ago, he got a big influx of cash—perhaps a bank loan?—but that almost immediately disappeared into the sea of red ink.

I flipped to the folder labeled "Personal" and discovered that he'd taken out a second mortgage on this house six months ago, which would explain the fresh cash.

It was unlikely David's financial situation had anything to do with the death of Anna Wentworth—although I wouldn't rule anything out—but it would explain the tension between David and Sheila, which Lauren had commented on, and the fact that

Sheila, who "liked nice things," couldn't buy new clothes when she'd put on weight.

I opened his email program. There was far too much for me to read in a short time, so I searched for a few keywords. "Garden" brought up an email from Sheila sent last week, reminding him (more like ordering him) to be out of the house all day Sunday. *Interesting,* I thought, *that they communicate by email.* "Anna Wentworth" and "Mike Nixon" produced no results. One email subject line was "Final warning." I opened and read it. The letter was from an independent contractor David had hired to do a job, telling David—in very blunt, very nonlegal terms—that if he didn't pay monies owned by the end of the month, the matter would be handed over to the lawyers.

Last of all, I found an email folder organized by month. It was a record of airline, train, and hotel bookings, and there were a lot of them. David appeared to travel to all parts of the United States and took trips several times a month. A year ago, he'd flown business class and stayed at luxury hotels. That had changed over the last few months to economy seats on red-eye flights and chain budget hotels.

How angry might he be at his reduced circumstances? Had he asked Sheila to economize and she'd refused to do more than not buy a new pair of shorts? Maintaining gardens of garden-tour quality wasn't cheap.

Might he have taken his anger out on his wife's garden?

The police would have asked David if he knew anything about the destruction to the garden. I had to assume he'd denied doing it. If he'd confessed, they wouldn't still be looking into it.

I leaned back in the comfortable, ergonomically correct chair and thought. I crossed my legs, and my foot hit something. I peered under the desk.

A trash can. Full of papers.

I lifted it up and put it on my lap.

Conveniently, David hadn't emptied his trash for a few days. I found the letter that went with the lawyer's envelope. He was being sued by a former employee for back wages. Another letter had been sent by Lauren's school, reminding him that fees were long overdue and had to be paid in full if her place was to be kept for next term.

I wondered if Sheila knew just how much financial trouble they were in.

Only one way to find out. By searching her computer.

I put the trash can back under the desk and switched off David's computer. I wiped down the keyboard and the computer's power switch with the hem of my shirt, but otherwise didn't worry about leaving my fingerprints. I had every reason to be in this house: I'd been invited in by a resident.

Soft voices drifted down the wide staircase, and I followed them. At the top of the stairs, I peeked into the first room on the right. Jayne and Lauren were sitting on Lauren's bed, their legs folded beneath them, with Snowball curled up on the girl's lap.

Jayne's short and petite, and Lauren's tall for her age. They looked like two teenagers having a sleepover.

"This is a smashing room," I said.

"Does that mean it's nice?"

I laughed. "More than nice. Brilliant."

Lauren smiled at me. "Thanks."

And it was. The double bed was covered with a rose-pink duvet and piles of gray, white, and pink pillows. The walls were a soft gray, and a fluffy white rug covered the floor. The dresser and desk were painted white, and the gray drapes were an exact match to the color in the pillows. "Live your best life!" was painted in sparkly gold paint above the bed.

It was a genuine young girl's room, lived in and loved. The laptop computer in the center of the desk was surrounded by papers and books, and pictures of a smiling, laughing Lauren posing with girls of a similar age, filled the side tables and were pinned to the corkboard over her desk. Irene Talbot was in one, the picture showing her and Lauren in swimming costumes with the beach in the background. A photo of Lauren with her parents sat on her desk.

I was delighted to see a bookcase so crowded that the books spilled onto the floor, and that the night table was stacked high. Her tastes ran to modern teen adventure and science fiction.

"Did you check to see if any of your mum's things are gone?" I asked.

"Gosh, no. We should do that, right? In case—" Her face froze as a thought crossed her mind. "In case someone took her."

"Gemma didn't mean that," Jayne said quickly.

But I had. It bothered me that I still hadn't heard from Ryan. I would have thought he'd want to talk to the girl.

Lauren led the way down the hall. The guest bedroom looked so unused, I didn't even suggest we go in.

The master bedroom was large, with an en-suite bathroom. The bedcovers and decorative pillows were scattered on the floor, the sheets rumpled. A towel was draped over a chair.

Lauren walked into the closet, and I said, "Give me a minute."

I stroked my right cheek as I studied the room, trying to get an impression. A framed picture sat on the nightstand to the right of the bed. This was the first picture I'd seen in this house of Lauren with her parents, and it had been taken recently. The book on the table was a biography of Franklin Roosevelt. David's side.

Sheila's night table had a book on formal gardens of Great Britain, as well as a catalog from a travel company. I flicked through the glossy catalog, seeing castles and beautiful houses and gardens and luxury hotel rooms. One page was dog-eared: a garden tour of the stately homes of England.

"Was your mother planning a vacation?" I asked.

"She wanted to go to England," Lauren said, "but Dad said we can't afford it."

"What did she say to that?"

"That she'd go without him. Do you think . . .?"

"Maybe."

I opened the drawers of the night table.

"Gemma!" Jayne said.

I ignored her. Gardening magazines, more travel brochures, a jumble of costume jewelry. I'd seen the good jewelry on the dressing table under the window. I closed the drawers.

"One of the suitcases is gone," Lauren said.

"Are you sure?"

"Pretty sure. It's a small one. Red. Like those ones, but smaller."

One side of the walk-in closet had men's clothes, the other women's; far more of the latter than the former. Two matching hard-sided red suitcases sat against the wall underneath the winter coats. "Do you notice anything else missing?" I asked.

Lauren put her right hand to her cheek and studied the closet, not saying anything. I stood quietly and let her think.

Jayne remained in the hall, clearly uncomfortable prying into people's things.

I'm never uncomfortable prying into people's things. If they don't want me to pry, they shouldn't get involved in murders. And they shouldn't abandon their only child to my care.

"Maybe," Lauren said at last. "It's hard to tell, she has so much, but I don't see her pink and white dress or the red linen jacket. Or the white sandals or the red Keds."

"How about the number of items?" I asked. "Is this the normal amount of clothes to be hanging here?"

Lauren thought. "I don't come in here much, but I don't think so. There's a space there."

"So there is." Five hangers were empty.

"I'm pretty sure her jeans are gone. She only has one pair. Plus her blue sweater. And the white capris with gold stitching on the hem and pocket."

"Well done," I said. "You've a good eye for detail."

She beamed at me.

"Let's check the bathroom," I said.

The master bath was all shades of gray and cream with gold accents. A giant round tub filled the center of the room, a glass-enclosed shower stall was against one wall, and his-and-hers sinks lined the other. The soap dishes were of heavy gray stone, and the towels and the rugs were thick and fluffy.

Lauren pulled open a drawer next to the sink. "Oh yeah. A lot of her makeup's gone. And her traveling toiletry bag isn't here either."

Not proof positive that Sheila had left under her own free will, but combined with the early morning text to Irene, the missing suitcase, and empty hangers in the closet, close enough.

"Do you know where she keeps her passport?" I hadn't seen it among the detritus of her night table.

Lauren shook her head.

"Have you packed your overnight bag?"

"Yes."

"Get Snowball into her carrier then, and we can go."

She ran off, and I began opening drawers in the bathroom. Candles and matches, bottles of bubble bath, jars of skin lotion, fancy scented soaps, an assortment of different-sized fluffy gold towels. Cold medicine, cough syrup, a half-empty bottle of headache tablets. I wouldn't know if they actually were headache tablets without having them tested, but for once I decided to take something at face value and put the cap back on the bottle.

"What are you looking for now?" Jayne asked.

"I won't know until I find it. And I'm not finding anything. I don't see shaving equipment or men's deodorant in here. David must use another loo. Why do you suppose they make different deodorants for men and women anyway?"

"So that a married couple will buy two bottles, not one?"

Two more doors led off the hallway, and I headed for them. The first was another bathroom, obviously used by the man of the house. A quick search turned up nothing out of the ordinary.

Lauren screamed. Snowball screeched. Something fell to the floor.

Jayne whirled around. "Lauren! Are you okay?"

"She doesn't want to go into her carrying case," Lauren cried. "Ouch, that hurt!"

More screeching.

More screaming.

"Perhaps you should try to help, Jayne," I said. I never take Moriarty to the vet myself; that's strictly Uncle Arthur's job. He comes back covered in scratches, but he always tells me all has gone well.

"Perhaps I should." Jayne ran off.

The second door led to, as I'd hoped, a study. Two paintings hung on the walls, both watercolors of lush gardens at sunrise. The wall behind the desk was filled with framed photos of Sheila admiring plants. Every book on the shelves had to do with gardening. I read the spines quickly and noticed that two of the books were by Anna Wentworth. A dust-rimmed empty space took up the center of the big desk, almost certainly where the computer had sat before being confiscated by the police. A chair matching the one in David's office had been shoved up against the wall. I rounded the desk to have a look at the picture in the silver frame beside where the computer had been.

A photograph of Lauren among Sheila's things. At last. I was so pleased to see it, I felt tears gathering in my eyes. The girl's smile was huge, her eyes full of the sort of joy that should be a child's whole life. I'd seen that joy when I'd returned Snowball, but not again.

I hoped it would return. And soon.

I checked the dust bin under the desk. Empty.

I dropped into the chair and looked around, studying the room. Even in the absence of the computer and the trash, I should be able to find *something* that would give me a peek into the state of Sheila's mind. Judging by the pattern in the carpet made by the wheels of the chair, Sheila sat here a good deal and had done so within the last few days. The photo of Lauren was recent, perhaps taken this spring. The flowers in the glass vase on the windowsill were fresh, and judging by the lack of dust on the package, the ream of computer paper next to the printer had recently been opened. I ran my fingers over the printer. The tray had no dust on it, but the crevices at the back were thick with it.

I opened the desk drawers. The police had been here before me, so I didn't expect to find much.

The top drawer contained a jumble of envelopes, pencils, pens, yellowing papers, paper clips, elastic bands, return address stickers, a stapler and box of staples, a broken ruler. All the usual junk found in an office desk. Come to think of it, the top drawer in my desk at the Emporium contained much the same stuff.

The next drawer held a stack of papers. I pulled them out and flicked through them. The text was double spaced and wide margined, probably printed on the printer next to the desk. It looked as though Sheila was writing a book or a series of articles. All to do with gardening, of course. Her name was printed at the top of every page. I saw chapter headings such as "Maintaining a Successful Seaside Garden" and "Tough Plants That Thrive in Your Sandy Soil."

The topmost pages were crisp and clean, but as I dug down, they seemed older, although none of them were crinkly and yellowing. The oldest, I estimated, had been printed two or three years ago.

Was Sheila writing a gardening book? It looked like it. I glanced at the bookshelf. My eyes settled on Anna Wentworth's books.

If Anna was being published and Sheila wanted to be but was not, all the more reason for Sheila to be resentful of her former friend.

I didn't find a passport. If Sheila wanted to go on a tour of the stately gardens of England, she'd need one. Either she'd taken it with her or the police had confiscated it for the time being—or maybe it was someplace I hadn't yet searched.

The screaming and screeching had died down, to be replaced by a low rhythmic whine.

Snowball was ready to leave.

I found Snowball, Jayne, and Lauren waiting for me in her room. Snowball wasn't shy about expressing her displeasure at being confined to the cat carrier.

Lauren jumped to her feet when I came in. "Did you learn anything?"

"Learn?"

"You're detecting, right? You're looking for clues. Aunt Irene said—"

"Never mind what Irene said. Ready to go?"

"Yes."

"I want to have a quick stop in the kitchen."

"In case there are any clues there, right?"

"For a glass of water," I said. "I'm thirsty."

Tiny claws stuck out of the bars of the cat carrier, scratching at the air, and the steady whining continued. Snowball was not a happy kitten.

"Not much longer, sweet thing, and then I'll let you out," Lauren cooed to Snowball as she picked the carrier up by its handle. With her other hand, she hefted a tote bag containing cat litter and food. Jayne picked up the litter box and carried it in both arms, leaving Lauren's small pink suitcase for me. The cat needed more supplies than the child.

We left Snowball and the bags by the door and went into the kitchen. I took a quick peek at the devastated garden. Nothing appeared to have been touched since I'd last been here.

"Did your mum say anything about repairing the damage?" I asked.

"She's getting quotes from landscaping companies. Dad says we can't afford it and she'll have to do all the work herself. She said all right, but she wants to hire a gardener to do the heavy work, and he said no. They had a big fight over that."

"I'm sure."

I glanced around the kitchen but could see nothing of interest. Everything was clean and tidy except for a single plate and one glass on the draining board and a peanut butter–smeared knife in the sink. Lauren had made her own breakfast.

I checked the garbage can under the sink. It was empty except for a broken plate. Most of the food residue went into the composting bin on the counter, to be used to feed the garden.

The kitchen had been painted six months to a year ago, but a single chip in the wall, about an inch off the floor, caught my eye.

I crouched down and touched it. No dust. "What happened here?"

"Mom threw a plate against the wall when Dad asked her what happened at the police station Sunday night."

"Does she do much of that?" I asked. "Throw things? Does she ever throw things at you?"

"Nope. She and Dad yell at each other a lot, and when they do, I go up to my room."

I swung around on my heels, ready to stand up, but something caught my eye, and I duck-walked across the room. At this level, I could see a scrap of paper under the fridge. I pulled it out and read it. The paper had been roughly torn from a pad of paper. The handwriting was in black ink.

Lauren, I called Irene. She'll pick you up this morning, and you can stay with her. I've gone away for a few days. Don't worry, I'll be back soon.
Love, Mom

"Looks like this is for you." I stood up and handed the paper to Lauren. As she read it, a small smile spread over her face. Jayne threw me a questioning look.

"Is that your mother's handwriting?" I asked.

"Yes," Lauren said.

I studied the layout of the kitchen, the distance from the island to the floor beneath the fridge. "She should have put the note under a saltshaker. I suspect it got knocked off the counter."

Whether she was confessing or not, Snowball's steady whine continued from inside the cat carrier.

Sheila might have left a letter on the counter, but she had still scarpered in the night, leaving her eleven-year-old daughter to fend for herself. Still, knowing she'd at least been thoughtful enough to leave a note made me feel fractionally better toward her.

But only fractionally.

"See," Lauren said to Jayne, "Irene was right. Gemma can figure things out. She's brilliant!"

"Only because I was down on the floor," I said. "Let's go."

"What else did you learn?"

"Give me your mum's phone number. I'll let her know you're with me."

Lauren rattled it off, and I entered the number into my mobile phone. I then placed the call, and was informed that the voice-mail box was full.

I wasn't surprised. If Sheila was on the lam, so to speak, she'd have turned her phone off so it couldn't be traced.

"I should call your dad too," I said. "Let him know you're with me."

Lauren pointed to the fridge, where a piece of paper with three phone numbers—Mom, Dad, Aunt Irene—was trapped under a magnet advertising the beauties of Cape Cod. I called David, got voicemail, and left a short, succinct, and not particularly polite message.

I took a pen out of my bag, turned the paper with Sheila's note over, and wrote on the back. I simply told Sheila or David that Lauren was with me and gave them my number. I placed the note under the saltshaker, and we collected the still protesting cat and the bags, and left.

When we'd arrived at the Tierney house, I'd noticed that the little red pole on the postbox at the end of the driveway was up, meaning the mail had been delivered. "Who brings in the post?" I asked Lauren.

"The what?"

"The mail."

"Mom or Dad. Whoever sees it first."

"Do you ever check?"

"No. No one writes me letters, Gemma. No one sends Mom or Dad letters either. They always complain that all they ever get is bills and flyers. And Mom's gardening magazines."

I opened the flap of the box and peered inside. It was stuffed with the aforementioned bills and flyers. I took them out and flipped through them. One of the flyers featured a picture of a hamburger and fries that appeared to be made of plastic and offered me a two-for-one deal. This same advertisement had been in my own postbox on Monday. Meaning no one had brought in the post since the weekend. Fair enough, considering the Tierneys had more important things to worry about.

Among the plethora of papers that would go directly to the recycling bin, I found an envelope. A plain white envelope, business-letter sized, mass produced, cheap and flimsy. It was sealed but had not been properly addressed and didn't have a stamp, meaning it had been hand-delivered. Two words were written across it in a rough scrawl—half cursive, half print—in black ink. *Sheila Teerny*. Sheila was spelled correctly, but Tierney was not. The *S* and *T* were dark and clear in big print, but the smaller letters ran together.

"What's that?" Lauren said.

I pulled at one corner of the flap. The envelope was cheap and the glue poor, and it opened without tearing.

"You can't read that," Jayne said.

"Why not?"

"It's someone's private mail."

"Someone who involved me in her private affairs, thus inviting me to do so."

"I think interfering with the mail is a federal offense," Jayne said.

"Gemma has my permission to read it," Lauren said.

She sounded so self-important, I hid a grin.

The single sheet of paper inside appeared to have been torn from a larger piece. The writing was in the same ink as on the envelope and had been made by the same hand.

Sheila. I told you no. Please do not bother me again. M

Chapter Twelve

I stuffed the letter and the envelope in my pocket and put the junk mail back into the postbox. This envelope had been underneath the flyer for the fast-food restaurant, meaning it had been delivered before the mail came on Monday.

"What time is your post delivered?"

Lauren shrugged. "I don't know. Sorry. I'll pay more attention to that sort of thing from now on. Like you do."

"What does it say?" Jayne asked.

"Can I see it?" Lauren asked.

"Meow," Snowball said.

"Nothing important," I said. "Let's go. You must be starving, Lauren."

"Sorta," she admitted.

Jayne gave me The Look. The look she uses when she knows I'm hiding something. I didn't show Lauren the letter. The contents were polite enough, but an implied "or else" lay beneath.

The streetlights had come on, and we walked through the darkening streets toward home. I fell back, dragging the pink suitcase behind me, and let Jayne and Lauren, the latter carrying the cat box, go ahead.

I needed to have some time alone to consider what all this meant, but first I was starting to be seriously worried about not hearing from Ryan. I gave him another call as we walked, and voicemail picked it up again.

"Ryan, it's Gemma. I need to talk to you about Sheila Tierney. I know you're mad at me for interfering, but that doesn't matter right now. She's skipped town. Surely you want to talk to her daughter about that, and the girl's with me. We'll be at my house in about two minutes."

I hung up. It was possible Ryan had been called away on another matter. The police didn't deal with only one crime at a time. As far as I knew, there hadn't been another murder in West London recently, so I'd have thought his priorities would lie with the Wentworth case.

Maybe not.

If Ryan had gone to work on something else, he'd have handed the Wentworth case over to another detective. And that meant Louise Estrada.

Nothing I could do but give my archnemesis a call.

Jayne and Lauren's light voices, accompanied by the steady, unvarying whine from Snowball, drifted toward me on the warm, salt-filled night air. Jayne was asking Lauren about school, and Lauren told her she was on the baseball team and in the drama club, and took tennis lessons outside of school.

Louise Estrada answered her phone on the first ring.

"Good evening, Detective," I said cheerfully. "It's Gemma Doyle here."

"What do you want?" she snapped.

"I've been trying to get Ryan, as I have some news about the Wentworth murder."

"Have you never heard the expression 'silence was the loud reply'?"

"What does that mean? I don't mean what does the expression mean, I mean why are you telling it to me?"

"If he hasn't called you, it's because he's been busy. It's not my job to run his romantic affairs."

"That's not—"

"If I must. Hold on."

I heard mumbling, and then Ryan came on the line. "Gemma, sorry I didn't get back to you, but things got ahead of me. I got your message, thanks. Is the girl still with you?"

Up ahead, Jayne and Lauren were turning into my driveway. "Yes. I went to her house to get some of her things and found a note her mum left her, saying she'd be away for a few days. The cat had knocked the note to the floor and it went under the fridge."

"Why were you looking under the fridge?"

"I wasn't actually looking under the fridge, but I was crouched down on the floor and—"

"Be right there!" he called to someone. "Sorry, Gemma. Gotta run. Talk to you later. Are you going to be home tonight?"

"I should be. Lauren's staying with me."

"If I get a chance, I'll drop by. Would that be okay?"

"Yes. But—"

The call disconnected as he hung up.

I unlocked the back door and we went into the mudroom. Violet came running toward us, all ready to offer profuse greetings to our visitors. She did a double take as she caught sight of the cat carrier, smelled the animal inside, and heard the increasingly frantic cries coming from within.

"You have a dog," Lauren said. "That's smashing. Snowball loves dogs."

"Has she been around many dogs?" Jayne asked.

"No, but I'm sure she'll love them. Can I pat yours?"

"Why don't you put Snowball down first?" I said. "I'll put Violet into the yard, and you can open the carrier. Let's let Snowball explore her surroundings for a few minutes before introducing them."

"Okay."

I had to force Violet out the door. Once that was done, I slammed it behind her and said, "You can let Snowball out now."

Lauren opened the door of the carrier. A streak of white fur, accompanied by a screech loud enough to wake the dead, flew across my kitchen and disappeared into the hallway. Lauren ran after her.

"I don't suppose you want a child and a cat," I said to Jayne.

"I'd love to take her home, but she won't want to go with me. Not when she can stay here."

"Why? Looks to me like you two are getting on great."

Jayne grinned at me. "You're her idol, Gemma, not me."

"Rubbish."

"You haven't noticed?"

"Noticed what?"

"You are so amazingly observant about other people but totally oblivious to anything that concerns your own life. Lauren's already taking on an English accent, everything's 'smashing' and 'brilliant,' and she strokes her cheek when she's thinking in a way that is totally you."

"Rubbish," I repeated. "You're imagining things."

"I am not, Gemma. She wants to be you."

I thought about that for a moment as I consciously folded my hands together behind my back.

"What's for dinner?" Jayne asked.

"I have absolutely no idea."

"In that case, let's order a pizza. Kids love pizza."

"You love pizza."

"What a coincidence," Jayne said.

"You make the call while I show Lauren to the guest room. First, though, I'll let Violet in. I hope we're not going to have running battles throughout the house all night."

I opened the mudroom door, and the dog came in. She ran directly to the open cat carrier, took a couple of sniffs of the air, and charged out of the kitchen, her nails scrambling on the tile floors.

I followed the sound of Lauren's voice. An almighty shriek sounded, a dog yelped, and Violet hurtled past me, heading back toward the mudroom.

I found Lauren and Snowball in the den. The cat was crouched on the top of the bookshelves, eyes narrowed, tail twitching slowly, back hunched, fur standing at attention.

"Your dog came in," Lauren said, "but Snowball yelled at her and she ran out again. Do you think I should bring Violet back and introduce them?"

I had images of emergency calls and racing ambulances. "Probably not a good idea. Let them find their own way as and when—and if—they like. Jayne's ordering pizza and it'll be here soon. Let me show you to your room. I live with my uncle Arthur, but he's away right now. His rooms are on the second floor, so please don't go up there."

We left Snowball perched on the bookcase.

By the time Lauren had settled herself in, the pizza had arrived. As we ate, she chatted happily about school and her friends and her plans for the future.

"Time for me to be off," Jayne said as I was putting the last two slices of pizza in the fridge for breakfast. "Come into the tearoom tomorrow, Lauren, and I'll show you what I do all day. Do you like to bake?"

"I don't know. I've never tried."

"You've never tried? You mean you and your mom don't make Christmas cookies or birthday cakes?" Jayne looked truly shocked.

"That's what bakeries are for, Mom says."

"Wow! You really have had a deprived childhood. It's time you learned. See you tomorrow, Lauren. 'Night, Gemma."

"Good night," we said.

When Jayne had gone, I turned to Lauren. "What time do you normally go to bed?"

Her eyes flicked to the side. "At eleven o'clock."

"No, I mean what time do you *normally* go to bed. Not what time do you *want* to go to bed tonight."

Her eyes narrowed as she studied my face. "How'd you know that wasn't true?"

"I have my methods." I wasn't going to tell her that not only had she avoided looking at me when she lied, but she'd spoken more formally than she usually did. If she hadn't been lying, she would have just said, "Eleven."

"I think now would be a good time," I said. "It's late and you've had an emotional day. Get yourself ready and settled, and I'll come in and say good night. You can read for as long as you like once you're in bed. Did you bring the book you got at the store?"

"Sure." She ran off, Snowball cradled in her arms. While we'd been eating, the little cat had ventured cautiously into the kitchen. Violet, who'd been curled up under the table with one eye watching for the intruder and the other for falling pieces of pizza, had scrambled to her feet and barked. Snowball hissed in return and jumped onto the table. As Jayne snatched her plate out of the way, Lauren, without being asked, lifted Snowball off the table and put her on the floor.

For the remainder of the meal, Violet and Snowball eyed each other warily. A truce appeared to have been called. I could only hope, as between Louise Estrada and me, it would continue.

My phone rang as I was rinsing the plates and putting them in the dishwasher.

"Sorry about earlier," Ryan said. "Louise was breathing down my neck, and I couldn't talk."

"Where is Sheila Tierney?" I asked.

"Why do you think I know?"

"Because it's totally obvious." That neither Ryan nor Louise Estrada had reacted when I told them Sheila had apparently disappeared, or had bothered to question Lauren as to the possible whereabouts of her mother, or had searched her house for clues to indicate whether or not she'd been abducted, made it apparent they knew exactly where she was.

She had not been arrested, because they couldn't keep that secret. It was unlikely they would have allowed her to leave West London, so she had to be somewhere in town.

"She left her eleven-year-old daughter wandering the streets," I said.

He sighed. "Yeah. I feel bad about that. I thought the kid was being looked after by Irene. I should have checked."

"Irene's out of town, and Sheila didn't even bother to ask if she'd be okay taking the girl. I don't think I like Sheila Tierney very much, but I do like Lauren a great deal."

"Likeability doesn't come into it," he said.

"It would make life a good deal easier if it did."

He chuckled. "I've done all I can do here for today. Can I pop around for a drink?"

"As much as I'd like that, I don't think it would be a good idea. Not tonight. I have the girl here, and she's not likely to be well disposed toward the police in general or you in particular."

"Fair enough," he said.

"What did the autopsy have to say?"

"Nothing unexpected."

I put my free hand in my pocket and touched the letter I'd pulled out of the Tierney postbox. "I found something you might be interested in when I was at the Tierney house getting Lauren's cat and her overnight things."

"What?"

"A letter— more of a note—left in the postbox for Sheila."

"You've touched this letter, I assume?"

"I didn't know what it was."

"Be there in five," he said.

I went down the hall and tapped at the guest room door. "I'm taking Violet out for a quick walk. Be back soon."

"'Kay," Lauren called.

Violet and I waited in the backyard for Ryan. When his headlights washed the front of my house, I went to meet him.

He got out of the car and glanced around. "Your visitor inside?"

"Yes," I said.

He put his arms around me and pulled me to him. I snugged into his broad chest and listened to the beating of his heart.

"Just once," he said. "Just once, I'd like to have a case that doesn't involve you."

"You'd miss my insights and my keen wit."

He pulled back and smiled down at me. "I'd miss nightly assignations like this one. What have you got?"

As soon as I'd arrived home earlier, I'd slipped the envelope into a plastic freezer bag. I handed it to Ryan now. "I found this in their postbox. Judging by the other material in the box, it would have been put in there sometime before midday on Monday."

He held it up. "Was it in this bag?"

"No. I did that. I took it out of the postbox, and I'm sorry I didn't think to put on gloves. Not that I had any gloves on me at the time. Despite what some people might think, I don't consciously go around hoping to stumble upon a crime scene. Quite the opposite: I'm relieved when I don't. The note was in that envelope, and I opened it. In my defense, it was addressed to Sheila, and Sheila has left her child in my care without asking me if I wanted the responsibility, so I've a right to be curious."

"If you want to put it like that."

"I do. My prints will be on both the envelope and the letter, and I put it in my pocket before wrapping it in plastic, but I didn't let anyone else touch it."

He peered into the bag. "Someone who doesn't know how to spell Sheila's last name."

"Because they've never seen it written, only heard it spoken. Not anyone of Irish heritage. It's a not-uncommon Irish name."

"I don't know about that," he said. "I'm of Irish heritage and I can't make head nor tail of some of the names they come up with. What does the note say?"

"It's short and to the point. Someone with the initial *M* is asking Sheila to leave him or her alone."

"That's interesting," Ryan said.

"Isn't it just? Have you come across anyone with the initial *M* in this case?"

"I might have," he said. "I might not have."

"Anna Wentworth's husband is named Mike."

"So he is. What are you going to do about the girl?"

"It's up to her. She can stay here as long as she wants. Irene might be back tomorrow, and Lauren can go there if she'd prefer." I took a step backward, taking myself out of reach of Ryan's arms. I studied his face. The stubble on his jaw was thick, his cheekbones high and sharp in the light cast by the streetlamps, and his blue eyes formed dark, unreadable pools. "Do you think her mother killed Anna Wentworth, Ryan? In the short time I've spent with the girl, I've come to like her a great deal, and such a thing can break a child. Particularly as I don't see her father being of much support."

Ryan ran his fingers through his short hair. "I wouldn't tell you if I thought she had. And I wouldn't tell you if I thought she hadn't. So all I'm saying is, I don't know."

Meaning they didn't have any hard evidence pointing to Sheila's guilt. But they were looking for it.

"Are you going to tell me where Sheila is?"

"No." He pulled me into his arms once again. "You can tell Lauren she's safe."

I lifted my chin and he kissed me long and hard. Then he pulled reluctantly away. "Good night, Gemma."

"Good night."

He got into his car, gave me a wave, and drove away. I watched until the red lights turned the corner and then called to Violet, and we went inside.

Lauren was sitting at the kitchen table, dressed in her pajamas, Snowball on her lap. "Why were you kissing him? He's with the police."

"He's also my boyfriend. He's a good man. He says you're not to worry: your mum's safe and she's not been arrested. She just needed some private time. I thought you were in bed. You shouldn't be spying on people."

"Hardly spying as you were standing right there in the middle of the driveway. I have the right to know what's going on."

I couldn't argue with that, so I didn't try. "Go back to bed. I'll be in to say good night in a minute. If you need anything in the night, help yourself."

"Thanks, Gemma." She got up and left, carrying her cat.

My phone rang once again. It was a number I'd called recently. David Tierney.

"Is that Gemma Doyle?" he said.

"Yes. David, where are you? Why haven't you called me before now?"

"Sorry 'bout that. I've been in meetings all evening, and I just checked my messages. What's happening?"

"You've been in meetings? It's almost eleven o'clock."

"Important business meetings don't always follow the clock."

Important business meetings held in a bar, judging by the slur in his words and the roar of men's laughter in the background. "Is Lauren there?" he asked.

"Yes, she's here. With me. At my house. Are you aware Sheila's gone . . . somewhere?"

"Not until I got your message. I can't believe she'd skip out like that. No clearer indication of guilt, is there?"

Not exactly a subtle question, but he'd opened the door so wide, I'd be a fool not to walk through it. "Do you think Sheila killed Anna?"

"What? No, of course not. She's just . . . impulsive. She doesn't always think things through."

"Do you want to speak to Lauren?"

He hesitated. In the background, a man shouted and another laughed.

"You should," I said. "She's frightened and confused."

"Yeah. Okay."

I knocked on the guest room door, and Lauren called, "Come in."

She was in bed, reading, propped up on pillows, with Snowball curled at her side. Violet had followed me in. The dog and the cat eyed each other, and then Violet dropped to a sit, lifted a rear leg, and scratched behind her ear. Snowball relaxed.

"It's your father." I handed Lauren the phone.

She grabbed it. "Dad!"

I called to Violet and we left the room. I didn't even try to listen. This conversation was definitely none of my business. I went into the den and rummaged through the secretary. I found what I was looking for under a stack of papers I intended to get around to sorting one day. When I returned, all was quiet in Lauren's room, and I knocked lightly. She called, "Come in."

Her eyes were wet. She handed me my phone with one hand and wiped at her cheek with the back of the other. "My dad wishes he could be here, but he's super busy with work."

I sat on the edge of the bed and handed her the photo of Benedict Cumberbatch. "Here you go. It's signed to me, but you can have it if you like."

She gave me a strained smile. "Thanks. Are you sure?"

"Absolutely. I want you to have it."

"Thanks." She showed the photo to Snowball. Snowball didn't seem overly impressed.

I'm not accustomed to dealing with children, so I decided to talk to Lauren as I would any other person. "Where's your dad? Did he say when he's coming home?"

"Raleigh, North Carolina. He's going to try to get a flight tomorrow."

I'll believe that when it happens, I thought. I gave Lauren a smile, but even I could tell how fake it was. I was absolutely furious with the man. His wife in hiding because everyone thought she was a killer, his daughter forced to stay with a virtual stranger, and he was hanging out in a bar in Raleigh, North Carolina, probably telling all his mates how hard done by he was.

"Irene will be back soon, but if you'd rather stay here, you're welcome. It won't be much longer, I'm sure, until your mum comes home. A lot of things have been happening to her: the garden, the death of her friend. She has some heavy stuff to deal with, and she doesn't want to bother you."

"But I want to help," Lauren said, "if they'll let me. Mom and Dad still treat me as though I'm a *child*."

I repressed a smile. "I'm surprised you don't have a phone of your own. Don't most girls your age want one?"

"I'd like to have one, sure, but my school tells the parents that kids need to be twelve or thirteen before they get their own phone. Not many of my friends have one."

Wise school, I thought. "Do you like your school?"

"It's okay. I used to go to the public school. This one's better." I thought of the letter from the school on David's desk, telling him to pay up or Lauren wouldn't be welcomed back.

"My best friend's named Brooklyn. She's gone to Quebec for the summer to learn French. I wanted to go too, but Dad said we can't afford it."

"Sounds like your dad can't afford a lot of things."

She shrugged. "That's okay. Brooklyn said she'll help me with my French when she gets back."

Snowball shifted position and wiggled her tiny body between us. Violet put her chin on my leg and wagged her tail. She and Snowball had accepted each other.

"See," Lauren said. "I told you they'd be friends. Friends are important, aren't they, Gemma? You and Jayne are friends, right?"

"We certainly are," I said.

"My mom hasn't been happy since she and Anna stopped being friends."

"Were they good friends?"

"Yeah. Anna was at our house a lot of the time, or Mom went over there. Anna always brought Peony when she came to visit. Peony's her dog, and she'd let me play with him. I was hoping we could get a dog too, but Mom says a dog's too much responsibility, even a small one like Peony. They mess in the garden. Mom doesn't like that."

"When did Anna and your mother stop being friends?"

"I don't remember exactly, but it was before school let out. Anna came to our house one day, and they had a big fight, and Mom started throwing things. She broke a plate that belonged to her grandmother, and then she got all mad at that."

"What did they fight about?"

"The book."

"What book?" I asked casually, as though every neuron in my brain hadn't pricked up.

"Some dumb gardening book. I was in my room with Brooklyn and Madison; she's my other best friend. It was real embarrassing, but Madison said that's nothing. Her mom fights with her sister all the time, and her aunt once came around with an ax and chopped a hole in the front door 'cause her mom wouldn't let her in."

I didn't know any girl named Madison, but if ever I made her acquaintance, I'd be sure to stay well away from her family.

"Sometimes," Lauren said in a low, sad voice, "I think my mom loves gardens more than she loves me."

I reached out and folded the girl in my arms. "I'm sure that's not true," I said, thinking that it probably was.

I struggled to come up with something more cheerful to talk about. "I heard you tell Jayne you're in the drama club at school. Have you been in any plays?"

She pulled out of my arms and looked at me with sparkling eyes. "Oh yes. We did *The Importance of Being Ernest* last year. I was just an extra 'cause I was only in sixth grade, but Mom said it's important to start off by getting familiar with being on the stage before having lines to say. She helped me with my makeup and told me how to walk and how to stand. That was fun."

"Was your mother an actor?"

Lauren shook her head. "No, but when she was a teacher at West London High, she was in charge of the drama club there. She taught American history, but she didn't like it. She complained about it all the time. When Dad's company started making enough money so she could quit, she was really happy."

"When was this?"

Lauren shrugged. "A couple of years ago. She quit the garden club last night. I wasn't surprised. She's been saying mean things about them for a long time."

"What sort of things?"

"She says the West London Garden Club isn't serious enough, but Anna said it was important for them to have local connections. Mom thought they were cheap. She doesn't like cheap things."

I refrained from comment.

"Like the time the club wanted to move their meetings from the Harbor Inn to the Beach Front Hotel. Mom went to the hotel to check out the meeting room and took me with her. I thought it was okay; they were only going to have a meeting, not live there. But she was horrified. She said the whole place smelled like bleach and disinfectant, and she walked around with her nose in the air, sniffing all the time. She said it would do the image of the club no good to be seen there. Mom cares about her image." Lauren yawned.

"Time for me to go to bed too," I said. "Do you want me to turn out your light?"

She put her book and the photo of Cumberbatch on the nightstand and wiggled further under the covers. "Yes, please. Gemma?"

"Yes, love?"

"Good night."

"Good night, Lauren."

I called to Violet and we slipped out of the room. I turned the light off as I went.

Chapter Thirteen

The next morning, I skipped the leftover pizza and took ingredients out of the fridge and pantry to make a hearty, traditional English breakfast for Lauren and me. When the sausages were grilling and the bacon in the oven, I knocked on her door. "Time to get up. Breakfast in fifteen minutes, and then we're going to the Emporium."

Muttering came from the other side of the door, so I knew my house guest hadn't absconded in the night.

I went back to the kitchen to finish cooking. I heard doors opening and water running, and ten minutes later, Lauren came in. She'd tied her long hair into a high, bouncy ponytail and put on shorts, a T-shirt, and white trainers. She looked rested and refreshed, ready to dive eagerly into another day. Whereas I probably looked anything but. I'd sat up for a long time last night, thinking things over.

I had sufficient information to start tracking Sheila Tierney down and to begin formulating some theories about the death of Anna Wentworth. Sheila would not want me tracking her down, but I didn't much care what the fool of a woman wanted.

Ryan wouldn't want me doing that either, but I didn't intend to tell him.

A Curious Incident

Lauren and I had agreed that Snowball's food and water dishes could be kept on top of the chest freezer in the mudroom to keep them out of reach of Violet, and the first thing Lauren did before coming to the table was to refill the bowls. While Snowball ate, Lauren settled herself at her place. She eyed the mountain of food on the plate in front of her. "Gee, Gemma. That's a lot."

"Is it? That's what English people eat for breakfast."

Three rashers of bacon, a plump sausage handmade by a local butcher, grilled tomatoes and mushrooms, two fried eggs, toast with butter and jam.

"I usually have cereal," she said.

"Oh. I have some muesli in the cupboard if you'd prefer." I also normally had cereal, sometimes with fruit and yogurt, but I thought children needed a hearty cooked breakfast.

"No. This'll be good." She picked up her knife and fork and dove in.

I have to admit, I dove in myself. Nothing like a traditional English breakfast to start the day.

On the rare occasion I've given a thought to someday having children of my own, I've always decided it isn't for me. I'm not much of a baby person. Other women—Jayne comes to mind—will ooh and coo over every infant and toddler that comes in reach, but I've never seen the appeal: crying, messy creatures with plenty of demands and poor conversational skills.

Without trying to be too obvious, I studied Lauren as she made her way through her breakfast. *Yes*, I thought, *I'd like to have a daughter just like her. Smart and kind and beautiful, with a world of possibilities ahead of her.* As though she knew I was thinking about her, she looked up suddenly and gave me a wide grin.

I stuffed food into my mouth. "I usually walk to work," I said around a mouthful of apple-and-sage pork sausage, "but today I'll take the car because I have an errand to run as soon as my assistant comes in. You can spend the day in the shop and the tearoom, and in the mid-afternoon, if you like, I'll give you a key to the house and you can come here and take Violet for a walk. She'd like that."

"Okay. Can Snowball come to work with us?"

"Probably better not. She and Moriarty might not get on too well, and we don't want to worry about her trying to get out the door into the street."

"Okay. Snowball and Violet can play here."

I didn't know how much playing would go on, but the two animals seemed to be getting on by ignoring each other. Snowball had disappeared after finishing her breakfast, and Violet was under the kitchen table, hoping for scraps to fall.

"This is good," Lauren said, scraping up the last of her egg yolk with the end of a piece of toast. "I've never had bacon before."

"You've never had bacon! How is that possible?"

"Mom says it makes you fat."

"In my house, you can have a treat now and again." I brought up a mental image of Sheila. To be impolite about it, she didn't look like a woman who dieted constantly.

Lauren seemed to read my mind. "Mom's put a lot of weight on over the last couple months. She says it's 'cause of all the stress. She thinks I don't know she has bags of chips and chocolate bars hidden in the pantry for after I'm in bed when Dad's away."

Breakfast finished, we headed into town.

* * *

Ashleigh arrived for work at eleven, wearing an outfit I hadn't seen before: a red-and-blue plaid skirt that fell to her knees, a white shirt under a blue cardigan, and flat brown shoes. Her hair curled up at the edges just below her chin.

I hated to ask, but I did anyway. "What are you dressed as today?"

She threw a quick glance toward the reading nook, where Lauren was nestled with book in hand and shop cat on lap. "Nancy Drew. Girl Detective."

"An interesting choice," I said.

"I'm glad you like it," she said.

"I have to go out. I hope not to be too long. I've given Lauren some money so she can buy lunch in the tearoom. Let her have any book she likes, and pay for it out of petty cash."

"Don't give us another thought," Ashleigh said. "Lauren and I can manage fine without you."

I didn't care for the sound of that, but I called goodbye to Lauren anyway. She threw me a wave without taking her eyes off the page in front of her. Moriarty ignored me, as was his custom unless it was dinnertime.

My first stop was the West London Library. The woman behind the circulation desk gave me a big smile when she caught sight of me and cheerily said, "Good morning, Gemma. What can we do for you today?" The library and I often work together when authors who write the sort of books I feature come to town or a local author has a new book out. I didn't carry any of Anna Wentworth's books, and that was an oversight on my part. I usually do what I can to help promote local writers, even if their books don't suit the mandate of the Sherlock Holmes Bookshop and Emporium.

"'Morning, Teresa. Do you have anything by Anna Wentworth? She wrote a couple of books about gardening."

"I know the ones you mean. I'll check if they're in." She turned to the computer. "Terrible about what happened to her."

"It is."

"Her books are very popular, and we often have a wait list, but you're in luck. Her second, *Foundations of a Cape Cod Garden*, is available. Can I find it for you?"

"Please."

I soon had the big book in hand. The cover picture showed a line of wheat-colored pampas grasses outlining a flower bed, with the open ocean calm and peaceful in the background.

I thanked the librarian and left. The back of the West London Library has a pretty little garden with picnic benches, where office workers often sit to enjoy their lunch. It was a nice day, warm and sunny but not too hot, so I took a seat and flicked through the book, seeing plenty of pictures of beautiful flowers and lush gardens. The book seemed to be organized around problems. Chapters had names such as "Sandy Soil," "Salt Spray," "Heavy Foot Traffic." One was titled "Dangerous Plants." I scanned a few paragraphs at random. I don't know much about gardening, and I don't know anything about writing gardening books, but the prose was clear and well presented. If I had a problem with my sandy soil, I could see this book coming in handy.

If I had a problem with sandy soil and didn't have Mrs. Ramsbatten and her team to deal with it, that is.

The word *peony* caught my eye, and I remembered that was the name of Anna's dog. I admired the pictures of the tall bushy plants, the lush pink and white blooms. Come to think of it, I have one of those in my backyard. I'd never known what it was called.

I turned to the back leaf. I'd never met Anna Wentworth, but I'd seen a picture of her in the *West London Star*. This one was more of a glamour shot: professional lighting, head cocked in a stiff pose, pasted-on smile, hair and makeup perfect. Nothing of her personality came through. The author bio mentioned that she lived in West London and was a popular author, blogger, and lecturer on all things gardening.

I closed the book, got into my little red Miata, and headed to the outskirts of West London.

I had a pretty good idea of where to start my search for the elusive Sheila Tierney. Ryan knew where she was, so considering she was still the prime suspect in a murder investigation, she was almost certainly in West London.

She had, according to her daughter, no friends, so it was likely she wasn't close enough to anyone to ask them to give her shelter in their home. I'd texted Irene this morning to inquire whether she'd heard from her stepsister. "No" had been the reply. I asked if Sheila had a key to her house, and she'd answered that in the negative as well, followed by a string of exclamation marks.

If Sheila was hiding out, not wanting to be the subject of any more gossip, she'd almost certainly not go anywhere she'd expect to see neighbors or acquaintances. Which eliminated places such as the Harbor Inn and other upscale hotels and inns.

Last night, Lauren had told me her mum had sneered at the Beach Front. What better place to go if one was trying to be unfound?

The Beach Front is not one of West London's finer establishments, but it's clean and serviceable and most of all cheap. For Cape Cod in summer, anyway.

At this time of day, the parking lot was mostly empty. I parked close to the doors and settled a pair of enormous sunglasses on my face, wrapped a summer-weight cotton scarf around my neck, and tied my curly hair back with a rhinestone-encrusted clip. Not much of a disguise: anyone who knew me would recognize me instantly, but I was hoping that if I encountered someone who'd only seen me around town or shopped in my store, they'd look straight past me.

Uninspired is the word I'd use for the hotel's decor. This was part of a chain, the furniture and decorations mass produced and showing signs of use and age. The breakfast room off the small lobby was shrouded in darkness. The place did smell of bleach.

"Hi, welcome to the Beach Front," said the young man—more of a boy really—behind the desk. "Are you checking in?" He was long and gangly with a bobbing Adam's apple, bad skin, big ears, and teeth too large for his mouth. His white dress shirt was too short for his arms, and bumpy wrists peeked out. He was still in his teens, and this was no doubt a summer job. Perfect for my purposes.

"No, thank you," I said in my best New England accent. "This is going to sound sort of funny." I giggled. "But I've lost my sister."

"You lost your sister?"

"Yeah. Silly, eh? Of course, I haven't really lost her so much as misplaced her. She's staying here, but she's not answering her phone, and I don't know what room she's in."

"What's her name?"

Another giggle. "That's the thing. I don't know."

His eyes narrowed. "You don't know your sister's name?"

"I know her name. Of course I know her name. But I don't know what name she's using here." I glanced quickly around the empty lobby, as though ensuring no one was listening, and then I leaned over the desk. Instinctively, he leaned toward me, all ears.

"She's left her husband, you see, and his family is . . . well, let's just say they're the sort of *family* you don't want to cross."

His eyes widened.

"They're from *New Jersey.*"

"Right." He winked. "I get it."

"She checked in very early yesterday morning. Were you here yesterday? What time did you start?"

"Six."

"Oh good, you would have seen her then. She's older than me, about the same height but maybe forty pounds heavier. We don't look much alike. She's on her own, and she had one red carry-on-size suitcase. She has blonde hair, and she's . . . well, she doesn't look too good these days. Things have been rough, you know. She's kinda tired looking." Lauren had told me her mother had been a drama teacher and she'd done Lauren's makeup for the school play. I took a chance she'd have put on some sort of disguise. "Maybe she was wearing her sunglasses, even though it was early morning when she came here. She's been crying a lot, you see."

"I think I know who you mean," he said. "I checked in a woman on her own, and she had a red suitcase. She didn't have a reservation, but we're not full up, so that was okay. Yeah, she was wearing sunglasses. She came down for breakfast this morning, just got her coffee and a muffin and went back upstairs."

As the hotel only had two floors, he'd narrowed her location down, which would be helpful if I had to knock on every door.

"Oh, good. I'm so relieved. What room's she in?"

"I can't tell you that. It's against the rules."

I leaned further across the desk. I lowered my voice. "I promise I won't tell anyone you told me. She wants to see me. She called and asked me to come, but I forgot the room number. I guess I was so worried about her, it slipped out of my mind." I attempted to look plaintive and slightly absent-minded.

He hesitated. I smiled at him, but he took a deep breath and shook his head. "Sorry. No can do. The boss is very strict about that." He put on a serious expression.

"Okay, I understand. Can you call her room and tell her I'm here?"

"Yeah, I can do that. No problem." He pressed a few keys on the computer then picked up the phone on the desk. I smiled as he pushed buttons. I kept smiling as the phone rang on the other end.

"Hi. It's the front desk. Your sister's here. You should give her a call. 'Bye!" He hung up. "Sorry, not answering."

"That would be because she's afraid someone tracked her down. That's just like Susan. Is she using her real first name?"

He glanced at the computer. "Yeah."

Another guess on my part. When people use a fake name, they almost always choose one that has their initials. Easier to remember that way. Susan, Sandra, Sophie. I simply chose the likeliest option.

Susan Turner would be my next guess. But even having the name wasn't going to get her room number out of him. "Gosh, there's my phone now. I bet that's her." I turned around and walked across the lobby. I peered into the breakfast room, dark and clean and ready for tomorrow, as I pulled my phone out of my pocket. "Thank heavens!" I cried. "Are you okay, Susan? Great. Be right up!"

I put the phone away. "Thanks so much for your trouble," I said to the clerk. "I'll tell Susan to tell your manager you were respectful of her privacy."

He grinned at me.

He'd punched 9213 into the phone when he made the call, and it was to room 213 that I went. I didn't wait for the elevator but took the stairs two at a time. Sheila might not be in her room; the woman who'd checked in yesterday morning with a red suitcase might not even be Sheila. If so, this would be a wasted trip, but I assumed that if it was Sheila, and if she was in hiding, she'd be unlikely to go for a stroll through the streets of West London. She might do that if she got bored enough staying in a cut-rate hotel, but she'd only been in hiding one day.

I could hear the murmur of the TV in room 213. I gave the door one firm, loud knock. "Housekeeping!"

The door opened a fraction. Sheila Tierney peered out. She blinked. I stuck my foot in the door, and said, "Hi. Can I come in?"

"You're not housekeeping."

"No, I'm not." I pushed at the door. Sheila stepped back and I walked past her into the room.

"You're the woman from the bookstore in town. The one who found Lauren's cat. What are you doing here? Did the police tell you I was here?"

"No, they didn't. I figured it out myself. You weren't hard to find."

One of the twin beds was unmade, and an open suitcase lay on top of the other, a pink and white dress and red jacket spilling out. Red Keds were on the floor, and a damp towel had been tossed over the chair next to the small desk. On the TV, four women were shouting over each other.

"Can you turn that off, please," I said, "so we can talk."

"I don't have anything to say to you. I don't even know you."

"Be that as it may, I know you. Far better than I would like. Do you know where your daughter is?"

"Lauren? She's with her aunt Irene."

"No, she's not. Irene's in Boston at a conference. Your husband, Lauren's father, is in Raleigh. If you turn off the TV, I'll tell you where Lauren is."

Sheila crossed the room in two angry strides. She looked, I thought, awful. She was dressed in jeans and a T-shirt, both of which had been bought before she'd put on weight and were no doubt what she wore to work in her garden. The jeans were worn at the knees, and a grass stain on the seat hadn't come out in the wash; the bright colors of the flowers on the white T-shirt were fading to a dull pink. Her hair was beginning to show its brown and gray roots, and it hung limply around her pale, makeup-less face. Lines of stress were carved into the delicate skin around her mouth, and the bags under her eyes were dark and heavy. She picked up the remote, pushed a button, and blessed silence filled the room.

"At the moment," I said, "Lauren's at my store, reading in the company of my shop cat. She spent the night at my house."

Sheila let out a puff of breath. "Thank you. I knew she'd be okay; she's a resourceful girl."

"She's eleven years old, and no one at that age is resourceful unless they've lived the life of a Baker Street Irregular or the Artful Dodger. She showed up at my shop around three yesterday afternoon. She woke up and you were gone. She waited all day for you or her father to come home. She was worried and frightened and had nowhere to go. Her friends are on holiday, and Irene was at her conference and had her phone turned off."

Sheila had the grace to flush. "I'm sorry. I left her a note, telling her not to worry."

"Like telling someone not to worry ever helps. She didn't get the note. The cat knocked it off the counter, and it went under the fridge."

"How did you see it then? Have you been in my house?"

"Of course I've been in your house, Sheila." Suddenly I was angry. Truly angry. This selfish, self-obsessed woman didn't deserve a girl as wonderful as Lauren. "Your child is staying with me because she was abandoned by her parents. She needed to go home and get her things. Not to mention take care of her cat."

"I didn't abandon her. I thought Irene—"

"Yes, yes. You thought. Well, you didn't think enough. And I suggest you start thinking now."

She dropped onto the unmade bed, put her head in her hands, and started to cry. While Sheila cried her misery out, I amused myself by checking her belongings. She'd brought a couple of gardening magazines and a contemporary romance. Her cell phone lay on the desk, but I didn't see an iPad or laptop. The light on the room phone was blinking. An open toiletry bag was on the bathroom shelf, and pots of makeup were spread across the counter.

"How long were you planning to stay here anyway?" I asked.

"I don't know," she sobbed. "You're right. I wasn't thinking. I got a phone call the night before last around ten. It was one of my so-called friends from the garden club. She hadn't been able to make the meeting, she said, and she wanted to know how it went. She'd heard I was accused of killing Anna. She had the nerve to ask me if I'd done it. I was so mad I went into the kitchen for a glass of wine, and I saw people in my yard! Scared the life out of me. They were poking around, looking at all the"—she let out a strangled sob—"damage. I opened the door and yelled at them. It wasn't even kids. I wouldn't have minded so much if it was just kids being kids, but it was people I recognized. My neighbors. I sat up all night, afraid to go back to bed. I needed to get away for a few days. Have some time to myself, stay out of sight, let the gossip die down."

She looked around the room. "Not exactly the destination I would have chosen, which would have been an exclusive Caribbean island, but the police told me I can't leave West London. So I came here, thinking no one I knew would be likely to see me. But you found me."

"So I did. I doubt anyone else will track you down. Your voicemail box is full. You should clear it in case something happens. Like your daughter needs you. The front desk left you a message on the room phone. Your sister isn't looking for you. They meant me."

"I know you don't approve of me, but I don't care. You've no idea what it's like being the object of so much vicious gossip, being accused of murder."

I didn't bother to mention that I'd been a suspect in a murder case before, and I never much cared what gossip had to say about me in any event. "I don't see a computer. Aren't you planning to do any writing while you're here?"

"The police confiscated my iPad and my home computer." She looked up. "What do you know about that?"

"Lauren told me you're writing a book on gardening." I lied. Lauren hadn't said any such thing, but this was probably not the time to tell Sheila I'd searched her house and saw her manuscript. "I don't think Lauren knows you've already been published. You and Anna Wentworth."

"No one knows. How do you?"

"I make it my business," I said, "to know what other people do not."

I'd only had time for a quick glance at the manuscript in Sheila's drawer and at the book I'd taken out of the library, but the

similarities had leapt out. The chapter headings were different—
Anna's shorter and punchier—but the themes were the same, and
some of the lines were identical. Word for word.

"Anna and I co-authored her second book," Sheila said.

"But you didn't get any credit for it. Your name's not on it.
Everyone in town thinks Anna wrote it on her own."

Sheila threw up her hands. "That was Anna's idea. Of course, it
was Anna's idea. And I, idiot that I am, believed her. I'm a gardener.
I make things grow. I can make plants not only grow but thrive
where no one else can. I'm not a businesswoman, and I know absolutely nothing about the publishing world. Anna said that in order
to capitalize on the success of her first book, moderate though that
had been, the publisher insisted that only her name be on the cover
of the second book. Anna also said it would be okay if the contract
was in her name. Better not to confuse things."

I said nothing.

"The book has done really well. It far outsold Anna's first
book, and because of that, sales of the earlier book went up. When
I asked to see the royalty statements for our book, she wouldn't
show them to me. She said she was giving me half of what she got,
but that it wasn't much. Not after the agent took her cut and we
paid the photographer. I didn't believe her."

"Your husband's in business. Surely he told you that you
needed to get something in writing."

"I didn't talk it over with David. I . . . we . . . don't share much
these days."

No kidding.

"He doesn't take me seriously. He thinks my gardening's a
silly, frivolous, wasteful hobby. I'd hoped"—her voice broke—
"when I started making money from it, he'd appreciate me more.
Not only did I write most of the book, I was writing most of

Anna's blog posts too, but Anna put them up under her name. She said, as it was promo for the book, we shouldn't confuse things by crediting me. You must think I'm a fool."

"No," I said. *Yes,* I thought.

"Anna and I were friends. I *thought* we were friends. But more than that, she was a fellow gardener. I thought she was as passionate about gardening as I am, but I eventually realized that for her it was nothing but a means to an end. A means to make some money and pretend to be a big shot around town. Anna loved nothing more than being the center of attention."

Said as though Sheila hadn't stormed into the garden club meeting as dramatically as possible.

"Anna didn't even do most of the work on her garden herself." Sheila snorted. "She has a gardener do it all. I think he does the garden layout and design too."

She suddenly seemed to realize she was talking a bit too much. "You aren't going to tell the police this, I hope. I might not have liked Anna—to be honest, I came to hate her—but I didn't kill her."

I'm often amazed at how much people will tell me. Things they've tried to keep secret from everyone else in their life come pouring out at the slightest nudge. I don't think it's because I have a particularly trustworthy face or they assume I'm on their side, but when they realize I've figured out some details about them, they believe I can be trusted with everything.

A very foolish assumption.

"What a mess," Sheila went on. "If anything, I'm worse off now she's dead."

"Why?"

"My lawsuit probably won't go ahead. I might never get the money I'm owed. I'd decided to hire a lawyer and sue her. I can prove I wrote most of that book."

"How far did you get with that?"

"Not nearly far enough. I finally told David, and he hit the roof. Yelling and screaming and saying he didn't need any more legal problems. I tried to tell him I'd win my case, but he wouldn't listen to me."

The words "more legal problems" matched what I'd read in his office computer.

"You haven't hired a lawyer yet?"

She shook her head.

"How much of this does Anna's husband, Mike Nixon, know?" *Mike, with an M.*

For the first time, a small smile crossed Sheila's face. "Mike. He's such a sweetie. A really nice man. Much nicer than Anna deserved. They don't get on very well, haven't for a long time. If Anna was a crook and a cheat, it wasn't his fault. I didn't want to bother him with this." She broke into a smile. "Now that she's out of the picture, I bet he'll be willing to help me. To ensure I get what's mine. I'll talk it over with him. After the funeral, of course. I don't want to appear too eager."

Her phone rang. She walked over to the desk, picked it up, and read the screen. Her face twisted and she threw the phone onto the bed. "Another one of my so-called friends wondering if I've been arrested yet."

"You should clear out your voicemail box."

"So you said. Look, are you okay with Lauren for another day or two? She's a good girl."

"She's a lovely girl, and I'm happy to have her. But my house is not her home, and I'm not her mother."

"I'll call David and tell him to get back here."

Not exactly what I'd meant.

"Was your husband having an affair with Anna?"

"You're very blunt, aren't you?"

"When I want to be. You told people you suspected he was."

"And wasn't that a mistake? Easier to start a rumor than to stop one. I overreacted, okay. I jumped to conclusions, and I regret it. He's been traveling a lot, like all the time. Things haven't been easy between us for a while now. I didn't . . . I didn't understand how desperate he is to find new financing for the company. He was away all the time, and then one afternoon, I saw his car parked in Anna's driveway. I thought . . . You know what I thought. I went home, called one of my so-called friends, and cried it out. I stewed about it for a couple of weeks, and then Anna came to my house one day to work on the book. I ended up confronting her about everything, and I let her know what I thought of her."

That must have been the argument Lauren overheard when she was upstairs with her friends.

"Anna and I never spoke again. I later found out that David had stopped at their house on his way home from the airport to tell Mike about a lead he had for a job for him. The job never came through, and the story about my suspicions was out of my control."

Sheila suddenly reached out and grabbed both my hands in hers. I almost yelped in surprise. She stared deeply into my eyes. "Anna Wentworth wrecked my garden because she was a petty, vengeful, jealous woman, but I didn't kill her, and I don't know who did. The police haven't arrested me, have they? But everyone in this town is ready to see me hung from the nearest lamppost. I had to get away. I have to stay away. You understand, don't you? You're obviously a highly intelligent woman, and I can see how much you care for my daughter. Right now, Lauren's better off with you or Irene than with me, with so much on my mind." She forced out a smile.

I snatched my hands out of hers. "You can do whatever you like, Sheila, but don't try to manipulate me. My phone number will be in your record of recent calls, so keep it. You can call your daughter at my shop during the day or on my phone after hours. I'd suggest you call her now and tell her you're safe. She came to me and asked for my help because she loves you and is worried about you. It's long past time you remember that."

"Thank you," she said. "I owe you big time."

"As we say in England, sod off, Sheila." I walked out of the room.

As I crossed the lobby, the young man behind the desk beckoned me. "Everything okay?"

"Fine, thanks. She's resting."

He glanced around the empty lobby to ensure no one was listening and spoke in a low, serious voice. "Should I alert the cops?"

"What? Why?"

"In case her family"—he made quotation marks in the air—"comes to get her. I won't tell them what room she's in, but . . . maybe they'll try to get it out of me." He looked almost pleased at the idea. He'd seen too many action movies and had visions of himself heroically holding off the invading hordes of New Jersey mobsters.

I patted my right hip in the approximate location at which I'd carry a gun, if I was so inclined, and gave him an exaggerated wink. "We're on it."

His mouth flapped open and his eyes almost popped out of his head.

"You're providing good security." I gave him a finger wave as I left the hotel. "Keep it up."

I drove back to Baker Street full of thought.

Sheila had played the poor-persecuted-me card to the hilt. It would have had more effect, though, if she hadn't come to the garden club meeting the other night, determined to be seen in all her righteous indignation. She'd always loved the limelight, and when it got too much to handle, she'd abandoned her daughter and fled.

Sheila had reasons, if what she'd said was true, to be angry with Anna. To be murderously angry. She didn't strike me as the sort of woman to be so naive as to have agreed to help write the book and have it published without some legal safeguards, but she might have been. Especially if she'd trusted Anna. Lauren had said the two women had been close friends. Sheila was a gardener and a former high school teacher, not a businesswoman, and she and her husband, who could have advised her, had trust issues.

If she'd trusted Anna and then been betrayed by her, all the more reason to want to kill the woman.

Then there was the matter of Mike Nixon, Anna's husband. "Dear, sweet Mike" and possibly the unknown *M* who wanted Sheila to keep away from him. The true state of Mike and Anna's marriage didn't matter one bit, not if Sheila thought it was on rocky ground.

I pulled into the alley behind the Emporium and Mrs. Hudson's. I switched off the engine but stayed in the car, thinking.

Irene, who knows Sheila as well as anyone, had been adamant that it was not in Sheila's character to kill, at least not in the way Anna had been murdered, and at the time I'd agreed with her.

But I had to remember, people are often not what they seem. In times of great stress or great anger, they can do things completely out of character. My own impression of Sheila, from what I'd just seen, agreed with Irene's. Sheila was a woman who angered easily and lashed out when angry. Not the sort to calmly stalk her rival through the darkened streets, attack her, and slip away, leaving no evidence behind.

I have been wrong before, and I mustn't forget that. I'd barely started looking into Sheila Tierney's life, but I'd already found three reasons for her to have killed Anna: revenge for the destruction of her garden, anger at being cheated over the book, and in an attempt to get Anna's husband.

She had three reasons—and no alibi for the time of Anna's death.

The police would consider only the facts of the case, not people's impressions of what Sheila might or might not have done. If I was to do the same, I'd have to conclude that it was entirely possible Sheila Tierney had murdered Anna Wentworth.

Chapter Fourteen

B ack at the Emporium, I found Lauren at the Young Adults section, helping a girl close to her age choose a book.

As I usually do when I've been out, I did a quick scan of the store to see what had been sold in my absence. A good number of books, a collection of the ever-popular "I Am Sherlocked" mugs, a couple of the Jeremy Brett DVDs, a *Mind Palace* coloring book, a Sherlock wall calendar for next year, and several copies of the latest issue of the glossy new *Sherlock Holmes* Magazine. Not bad for one hour on a Thursday morning.

A small line had formed behind the sales counter, and I hurried to help Ashleigh. "Looks like you've been busy," I said when the customers had been served and sent happily on their way.

"We have. It's been nice to have some help."

"Sorry," I said. The young customer put the entire set of Enola Holmes books by Nancy Springer on the counter. "I'll take these, please. We're going to Kansas to visit my grandparents, and it's going to be *sooooo* boring." She emitted a world-weary sigh. "Mom gave me money to buy books for the trip. I don't usually read mysteries, but Lauren said these are really good."

"I hope you enjoy them," I said.

When she'd left, I thanked Lauren for her help. "Most of your reading material seems to be science fiction or adventure. I'm glad you like mysteries too."

"That girl couldn't decide what she wanted, so I decided for her."

Ashleigh laughed.

"Imagine going to Kansas for summer vacation at your grandparents' house," Lauren said. "*Soooo* lame."

I laughed.

"She looked at some of the puzzles, too, but didn't buy any. I'll put them back." Lauren went to straighten the table.

A girl after my own heart. At home, my life and my possessions are a mess, but at the shop I need everything to be neat and tidy and well organized. Otherwise, how would I keep track of it all? My worst nightmare is people who take things out of their proper place and put them away incorrectly.

"What's the legal age for hiring summer students in Massachusetts?" I asked Ashleigh.

"Not going to tell you," she said.

"Lauren," I called, "let's go upstairs for a few minutes."

"Okay," she said.

We climbed the seventeen steps to the upper level while Moriarty ran nimbly ahead.

"Did you get yourself something for lunch?" I asked.

"No. We've been so busy."

We. I hid a smile.

"It's been smashing helping out here, Gemma. Absolutely brilliant."

"I'm glad you're enjoying it, but now that I'm back, you can get yourself something for lunch and then go to the house and take Violet for a walk. First, go around to the house next door, the one to the west, and introduce yourself to Mrs. Ramsbatten. If she sees you with Violet, she'll wonder what's going on."

"I think I know her," Lauren said. "A tiny old lady who looks like Mrs. Claus?"

"You notice people. I like that."

"She's been to my house on garden club business."

"Recently?" I asked, remembering my neighbor's late-night prowling.

"Not for a couple months."

I changed the subject. "I saw your mum."

Her entire face lit up. "You did? Where is she? Why hasn't she called me?"

I kept my comments brief and to the point. Her mum needed some away time because she was upset that people were poking around in her garden and talking about what had happened to Anna. She didn't mean to leave Lauren alone, but hadn't realized Irene was out of town. "She said you can stay with me for a few more days, if you want to. Do you?"

"Sure. It would be upsetting to Snowball to move her again so soon, don't you think, Gemma?"

"Absolutely. Do you have anywhere you need to be in the next couple of days that I should know about? Such as doctor or dentist appointments?"

"I have tennis on Saturdays and Tuesdays. I missed this week because of . . . things."

"You mentioned something about being in a tournament. Do you take lessons?"

"Yeah. I'm doing real good, my coach tells me. Saturday's the first round of our tournament. I have a doubles partner, so I really need to be there."

"Do you like the game?"

"I love it!" she said. "Tennis is my life. Working in a book-store is my life now too, right?"

"Right. If you're still with me on Saturday, I'll see you get to your game. Where is it?"

"West London Country Club. Two thirty." Lauren headed off for lunch and her dog-walking duties. Moriarty went downstairs with her, and I picked up my phone. Ryan needed to know about Anna and Sheila and the gardening book. Sheila had asked me not to tell, but I had absolutely no intention of doing anything of the sort. I wouldn't tell him my impressions or my conclusions. I'd simply lay out the facts as I'd been told them.

"I paid a call on Sheila Tierney this morning," I said once he answered.

"Has she left the hotel? She's supposed to notify me of her movements."

"No, she's still at the Beach Front. Still in hiding. She didn't know I was coming."

"I shouldn't be surprised that you found her, but I am. I won't even ask how you managed that. What did she have to say?"

"That she wrote most of Anna's latest book, and if you have someone compare the manuscript that I didn't see in the bottom of her office drawer—although I was in her house at the invita-tion of her daughter—with the book that I did take out of the library, you'll see she's right about that."

"It's going to take me the rest of the day just to parse that sentence."

"Sheila can prove she wrote much, if not most, of the book. Anna didn't acknowledge Sheila's contribution or give her a fair share of the profits, and Sheila was planning to take her to court over it."

"That is interesting. I knew they'd been friends for years but had a falling out a few months ago. No one I've spoken to could say for sure why they argued, and Sheila herself said something about a disagreement that got out of hand and both of them too stubborn to apologize. But you, who didn't even know the two women until this week, found out."

"Because I listen to what people are saying, not only what comes out of their mouths."

"I don't quite know what that means, but I believe you."

"Sheila would have realized that being cheated by Anna might be interpreted as potential grounds for murder, so she didn't want to admit outright what happened between them. I also found out that Sheila is . . . fond might be the best word . . . of Mike Nixon. The word she used when talking about him was 'sweet.'"

"Might be interesting. What was your take on him?"

I thought for a while. "I don't have much of a take. He's been in the Emporium a few times, but we didn't talk about anything other than books. Outside the store, I've only met him once, but I liked him. I felt sorry for him. He seemed to be genuinely grieving Anna and confused at his loss. That, of course, doesn't mean anything."

"Anything else?"

"No. Lauren's going to stay with me for a few more days, at least until one of her parents wants to claim her."

"Thanks, Gemma. Take care."

"Don't I always?"

He hung up with a bark of laughter.

I went downstairs to spend some time on the shop floor. I believed Sheila might have killed Anna, but it wasn't my job to prove it either way. I'd told Ryan what I knew, and I trusted him to put the pieces together.

* * *

A Curious Incident

At twenty-two minutes to four, as Lauren was ensuring the books on the bottom row of the gaslight shelf were property filed alphabetically by author, I said to her, "Jayne and I have a partners' meeting at this time every day."

"You can set your watch by it," Ashleigh said. "I do. Rhetorically speaking, as I don't wear a watch, and if I did, it wouldn't need setting."

I ignored my assistant. "Do you want to join us?"

Lauren grinned at me and leapt to her feet. "Yeah. That would be good. Are you partners? I didn't know that."

"We're business partners. My great-uncle Arthur and I own half of the tearoom. Jayne owns the other half."

"Cool."

We went into Mrs. Hudson's to find Jayne seated at our favorite table in the window alcove. The tearoom closes at four, and only a few guests remained, lingering over the remains of their afternoon tea.

Jayne smiled at us as we approached the table. "How was your day as a shop clerk?" she asked Lauren.

"Brilliant! I'm going to own a bookshop when I finish college. Did you go to university to learn how to be a bookstore owner, Gemma?"

"I went to the school of hard knocks," I said.

"What does that mean?"

"It means I learned on the job. I used to have a mystery bookstore in London before I came to Cape Cod to help Uncle Arthur run the Emporium."

Jayne checked the time on her phone as Lauren asked, "What does your uncle do?"

"As little as possible. He's what we call a silent partner." I suppressed a shudder as I thought back to January, when Uncle

Arthur and Ashleigh ran the shop while Jayne and I were in London.

I'd been lucky to have a business to return to. He'd made it up to me by inviting the son of longtime friends to drop into the Emporium for a visit. That son goes by the name of Benedict Cumberbatch. As well as the life-sized cutout in the Emporium, a photo of Benedict as Sherlock, signed to Jayne and complimenting her on the quality of her scones, now hung in pride of place next to the shelf of assorted tea paraphernalia we offer for sale.

Fiona put a plate on the table. Today we had egg and salmon tea sandwiches as well as raspberry tarts, mini coconut cupcakes, and bright red macarons. We always got the day's leftovers at the partners' meeting—one of the joys of being a silent partner in a tearoom. And I am very much a silent partner. Unless I'm making a traditional English breakfast, a kitchen is not my natural habitat. The teapot and two place settings were already on the table, and the scent of warm, spicy Darjeeling rose from the pot.

"Would you like something to drink, Lauren?" Jayne asked.

"Can I have tea?"

"Another cup and plate, please, Fiona." Jayne checked the time again. "And maybe a few more sandwiches, as we have a guest."

"I have nothing of significance to report," I said as I poured my tea, "so you'll be able to meet Andy for your walk and picnic at four as planned."

"How'd—? Never mind. I don't want to know how you know."

"Sure you do. Andy went away for a few days to visit his family, but it would appear he's now back, unless you've found another beau?"

"I haven't."

"Glad to hear it. You're checking the time as though anxious that time is passing, although I'm not at all late. You've refreshed your makeup and brushed your hair, which you never do after work; and if I'm not mistaken, you're wearing nicer trainers than the old ones you wear in the kitchen, but not the flimsy sandals you put on if you're going to the shops on the way home. You've pushed aside the food plate, although you always have something at our meeting, which indicates you're planning to eat shortly."

Jayne shook her head. Lauren looked under the table, checking out the aforementioned shoes.

"We might be going to a restaurant for an early dinner, you know," Jayne said.

"No, otherwise you'd have better shoes and you'd have changed into a fresh outfit, not kept on your work jeans. A walk after work is romantic. A picnic, even better."

"Okay. He's bringing the food and drink, and I've done some desserts."

I mentally slapped my forehead. "I missed that. Macarons. You don't normally make them. You've been trying something new, and the beginning of the season is not the best time to experiment. The red color is presumably intended to be romantic."

"Andy's working tonight, so we're having an early date. A walk in the woods and then a picnic." Jayne sighed happily.

I tried one of the macarons. Absolutely delicious. The deep red color came from fresh raspberries.

"My mom says I can't date until I'm fourteen." Lauren selected a salmon sandwich.

"If I were your mother, it would be twenty-five," I said.

Jayne caught my eye and then raised one eyebrow and jerked her head in the direction of Lauren. I nodded and lifted my thumb to indicate all was okay as I picked up my teacup. Sheila had called the shop earlier in the afternoon, asking to speak to her daughter. I'd sent Lauren up to the office to take the call, and when she'd come back down twenty minutes later, she'd been smiling.

* * *

The Emporium closes at nine on Thursdays, so night was gathering as Lauren and I walked up Blue Water Place to my house. She seemed to have enjoyed her day and chatted happily about the delights of working in a bookshop. "I hope you're not too hungry," I said to her. "It's late for someone your age to have dinner, but I like to relax over my meal at the end of the day, not wolf it down on a quick dinner break and then hurry back to the shop."

"I had plenty to eat at tea with you and Jayne, Gemma. Those sandwiches were so good."

"Glad to hear it. That is, after all, the purpose of afternoon tea, to tide one over until dinnertime."

I let Violet into the enclosed yard, and Lauren fed Snowball and cleaned the litter box. Important tasks done, I took a beef stew out of the freezer and reheated it in the microwave while Lauren threw vegetables together to make the salad.

When dinner was over, we washed up and then took Violet for a walk. Lauren had given the dog a good long walk in the afternoon, so we didn't stay outside for long and were home before ten thirty. I sent Lauren, yawning heavily, off to bed along with Snowball, who was also yawing heavily despite having not spent the day working.

I was settling myself down in the den with my book when Jayne called.

"How'd it go?" I asked her.

"Heavenly," she breathed. "I can't believe Andy and I have been such good friends all these years and I didn't realize how absolutely marvelous he is before now."

It was an effort but I refrained from saying, "I told you so."

"Did you just get home? I thought Andy had to work."

"He did. I went around to my mom's after, and then I thought you'd be busy having dinner and stuff."

"Which I was. Lauren's in bed now."

"How's that working out?"

"Having her here? It's been marvelous. It's fun to see the store through eager young eyes."

"Mom told me everyone in the garden club's saying Sheila's skipped town. Some people are saying that's proof of her guilt. No one knows where she is. I'm assuming you do?"

"I do. Ryan knows, so she's not proving she's guilty of anything. She doesn't want to talk to anyone, and the fact that the garden club people know she's not home is proof enough that they've been going around there. Probably under the pretext of offering sympathy."

"That sounds about right. Sheila and Anna used to be good friends, Mom says, but then they had a terrible fight and could barely stand to be in the same room. I'm assuming you know about that."

"I do."

"Okay, keep your secrets. Except for one: Was Anna having an affair with David Tierney?"

"I don't think so. I'd say his business problems are all consuming these days." *More likely,* I thought, *that Sheila wanted an affair with Anna's husband but was getting nowhere on that front.* I sucked in a breath.

"What?" Jayne said. "You've thought of something, haven't you? I love it when that happens, even though I never have a clue what it was I said."

"You reminded me of something. Good night. Gotta run."

When Sherlock Holmes was faced with a complicated case, he lit his pipe (or prepared his seven percent solution), then either played his violin or leaned back in his comfortable arm chair at 221B Baker Street, closed his eyes, and considered the case.

On the other hand, I have a business to run, a lively dog to care for, an eleven-year-old to temporarily mother, and a friend's romantic entanglements to guess at. Never mind trying to manage my own romantic entanglements.

I had let aspects of this case slip out of my mind, and that would never do.

The mysterious M.

Faced with the evidence I had, I'd concluded it was possible Sheila was guilty of the murder of Anna. Whether she was or not, I mustn't forget about the other complications.

Jayne's mention of garden club gossip reminded me that it was rumored Anna had been having an affair with her gardener.

What was his name?

Manuel. *M.*

How likely was it that Mike Nixon couldn't spell Sheila's last name? Not very. His wife and Sheila had been good friends as well as writing partners, which means they would have spent a lot of time together.

If Mike had sent the note, he might have deliberately misspelled her name, but I could see no reason for that. How likely would it be that a man like Mike Nixon would stick a note in the postbox anyway? Surely, if he wanted to tell Sheila to back off, he'd have sent a text.

If Anna was having an affair with Manuel, as garden club gossip said, wouldn't that put her husband on the suspect list?

Did Sheila want the gardener for herself? If so, that was yet another reason for Sheila to have bumped off her rival.

Another nail in her coffin.

I told myself to slow down. Someone with the initial *M* asked Sheila to leave him—or her—alone. My natural assumption had been that Sheila had been pursuing this person for romantic reasons, and the feeling was not returned. I suppose it could be about something else, like Sheila wanted them to cut her lawn, but who slipped a note worded like that one into a mailbox to refuse a job cutting grass?

Do not bother me again, it had said.

I didn't know everyone in Sheila's life. There might be plenty of people with the initial *M*, but the only ones I'd come across were Mike Nixon and Manuel the gardener. The young, handsome, muscular gardener. Sheila had been quick to jump to the assumption that her husband was having an affair. Was that guilt talking? Because Sheila was having an affair herself, or she wanted to?

Which brought me to another train of thought.

I put my book aside and got my iPad out of the reproduction antique secretary.

Divorce laws were loosening by Sherlock Holmes's time, but before then, ending a marriage might well have been a matter of murder, and often was. Arsenic was commonly used to rid oneself of an unwanted spouse in the days of limited divorce.

But in Gemma Doyle's time, divorce isn't rare, needn't be complicated, and isn't the least bit scandalous.

However, it can be expensive, which is particularly difficult for those already having financial troubles.

I started my search with David Tierney and dug deeper past what I'd already learned. Ten years ago, he'd left the high-tech company he'd been working for and started D&S Restaurant Consultants to advise fast-food restaurants on using technology to improve the time it took to take customer orders. Computer industry buzz had been very excited. I recognized some big-name coffee chains and fast-food restaurants among his stable of clients. Pictures appeared of him shaking hands with important people and of him and a beaming Sheila greeting the rich and famous at charity benefits and convention banquets. Industry news called his company "innovative," "brilliant," "groundbreaking," and even "future-creating." Whatever that means.

Over the previous year, things started going downhill and, like an out-of-control toboggan on a snowy hill, fast.

As I'd deduced from the contents of David's computer, his company was in severe financial difficulties. He'd vastly overextended himself, taken on too many clients too fast, promised more than he could deliver, and had then been forced to hire staff who didn't have the cutting-edge qualifications he needed. He'd failed to complete some contracts and had done a shoddy job on others. He'd been sued more than once, not only by his clients for failure to deliver as promised, but also by his employees for not paying them. He was searching for fresh funding, basically carrying his begging bowl all around the East Coast in search of new investors. His recent history should have been the kiss of death to any attempts to rebuild the company. That he hadn't been outright shown the door by prospective partners was because his work was still being called "original" and "potentially groundbreaking," although no longer "future-creating." It was obvious that if anyone did go into partnership with him, that person would take control of almost everything, and David would be relegated to being a junior partner. If that.

I own one bookstore in conjunction with my great-uncle, who is almost ninety and would rather be at sea than worrying about the business, so I'm not exactly a titan of industry. But if David

Tierney asked for my advice, it would be to consolidate what he had and simply get the job done. Take contracts he could handle on his own, with one or two assistants, and do them. He might even take the time to help his wife manage a fledging career as a gardening guru.

But none of that would bring in the kind of bucks that led to charity benefits and shaking hands with the CEO of the world's largest coffee chain.

Nor would it bring in the sort of money needed to allow his wife to spend all her time in her garden, or put a child in private school, or pay for membership at the West London Country Club.

About the last thing in the world David Tierney needed right now was a drawn-out, bitterly contested divorce.

If Sheila had been murdered, David would be at the top of my suspect list. But Sheila hadn't been murdered—Anna had. If David and Anna had been involved, so what? Once again, this wasn't Sherlock Holmes's time, where a spurned lover might have threatened to sue David for breach of promise or destroy his reputation.

I then went on to see what I could find about Anna's husband, Mike Nixon.

Was everyone in West London minutes from penury?

It still surprises me sometimes what a person with a bit of internet knowledge and a suspicious mind can find out. Sherlock Holmes had to send the Baker Street Irregulars fanning out across the back alleys and waterways of London as well as dispatching a flurry of telegrams to all parts of the Empire and beyond. I could simply curl up in my favorite chair, my dog at my feet, a cup of tea at hand, and dig deep beneath the public surface of the internet.

Mike Nixon had told me he was a medical supplies salesman. Turns out he's actually an out-of-work medical supplies salesman and had, according to the résumé he was currently sending all around Massachusetts, been out of work for more than a year. In fact, he was no longer sending his résumé out and seemed to have given up trying to find work.

Instead, he'd become a frequent visitor to Las Vegas.

I've never been to Las Vegas, but from what I've been told, it's not the best place for someone short of funds to spend their time.

Mike Nixon was another man who couldn't afford an acrimonious divorce. Rather than there being a reason for him to want to kill his wife, it was quite the opposite: Anna's books and blog seemed to be, from what I could find, the couple's only source of income.

If Sheila went ahead with her lawsuit and was successful, she might have done some damage to Anna and Mike's precarious finances. But again, Sheila hadn't been murdered. Anna had.

Had Anna been mistaken for Sheila?

I couldn't see it. It was nighttime, yes, but not completely dark. Still, a nervous person, a moment of panic. A mistake.

I picked up the phone and called Ryan.

"Ashburton," said a sleepy voice.

"Hi, it's me. Hope I'm not disturbing you."

"Gemma! Is everything okay?"

"Yes, all's fine. Just a quick question."

"Gemma, it's three thirty."

"It is?"

"Yes, it is. And honesty forces me to tell you that I got to bed, finally, around half an hour ago, and I have a meeting with the chief at seven tomorrow . . . I mean this morning."

"Sorry. Never mind. My question can wait."

"I'm awake now. You might as well spit it out."

"Are you sure?"

"Gemma."

"Okay. What did Anna Wentworth look like? I mean her body shape, not her face. I've seen the photos that were in the paper, but it can be hard to tell the actual body shape. Louise told me she was about Jayne's size. Is that true?"

"I won't even ask why you want to know. Anna was five foot three and weighed a hundred and twenty pounds. She played tennis regularly and was apparently good at it."

"Thanks. You can go back to sleep now."

"Like that's likely to happen."

"I love you, Ryan," I said. "I really, really, really do."

"Hearing that was worth waking up for." I could hear the smile in his voice. "Good night, Gemma."

"Good night."

So Anna was a good bit shorter and much thinner than Sheila. Unlikely anyone would mistake one for the other in the dark, no matter how nervous they were. Plus Anna was with her dog, walking near her home as she did most evenings, and there was no reason Sheila would have done that task for her.

I closed my iPad, called to Violet, and we went to bed.

Chapter Fifteen

Sheila Tierney came out of hiding on Friday. I don't know if she was bored at the hotel or had simply gotten over her snit and dared to show her face in public again. Probably both.

Or maybe she missed her daughter.

She arrived unannounced at the Emporium at two o'clock. Lauren had spent the morning in the tearoom, helping Jayne in the kitchen. She came back after lunch to tell me she'd decided she wanted to own a bookstore where she would serve afternoon tea to the customers. She could do that between her games on the professional tennis circuit and her medical studies.

"I'm here!" Sheila announced as she stepped into the bookshop, dragging her red suitcase behind her. Lauren squealed and practically flew across the room. Sheila wrapped her arms around her daughter and held her close. She wore the red and white dress and had done her hair and makeup as normal, no longer trying to be in disguise.

"Ready to go home?" she asked when Lauren released her.

"Oh yeah." Lauren turned to me. "Is it okay if I go home now, Gemma? I've enjoyed working here, but my mom . . ."

"Off you go," I said. "You're welcome to drop in any time."

"We have to go to Gemma's house and get Snowball, Mom."

Sheila looked at me. "Would you mind giving us a lift? I walked from the hotel, and that was more than enough."

"I don't have my car with me—sorry. My house is on the way to yours. I'll give Lauren a key, and she can get the cat and her things. You can drop the key here next time you're in the neighborhood."

"Thank you." Sheila swallowed hard. "For . . . uh . . . everything." She choked out the words. Gratitude didn't come easily to Sheila Tierney.

"Any time," I said.

"Guess what, darling?" she said to Lauren. "Dad's on his way home!"

"Yeah!" Lauren threw her arms up and sprang into the air. "Did you hear that, Gemma! Dad's coming home. We're going to be a family again."

Sheila had the grace to avoid my eyes.

I handed Lauren the key to my house.

"Do you think Violet's going to miss Snowball, Gemma?" she asked.

"Not as much as I'm going to miss you."

"You can bring Violet for a visit sometime, if you want."

"I might just do that."

"Will you come and watch me play tennis tomorrow? It's the tournament."

"What time?"

"My game starts at two thirty."

"I'd like to. If I can get away from the store, I will. Saturdays are busy in here."

"I can manage," Ashleigh called.

"Ask Jayne too," Lauren said. "I helped her make tarts and cupcakes, Mom. It was fun. I'm going to have a bakery when I grow up."

They left, Lauren still chattering about all the plans she had for her future.

I stood at the window and watched them walk down the street. Lauren had a bright life ahead indeed. If her parents didn't mess it up.

Irene had called me yesterday from her conference. She'd come back if she was needed, but . . . An editor from the *New York Times* was scheduled to speak, and everyone was saying he was prospecting new hires. She'd hate to miss the opportunity but . . .

I told her all was under control and Lauren was fine staying with me.

I texted Irene now to let her know Sheila was home and David was due shortly, and then I went back to work.

The shop seemed rather lonely for the remainder of the day.

* * *

"Let's do something fun tonight after the shop closes," I said to Jayne over a cup of English Breakfast and a scone at our partners' meeting in the tearoom.

"I like fun," she said. "What do you have in mind?"

"How about dinner? We can go to the Café, and Andy can take a break and join us. I'll ask Ryan."

"Sounds like a plan."

"I'll call for a reservation when I get back to the store. How about nine fifteen?"

Jayne took out her phone. "Why don't I do that now? You'll forget."

I was rather insulted. "I never forget."

"Gemma, you never remember."

* * *

Andy's place, the Blue Water Café, occupies one of the best locations on the West London waterfront. It sits half on the pier by the fishing dock, with an incomparable view of the boat-filled small harbor and the open Atlantic Ocean beyond. As it faces east, it doesn't get a sunset, but tonight the long orange and red rays drew lines on the water against a dramatic backdrop of the darkening sky. The restaurant is always busy on a Friday night in summer, but as we were having dinner with the owner, we got one of the best tables, tucked in a corner of the deck, perched high over the dark cool waters where small harbor seals swam and played.

Jayne had gone home for a nap after the tearoom closed, and I'd come straight from work. I was the first to arrive. I'd barely settled myself at a table for four before the waiter arrived with menus. "'Evening, Gemma. Get you something while you're waiting for the others?"

"I'll have a glass of sauvignon blanc, thanks. Can you tell Andy I'm here?"

"Sure." He put a menu in front of me, but I pushed it away. I always have the same thing when I come to the Café. Some people think that's odd, but I know what I like, so why take a chance on trying something new and being disappointed?

Ryan and Jayne arrived before my drink. Ryan crossed the deck toward me, but Jayne waved and then ducked down the hallway to the kitchen.

Ryan kissed the top of my head and pulled up his chair. "This is a good idea. I need some downtime." The waiter put my glass in front of me, and Ryan said, "I'll have a Nantucket Grey Lady, please." He turned to me. "Jayne told me Andy's hoping to get a break and come out and join us. Are things happening on that front?"

"Yes, and I'm delighted. Jayne's blissfully happy, and I know Andy's the perfect man for her."

"You aren't interfering, I hope."

"Me? Perish the thought." I refrained from saying that all my interfering had come to naught, and they'd found each other only after I'd given up. I decided not to speculate as to if there was a deeper meeting to that.

"I'm glad for them, and I hope it works with their crazy schedules. I can't imagine a tougher life than being a chef in a top restaurant," said the man who solved murder most foul for a living and often went days without sleep.

Speaking of going without sleep . . . I remembered last night with a twinge of guilt. When the poor man did manage to get to bed, someone had woken him up. I smiled at him. He smiled back.

"You don't look too bad," I said. Some of the tiredness had lifted from his eyes, he was freshly shaven, and his big warm smile was back, as was the twinkle in the blue eyes I loved so much.

"Gee, thanks, Gemma."

"I mean, you don't look as bad as you normally do."

"This is getting better and better."

"I mean," I floundered, "you look like you've had some sleep on the job. I mean, sleeping when not working. On the job. With

Louise. At nighttime. Sleeping at nighttime, and not with Louise."
I firmly shut my mouth.

"I'm glad we cleared that one up at least." His beer arrived and he lifted his glass. "Cheers, as they say in England."

"Cheers." We clinked glasses and grinned at each other.

"In answer to your inelegantly put question, I did get home and catch a few hours of sleep before coming here. I needed it because someone disturbed me during the night."

"Sorry about that."

"Not a problem. I've been woken up by less pleasant people. I assume you know Sheila Tierney has left the Beach Front Hotel and gone home?"

"She came into the shop to get Lauren. She said her husband's coming home too."

Ryan nodded. "I called at their house. David was there. I asked Sheila if she'd been having professional or monetary problems with Anna Wentworth. At first, she pretended not to know what I was talking about, but David told her that I obviously knew, so she might as well spit it out. Whereupon she fell all over herself telling me how hard done by she was regarding their cowriting the book and how nasty Anna had been to her. David finally had to interrupt to get her to stop talking. I think he thought she was about to incriminate herself."

"He thinks she's guilty?"

"Possibly. Or he didn't want me to be there all day. I took her manuscript away and also a copy of Anna's second book. I'll have someone compare them."

"They'll match," I said. "Do you think she did it? Killed Anna, I mean."

He sipped at his beer. "I'm not committing to anything, but I don't think so. Frankly, she's not too bright, Gemma, and judging by what more than a few people have told me about her, she's wildly impulsive. If she did it, she'd have confessed by now. I also have to consider that she has no police record more serious than a couple of parking tickets. Meaning, no record of violence."

"No record doesn't mean it never happened. She did attack Anna."

"In front of a couple of dozen ticket-paying citizens and garden tour guides. Hair-pulling and kicking and a heck of a lot of screaming. From all accounts, Anna gave as good as she got, and more than a few witnesses implied Anna egged Sheila on. If Sheila had killed Anna, I don't believe she'd have been able to be so cool about it and cover it up so well."

That was an aspect I'd not considered. I'd laid out the facts for myself as I saw them and hadn't been able to dismiss Sheila as a suspect. Ryan was probably right: she wouldn't have been able to keep up the pretense under police questioning. She'd have been more likely to want to justify herself.

"Then again," I said, "she *is* a drama teacher. Maybe she's a better actor than we thought. The outburst over the garden vandalism and the attack on Anna might have been premeditated. Designed to make it look as though she's a rash, impulsive woman."

"You've overthought it, Gemma. If you have one fault, that's it."

"Only one?"

"I said *if* you had only one."

"What about the vandalism? Any idea who did that?"

"We've sent some things found in Sheila's garden for fingerprint comparisons, but we don't have the results yet, and I'm not expecting much. The guilty party almost certainly wore gloves. At a guess, it was probably Anna. No one else that we know of had any reason to do it. A good number of the members of the garden club— and we've spoken to every one of them we can find—are more upset about the destruction of Sheila's garden than the death of Anna."

"Did Anna have that many enemies?"

He chuckled. "They're a single-minded bunch. They liked Anna fine, although they say she didn't have a lot to do with the club lately. I mean that, to them, the garden's more important than the woman."

"I can think of a few Sherlockians like that. Not about gardens, though."

"Right. Sheila's was the only place that got hit. Unlikely to have been teenagers or drunken college kids on a rampage, as no one else has reported anything like that, and we didn't find the usual detritus, such as broken beer bottles, near the scene. Sheila had been a high school teacher, and not a popular one by all accounts, but she left West London High five years ago. The kids would have gone on to other resentments long ago."

"What happens now?" I asked.

"Now? You mean about the murder? We'll keep the case open, of course, but the chief's inclined to believe it was a random thing, and Louise agrees. That's not a conclusion he comes to easily. Not in a tourist town at the beginning of the season."

"Louise agrees. You didn't say you did."

"All I can act on is the evidence I have. And I have none."

I shook my head. "No. The idea of a random attack is too much of a coincidence happening immediately after the blowup over the garden."

"Coincidences happen, Gemma."

"'The universe is rarely so lazy.'"

He raised an eyebrow. "Not Sherlock Holmes, I hope. I can't take the advice of a fictional detective to my chief as a reason for me to keep investigating."

"Holmes, yes, but not an original. The *Sherlock* TV show."

"Sorry we're late." Jayne slipped into the chair beside me, and Andy took the one opposite. "Last-minute problem in the kitchen."

"Everything under control?" Ryan asked.

"Yeah." Andy glanced around the restaurant deck. Even this late, every table was taken. The soft white fairy lights on the railing broke the dark, and candles burned in hurricane lamps on the tables. Waiters carried plates piled high, people chatted and laughed, glasses and cutlery clinked, and marvelous scents filled the air.

Ryan spread out his arms, taking it all in. "I don't know how you do it, Andy. Running this place, keeping everything moving smoothly and everyone happy."

Andy grinned at him. "It's what I do. I love it. On good days anyway." He couldn't help taking a peek at Jayne, looking beautiful and, above all, happy in a navy-blue and white dress and silver jewelry. "Most days are good ones."

"What's good today?" Ryan asked.

"Everything," Jayne said.

"What's particularly good then?"

"Try the scallops," Andy said.

"I'm going to," Jayne said.

When the waiter arrived, Ryan ordered a Caesar salad with his scallops, and Andy asked for a burger, saying he wasn't in the mood for seafood. I ordered my usual: clam chowder and stuffed sole.

A Curious Incident

"I'll just have a glass of wine, thanks. Whatever Gemma's having," Jayne said. "I ate earlier.

"Better bring her a platter of calamari," I said to the waiter as he collected the menus. "Otherwise, I won't get any of my own dinner."

"Now," Jayne said, "no talking about murder tonight."

"Has there been a murder?" Andy asked. "I didn't hear about it."

"Which," Jayne said, "is why I love you."

I thought Andy would die of pure happiness.

Chapter Sixteen

We had a lovely evening and made no more mention of murder. No crisis happened in the kitchen, and Andy was able to sit back and enjoy his meal and simply relax, for a change. He told some stories about life in a restaurant that had us holding our sides with laughter. When we'd turned down the offer of dessert and finished our coffee, he went back to work, and Jayne, who had to get up at four to start the day's baking, headed home. Ryan and I walked along the boardwalk, holding hands and watching the tourists watching everyone else.

"Ice cream?" he said to me as we made a turn in front of the lighthouse at the end of Harbor Road to head back. High overhead the light of the fourth-order Fresnel lens flashed its rhythm of three seconds on, three seconds off, three seconds on, twenty seconds off.

"After that giant meal?" I said. "Why not?"

We joined the lineup at the ice-cream counter at the candy store. Ryan ordered a triple rum and raisin for himself and a small French vanilla for me. Cones in hand, we stepped onto the boardwalk. I saw someone I recognized on the other side of the street, checking out the menu on the door of the Blue Water Café.

"Don't look now," I said.

"Like you can tell a cop that. What am I not to look at?"

"Louise Estrada's across the street. She's with a man. Do you know him?"

"How can I tell you if I know him if I'm not looking?" He looked. "Never seen him before."

"They're on a date."

"How do you know that? Maybe it's her brother or a friend."

"She's unlikely to put on a skirt that short or heels that tall for her brother, but in case she did, his arm is not around her in a brotherly way."

As we watched, the couple spoke to each other and then went into the restaurant.

"They weren't standing that close," Ryan said.

"True. And some families and good friends are physically closer than others. The cincher is her hair."

"What about her hair?"

"She's had it done. She didn't have those caramel highlights the last time I saw her."

"She didn't?"

"No, she didn't. Considering she's been working as hard as you have on the Wentworth case, and the first opportunity you had for some sleep was a few snatched hours last night and again this afternoon, I'll presume that she thought getting her hair done was more important than sleeping. Therefore, it's elementary to conclude she's done herself up for a date."

"Should I say something tomorrow? Tell her it looks nice?"

"No. That would make her suspicious."

* * *

Crime doesn't stop in West London just because the police have a murder to investigate. Ryan got a call first thing the following morning about a boat stolen from the Cape Cod Yacht Club. Once he'd left, I put the coffee on and took Violet for a walk.

Another beautiful Cape Cod day. I love living on the Lower Cape, but I only wish I could enjoy it more. Summer, of course, is the busiest time at the shop, so I rarely get the chance to escape for more than a few hours at a time. I'd love nothing more than to grab Jayne and jump in the Miata and drive up the coast with the roof of the car down and the salt wind blowing through our hair.

But that's unlikely to happen: Jayne works even harder than I do.

Over the winter, we have time to catch our breath, and we went to England this past January. But winter's not the same. Long walks in the crisp winter woods can be fun, and it's lovely and quiet when the tourists have left. But one doesn't exactly enjoy running barefoot across frozen sand with gay abandon or splashing through ice-rimed water.

Which put me in mind of Andy. Jayne and Andy. If their relationship moved up to a more serious level, as I suspected it soon would, Jayne would have even less time for me.

I didn't mind that. I wanted her to be happy.

Jayne had, in my humble opinion, horrible taste in men. She went from one unsuitable boyfriend to another, and the only saving grace was that none of them lasted long.

Andy, on the other hand, was genuinely nice and perfect for her. I hoped he'd last. Judging by the expression on his face last night when he looked at her—which had been all the time—he hoped so too.

Violet and I turned the corner into Blue Water Place. Mrs. Ramsbatten was sitting in the white wicker rocking chair on her front porch, enjoying a cup of coffee. She called out and waved at me when she saw us. The roar of a lawnmower came from the far side of her house, but I didn't see the truck belonging to the garden service company that did the heavy work in her yard as well as ours. Her car was parked at the bottom of her driveway, facing the street, a sign saying "For Sale" taped to the front window.

"Good morning!" I waved. Violet wagged her tail in greeting.

Mrs. Ramsbatten summoned me over, so I opened the gate, and we walked through it and up the path. Violet ran up the steps, tail wagging furiously, and Mrs. Ramsbatten leaned over and gave her a hearty rub across her back.

"How you are today, dear?" she asked me.

"Very well, thank you. Lovely day."

"So it is. Any news from Arthur recently?"

"He sent a text yesterday morning to say he's arrived in Italy."

"Oh yes. A text. Convenient, I suppose, but so impersonal."

"At least I know he's safe."

"And that is a comfort. Now that you're here, dear," she said, getting to the real reason she wanted to talk to me, "I'm wondering if there's any further news about the Anna Wentworth case."

"I haven't seen the news yet this morning. Why are you asking me?"

She winked. "I do believe I saw young Detective Ashburton—such a handsome man, isn't he?—leaving in the early hours."

I felt flames rushing into my face.

"He reminds me of Mr. Ramsbatten. He has kind eyes. My dear Joseph had kind eyes also. I believe you can tell a man's quality by his eyes."

The lawnmower droned steadily in the background. A hummingbird passed in a flash of color and dipped at the feeder at the end of the porch, its tiny wings a blur of motion.

"Ryan doesn't tell me anything about police business," I said.

She winked again. "Of course not, dear. The members of the garden club are still abuzz about it all. Everyone said Sheila Tierney had caught a flight to Brazil and would be fighting extradition, but then she turned up at her house yesterday, cool as a cucumber, acting as though nothing had happened."

I said nothing.

"Geraldine Gallant went to Sheila's house yesterday evening, supposedly to ask if Sheila wanted advice on repairing her garden. Sheila slammed the door in her face." Mrs. Ramsbatten chuckled. "I'm not surprised. Geraldine is a terrible busybody."

"How do you know all this?"

Another wink. "I might not be as active in the club as I once was, but I'm still connected. In this case, I can't pretend to have any inside knowledge. Geraldine couldn't wait to get home and blast out an email, pretending she's concerned about 'poor Sheila's' state of mental health. As well as being a busybody, Geraldine thinks she's an expert in the art of the sly dig. Before the door shut on her, she managed to ask Sheila if she needed any professional advice now that Anna was no longer available for private consultations."

"Did Anna do much of that? Private consultations?"

"She did some landscape design work, I believe. She was dreadfully expensive, though."

"Do you know if Sheila ever helped her with that? When they were friends, I mean?"

"Come to think of it, she might have. I don't know about helping, but when Anna went to the Evans home to give them a quote, Sheila was with her. She didn't get the job. It was more than Rosemarie wanted to pay."

The roar of the lawnmower increased as it turned the corner.

"I have to get off to work," I said. "Have a nice day. Come on, Violet." I turned and stopped in surprise.

Manuel, who'd been Anna's gardener, was cutting Mrs. Ramsbatten's lawn. He nodded politely to me.

I turned back to my neighbor. "Do you have a new lawn care service?"

"Just Manuel. Such a nice young man. He's your new gardener too, dear. I wasn't happy with that other bunch. They were becoming unreliable. I've heard others complaining about them. They've taken on more clients than they can handle this season. When I heard that Manuel was looking for work, I hired him for us."

"Looking for work? I thought he worked at Anna and Mike's house."

"That wasn't full time. Anna was very much a hands-on gardener. She employed someone only to cut the grass and do the heavy work. No, Manuel works for a few families around town as well as putting in a couple of days a week at the country club. When the garden club heard that Mike had let Manuel go, they put the word out."

"Mike let him go?"

"He's already put the house up for sale. Seems premature to me. When Mr. Ramsbatten died, everyone told me not to make any decisions for six months to a year. That was wise advice. You'd think that as Mike's trying to sell the house, he'd want the garden to look its best, but perhaps he's the sort who prefers to do things on his own. Keeping busy helps with grief." A cloud briefly settled over her face, but she bent over to give Violet another pat, and when she looked at me again, her usual bright smile had returned.

I tugged gently at the leash and stepped off the porch. I waved to Manuel to indicate that I wanted to talk to him. He switched off the lawnmower and gave me a big grin. "Good morning."

"'Morning. I'm Gemma Doyle. I live next door." I pointed. Violet sniffed at his legs. "So I guess you work for me now."

"I guess I do. Nice dog." He gave Violet a pat.

"She is, thanks. I don't have anything to do with our yard, so have at it. Mrs. Ramsbatten will let you know if anything special needs doing."

"Okay, thanks. You were at Anna's house the other day, weren't you? Mike and Anna's, I mean. Were you close friends?" Manuel spoke with a New England accent, only slightly rough around the edges.

"I didn't know her, but I had met Mike before. I went with my friend to offer our condolences."

I couldn't read anything in his face, which put me off guard, as I usually can tell a great deal by faces. He didn't show any excessive emotion talking about Anna, as he would have if they were involved. He'd said "Anna's house," and then quickly changed it to "Mike and Anna's," which was natural enough, as Anna, not Mike, was the garden lover in that family, and therefore the one Manuel would have dealt with.

He was in his mid-thirties, with thick black hair that fell to his shoulders and olive skin with a layer of tan; and he was heavily muscled, as befitted a man who worked all summer in gardens. He wasn't particularly good-looking—his chin was too small and his face too thin—but he had a certain casual charm, and his eyes, large and dark and thickly lashed, were exceptionally beautiful. Were they kind eyes? I couldn't tell.

"Do you work for Sheila Tierney as well?" I asked.

Shutters came down over those dark eyes. "No." He nodded politely and switched the lawnmower back on.

There was a story there, all right.

I called goodbye to Mrs. Ramsbatten. On the spur of the moment, I decided Violet hadn't had a long enough walk, and we went back the way we'd come.

A Curious Incident

A few streets over, a "For Sale" sign swung in the breeze on the Wentworth/Nixon front lawn. I studied the house while Violet sniffed at the bushes lining the walk. Mike was clearly in a hurry to sell. The interior of the house would need a lot of work, but work means money, and he didn't have much. Perhaps he was counting on the appeal of the garden to attract a buyer who was prepared to put up with an out-of-date house or renovate it themself.

As I stood there studying the house, wondering what sort of life insurance Anna had and concluding that I'd probably not be able to find out, the front door opened and a woman stepped out, locked the door behind her, and slipped the key into a small box with a combination lock attached to the railing. She might as well have had a sign hanging around her neck, saying "realtor." She was in her early sixties, her ash-blonde hair falling in a straight line, to curl slightly under her chin, and sprayed to within an inch of its life lest a strand escape. She wore a pale blue summer suit, stockings, high heels, gold earrings, and a heavy gold necklace, far too formal for a Cape Cod weekend morning.

She saw me watching and broke into an enormous smile that didn't crack the network of fine lines around her eyes. "Good morning!" she trilled.

"Good morning," I trilled back. "This house must have just gone up for sale. I didn't see this sign when I came by the other day."

"I hung it not more than an hour ago. I've been inside taking pictures to put on the internet."

"I love this garden," I said. "I've always admired it. I've never been in the house, though. What's it like?"

She hesitated and then lifted her left hand and tilted it back and forth. The light of the sun flashed off the row of diamonds.

"Slightly dated, but the house itself has excellent bones. The garden's the feature of the property—it and the expansive outdoor entertaining area positioned to get the maximum enjoyment out of the garden itself." She smiled at me.

I smiled back. I assumed that an outdoor entertaining area meant a patio.

"I'm Leanne Trummer of West London Realty." She stuffed her card into my hand.

I accepted it. "I'm Gemma Doyle from the Sherlock Holmes Bookshop."

"I've seen you there," she said.

Good thing I didn't try to pretend to be someone I'm not. I took a chance she knew nothing about my household arrangements. "I've been thinking of moving for a while. My apartment's starting to feel too confining, and I miss having a big yard where I can get my hands down and dirty, and a place where my dog can play. I love this neighborhood, and I often bring the dog here for a walk, but most of the houses around here are out of my price range." I attempted to look wistful.

"Then you might be in luck. Because the owner's aware that a new family"—she took a quick peek at my ringless left hand; if I'd known I was going to present myself as a potential home-buyer, I'd have worn a fake engagement ring or borrowed a baby to push in a stroller—"or an interested individual will likely want to do a minor amount of upgrading, he's set a very reasonable price."

"Is that so? Could I—I mean, if you've got time—have a look? Only if the homeowners aren't home, I mean. I wouldn't want to disturb anyone." No cars were parked in the driveway, and the house didn't have a garage.

"This would be the perfect time. He's gone out. Now, I have to tell you the house went up for sale very quickly, so the owner didn't do any staging at all. It's exactly as the happy family lived in it!"

What a concept.

"Why are they selling?" I asked as we climbed the steps.

"He's been recently widowed. So sad. The poor man. He's moving to be closer to his family."

"Is my dog okay to come in?"

She glanced at Violet for the first time and then looked quickly away. Obviously not a dog person. "Perhaps not. Now, I love dogs. Can't get enough of them, but the homeowner doesn't have a dog, so we don't want fur getting onto things."

"He doesn't have a dog?" I'd seen a dog here myself. A little white ball of fluff named Peony.

"No," Leanne said.

"I would have thought with this large a yard, it would be perfect for a dog."

"Perfect, yes! The property sits on a quarter of an acre, delightfully large for this part of town, isn't it? So much room in the back for the dog to run, and it's all fenced, as you'll see. No work at all to get him settled in." She forced a smile at Violet.

"My dog's a female." I tied Violet to a railing as Leanne unlocked the door. The house smelled of cleaning supplies, and everything was tidy. I assumed a storage locker somewhere was stuffed full of trinkets and excess furniture. I walked quickly through the house, trailed by the realtor, chatting away about the excellence of nearby schools and the proximity to the shopping district, and also about the quiet streets and friendly neighbors. Rather than hope I wouldn't notice the fading linoleum flooring, stained broadloom, and outdated color of the fridge and stove, she told me how easy it would be to upgrade because, as she said, "the house has good bones." I would have preferred if she'd left me alone to snoop, but she didn't so much as pause for breath.

Not a trace of Peony, Anna's Bichon Frisé, remained. If I hadn't seen the dog on Tuesday, I wouldn't have thought an animal lived here. Obviously, he didn't any longer, and I briefly wondered what had happened to him.

I stood at the windows in the TV room, looking out over the garden. Less than a week had passed since the tour, and everything was still immaculate. It truly was a stunning garden. If I was looking for a new house and if I had the time and the money (and the interest) to keep a garden up, I'd consider buying it.

"Thanks for your time," I said when we were outside on the porch and I was freeing Violet from the railing. "I'll be in touch."

She whipped out her phone. "Let me take your number."

"I'll call you, why don't I?"

"This house won't be on the market for long, you know. This neighborhood is highly desirable."

I waved goodbye over my shoulder.

Chapter Seventeen

At two thirty, I walked into the tearoom kitchen. Mrs. Hudson's had been satisfyingly busy all day, and every time I stole a quick look outside, I'd seen a line of eager afternoon tea drinkers patiently waiting for a table.

Jayne was folding dough to make scones, and Fiona was taking dishes out of the dishwasher. The scent of something truly marvelous wafted out of the oven.

"Hey." Jayne wiped at her face with a floury hand, leaving white fingerprints behind.

"Good day?" I asked.

"Oh yeah," Fiona said. "We had a full house almost all day. Soon as the breakfast eaters left, the lunch crowd arrived, and then the afternoon tea people descended."

I grabbed a poached chicken sandwich off a nearly empty platter and popped it into my mouth. I'm never too proud to eat leftovers. Not Jayne's leftovers at any rate.

"How about you?" Jayne patted the dough out with her hands and then picked up a round cookie cutter and began cutting shapes.

"Delightfully busy, considering it's such a nice day, so you'd think people would prefer to be at the beach. But who am I to chase them away? I'm going to pop out for a while. Want to come?"

"Where?"

"Lauren invited me to watch her tennis game."

Jayne laid perfect rounds of dough onto a baking sheet. "That might be fun. Fee, what's it looking like out there?"

"Slowing down. A couple of empty tables," Fiona said. "No one in line."

"We don't usually get a rush late in the day when it's sunny," Jayne said. "People linger at the beach. Can you and Jocelyn manage here okay until closing?"

"Sure," Fiona said.

"Okay, I can come." The timer on the oven dinged, and Jayne put on oven mitts and took out a sheet of chocolate brownies.

"Those look yummy," I said.

"Hands off," she warned.

Brownies out, she adjusted the temperature and popped the scones in. "Even if we do get a sudden rush, we've got enough food prepared for the rest of the day. If that happens, I can stay for a while tonight and bake for tomorrow. Take those out when they're ready, will you, please?"

"Sure," Fiona said.

"One order of afternoon tea for four." Jocelyn's head popped into the kitchen.

"Maybe I should stay," Jayne said.

I grabbed her arm. "Nope. You're only leaving an hour and a half early today. Let's go.

"We can manage," Fiona said. "Go with Gemma."

And Jayne did.

* * *

A Curious Incident

As I don't play golf and don't mix in the sort of circles that can afford the fees at the West London Golf and Country Club, I'd never been to the place before.

We drove up a long, sweeping lane toward the multilevel, shingle-roofed, gray Cape Cod clubhouse. Emerald-colored lawns, with the occasional hilly bump and hole full of sand, were surrounded by lines of tall, stately trees. I stopped to allow a red cart to bounce across the road; the occupants didn't bother to wave their thanks. To my right, middle-aged men with silver hair clipped short and wearing ugly pastel or checked (sometimes pastel-checked) trousers were standing in a circle, peering into a small hole in the grass. To the left, a fountain in the center of an artificial pond sprayed water high into the air, and a group of women, also middle-aged and also silver-haired, drove past in another red cart.

The parking lot was full, but I found a spot marked "Guests" near the building. I figured Jayne and I were guests.

"Nice place," Jayne said as we got out of the car.

"Do you know anyone who's a member here?"

"No." Before we left, Jayne had taken a moment to wash the flour off her face and brush out her hair. The blonde strands glowed in the sun. We climbed the wide concrete steps, lined by iron urns full of fountain grasses, red and white geraniums, and trailing vines.

Inside, more silver-haired, middle-aged people bustled about. I went up to the reception desk, and Jayne followed.

"Good afternoon," I said to a young blonde woman with excessively white teeth, who was practically bursting with friendliness. "We're here at the invitation of the Tierney family to join them at the children's tennis tournament this afternoon."

"Oh yes." She gave me such a smile, I was sorry I'd taken off my sunglasses when we entered the building. "We have a great group of kids this year! Go through those doors and down the stairs, and then turn left. You'll see the courts at the end of the clubhouse."

"Thanks."

The back of the building opened onto a view of more emerald lawns, sand traps, grassy bumps, and tall old trees. The sparkling blue waters of Nantucket Sound spread out in the distance. A long veranda dotted with red umbrellas was to our right. People sipped drinks, and young, fresh-faced waitstaff, clad in black shorts and white T-shirts emblazoned with the club logo, ferried food and drink to members relaxing after their game.

"I think that's a state senator over there." Jayne pointed to a silver-haired, middle-aged man taking a sip from a short glass filled with a dark liquid and plenty of ice. "What do you suppose membership costs here?"

"Fifty thousand a year for a family."

"How do you know that?"

"I never go into a place blind, Jayne. Unless I have no choice. I looked it up this afternoon."

"I wouldn't have thought they'd advertise their fees publicly, not at a place as exclusive as this."

"They don't," I said.

"Oh," she said. "Are we here investigating the murder? I thought we'd come to see Lauren play tennis."

"I can do two things at once, but no, I'm not investigating. I'm leaving it in the capable hands of the police."

"That won't last long," Jayne mumbled. "You can't leave a question unanswered."

I declined to reply. She was probably right. "I wonder if these people sometimes get each other mixed up. Do you suppose one of the wives ever goes home with a man who's not her husband

and doesn't realize it until she notices that he's not snoring nearly as much as usual? Or they meet friends here for dinner and in the middle of the meal wonder why the friends are talking about their son the oncologist instead of their daughter the brain surgeon?"

"They do look like they've been punched out of the same mold, don't they? Sorta like the boy and girl sugar cookies I make for Valentine's Day."

We found the tennis courts with no difficulty. There were three courts, and doubles games were taking place on them all. Lauren was in the center one, partnered with a skinny boy about her age. Two girls made up the opposite team.

Lauren was bent over, swinging her hips back and forth, her eyes focused on the ball in the opposing player's hand. The girl served and Lauren ran forward, ponytail flying, short white skirt twirling. She hit the ball with a resounding whack and returned it over the net, where, despite a flying leap from the other player, it hit the ground and bounced. A man wearing white trousers and T-shirt and a red cap with the golf club logo stood on the sidelines, watching every move. He shouted, "Game!" A man and a woman paced alongside the courts. I assumed they were the coaches.

Lauren threw her arms into the air, and the boy grabbed her around the waist. She hugged him back while the opposing players looked gloomily on.

When Lauren and her partner separated, she caught sight of Jayne and me. She yelled and waved her racket in the air. I waved back and gave her a thumbs-up. The players changed sides.

"Have you ever played tennis, Gemma?" Jayne asked.

"Once or twice."

"I assume that means you've played at Wimbledon."

"Never quite got that far. Not to center court anyway. I see people we know. Let's go and say hello."

213

A line of Adirondack chairs painted in primary colors was arranged along the edge of the courts so parents could cheer their young players on. Behind the chairs, a small table had been set up under a red sun umbrella, with freshly baked biscuits—what in America they call cookies—and icy pitchers of minty lemonade and iced tea.

David and Sheila Tierney gave us genuine smiles when they saw us. "Gemma! How nice of you to come. Lauren was hoping you would." Sheila was once again made up and accessorized, and some of the shadows were gone from her face. Nothing had happened in the police investigation, as far as I knew, but I suppose every day you weren't in jail was a good day.

"I wouldn't miss it," I said. "Sorry we're late."

"Running your own business," David said, "your time's never your own."

I introduced Jayne.

"Of the heavenly scones," Sheila said. "You've turned my daughter into a baker. We're going to be making cookies tomorrow."

Jayne grinned. "My work here is done."

Sheila smiled and David laughed. They weren't exactly sitting close together, but the distance between them wasn't the size and temperature of the Arctic Ocean either. Maybe they were making an attempt to repair their marriage for their daughter's sake. I hoped so. Pretending to be happy has a strange effect: it makes you happy.

Two other people I knew were in the little group. I hadn't expected to see either of them.

"Are you a member here, Mrs. Ramsbatten?" I asked.

"My late husband and I were," she said. "He was an extremely keen golfer, and I played to keep him company. My golfing days are over"—she indicated the cane propped against her chair—"but I drop in now and again for a drink on the veranda and a chat with old friends. I was doing that when I saw dear Lauren and her parents arriving. She told me about her game and invited me to watch."

"Gemma and Jayne, do you know Mike Nixon?" Sheila asked.

I reached out my hand, and Mike got to his feet and took it in his.

"I do. He's a regular customer at my shop."

"Also a scone lover," he said with a smile at Jayne.

She smiled back. "My condolences on your loss."

"Thank you. Please have a seat." He waved me into the chair between him and Sheila, and Jayne took the one on his other side.

Further down the row, another group of onlookers sprang to their feet, cheering, and I looked to see Lauren slinking dejectedly toward the net.

"You'll get the next one, honey!" David yelled.

"Mike didn't want to come out," Sheila said to me, "but I absolutely insisted, didn't I, David? Terrible tragedy what happened to Anna, but life does go on, doesn't it? It won't do him any good being cooped up in that house, wallowing in memories."

Mike grunted something noncommittal. I knew from Ryan that the police hadn't released Anna's body. Meaning Mike's wife hadn't even been buried yet. If he wanted to linger among his memories for a while, who was Sheila or anyone else to tell him he couldn't?

"Mike and Anna were always so fond of Lauren, isn't that right, David? Until Anna and I had our little spat, of course. We would have recovered our friendship soon enough." Sheila dabbed at her eyes.

I'd suggested to Ryan that Sheila might have been acting when she'd professed to know nothing about Anna's death. I changed my mind. She was a dreadful actor.

I glanced at Mike. His face was set, and he didn't look much like a man enjoying his day out. Could he be "M"? Obviously, he didn't want to be here. Whether because he was uncomfortable around Sheila or for other reasons, I couldn't tell.

We watched the game for a while. The two teams seemed to be fairly evenly matched. Lauren was a better player than her partner, and I could see her getting irritated at some of his mistakes, but she kept her cool.

On the far side of the courts, two men walked past. They obviously weren't members here, being dressed in the clothes of working groundskeepers and carrying garden equipment.

Sheila leapt to her feet. "Oh, look, there's Manuel. Yoo-hoo!" She waved. "Manuel! Over here."

Manuel glanced over and hesitated. The other man slapped him on the back and laughed, then walked away, leaving Manuel looking like a miscreant who'd been outwitted by Sherlock Holmes.

Sheila kept waving. Mrs. Ramsbatten joined in.

"Would you like a glass of lemonade, Mrs. Ramsbatten?" Mike asked.

"That would be very nice, thank you."

"Gemma? Jayne?"

I said, "Yes, please," but Jayne declined.

Mike got to his feet and poured the drinks. The lemonade was fresh enough that ice clinked in the jug among slices of lemon and leaves of mint.

Manuel walked around the court. "Good afternoon," he said politely. He so pointedly avoided looking at Sheila as she gushed over him, I had absolutely no doubt Manuel was "M."

"Sheila," Mrs. Ramsbatten said, "did you know Manuel's looking for work? You must need a gardener."

I almost laughed at the horrified look that crossed the man's face.

"We do!" Sheila said

"We do not," David muttered.

"I'm sorry," Manuel said, "but I've filled my schedule."

"That was quick," Mike said. "I told you you'd have no trouble finding something else. No hard feelings, I hope, buddy. I didn't see the point of keeping you on any longer."

"No hard feelings at all," Manuel said.

Mike held out his hand, and Manuel shook it.

"Great," Mike said. "Would you like a drink or a cookie?"

"No thanks, we're not allowed to socialize with the club members."

"Nonsense," Sheila said. "It's just a little lemonade on a hot day."

"No. Thank you," Manuel repeated.

Mike handed me a glass, heavy with ice cubes, a slice of lemon, and an abundance of finely chopped green leaves.

"But . . ." Sheila said.

"If the man doesn't want a drink, he doesn't want a drink, Sheila," David said. "Sit down and stop bothering him."

Mrs. Ramsbatten snickered into her glass. Sheila sat and pouted. David's mouth twisted in disapproval, and he gave his head a small shake. Manuel shifted awkwardly from one foot to the other.

"The set's over." Sheila jumped up again. "Lauren and Jason are talking to their coach. I'm going to take her a cookie. She seems to like these ones. Jayne, you're a baker. Do you know how to make these?"

"Oatmeal? We learned that day one in cooking school."

Sheila took two cookies off the platter, wrapped them in a napkin, and tucked her free arm into Jayne's. "Maybe you could come around to the house one day and show . . ." Her voice trailed off as they walked away.

"Don't pay any attention to my wife," David said to Manuel. "We're not hiring a gardener or anyone else. There are going to be some changes around our house, and she's having trouble realizing that."

"These are nice cookies," Mrs. Ramsbatten said. "But nowhere as good as the ones at Mrs. Hudson's."

I placed my untouched glass of lemonade under my chair and went after Jayne and Sheila. I wanted to tell Lauren what a good player she was.

She beamed when she saw me approaching. She had a towel draped around her neck and was munching on a biscuit. Her face was flushed, her eyes glowing, and her hair messed.

"Keep those feet moving," the coach was saying to her. "Every moment." Lauren's partner had gone to chat with his parents.

Lauren wrapped me in a hug. "Thanks for coming, Gemma. Are you enjoying the game?"

"Like sitting center court at Wimbledon." I returned the hug.

"Where Gemma's never played," Jayne said.

"Wimbledon," Lauren said wistfully.

"We can't stay much longer," I said. "I have to get back to the shop so Ashleigh can have her break, but I wanted to say how well you play."

She grinned at me.

"Jayne's going to come to the house tomorrow and help us make oatmeal cookies," Sheila said.

"I am?" Jayne said. "I mean, I can't. I have to work. Lauren's always welcome to help me in the tearoom if she wants."

"It's not quite the same, is it?" Sheila said.

"No. Which is rather the point," I said. "Jayne bakes for a living. You know, baked goods flowing out, income flowing in."

The referee blew his whistle, and the coach clapped his hands and called, "Okay, people. Jason, Lauren, back at it."

The four young people ran onto the court, and we returned to our row of seats. Manuel and Mike had left, quick to make their escape once Sheila was out of grabbing range. David had joined some of the other parents and was listening to a man who did a great deal of swinging his arms as he talked, no doubt pretending he was also playing tennis. Mrs. Ramsbatten's eyes were closed and her head bobbing.

"We have to be going," I said to Sheila.

She dropped into her chair. "Okay. 'Bye."

Jayne bent over and picked up my glass of lemonade. "Do you mind?" she asked.

"Help yourself," I said.

She drank deeply, finished it off, and put the plastic glass back on the table, among the others, as we passed. Only one lemon slice and a few soggy leaves remained at the bottom of the glass.

"Do you think Sheila's a bit bossy?" she asked me as we crossed the floor of the clubhouse.

"A bit? She's a total control freak."

"But you don't think she killed Anna?"

"I thought it possible for a while, but I've changed my mind." I explained my reasoning to her. "Although I have been wrong before."

"Not so as anyone ever notices."

I didn't bother to point out all the occasions on which I had been wrong.

"Are you coming to Baker Street, or do you want me to take you home?" I asked her.

"I'll go back to work. If they had many customers after we left, I'll need to get some prep done for tomorrow."

"You seeing Andy tonight?"

"No. Saturday's the busiest night of the week at the restaurant. I might drop in on my way home, though, and have a cup of coffee while I watch him cook."

"Nothing sexier than watching a man cook," I said.

"Can Ryan cook? I've never asked."

"Ryan is struggling to master the intricacies of the kettle. So far, I've managed to teach him that the water needs to be added to the teapot as soon as it comes off the boil. Not five minutes later. And that the drink isn't suitable if one neglects to add the tea bags."

Jayne laughed and threw her head back so her fine blonde hair streamed out behind her. I'd put the roof of the Miata down so we could enjoy the warm sun. "That was fun. Thanks for inviting me to come with you. I like Lauren. I'm glad you don't think her mom killed Anna."

"What I think doesn't matter," I said. "And things can change. I'll drop you in town and then go home and let Violet out for a little bit. Can you pop into the Emporium and tell Ashleigh I'll be another half hour?"

"Sure."

* * *

Manuel had done an excellent job on our lawn. The grass was cut, the edges trimmed, and the bushes clipped. I didn't have time to take Violet for a walk, but I let her sniff around the yard for a while and promised her we'd go out again later.

I then walked back to Baker Street. I arrived at the Emporium shortly after five. The only customer was Donald Morris, standing at the counter, chatting to Ashleigh.

"Hi, Donald," I said.

"Gemma—excellent. I'm wondering when you'll be getting more copies of *Villains, Victims, and Violets*, and Ashleigh doesn't know."

"You should have asked me to save you one, Donald. The book proved more popular than I expected. Ashleigh, you can go for your break now."

"Did you enjoy the tennis?" she asked.

"I did. Nothing nicer than sitting in the sun with a glass of lemonade and an oatmeal biscuit, watching young people having fun."

"I'll be back in an hour," Ashleigh said, "but if you need me for anything, call. I have my phone." She left through the door to the street.

"I think Ashleigh has plans for world domination," I said. "The little part of it that's two-twenty-two Baker Street anyway."

"She was telling me of her ideas for a franchise operation," Donald said. "How's that going?"

"It's not. And it never will."

"You went to a tennis match? You should have mentioned it. I would have liked to come with you. I played a great deal of tennis in my youth."

"You did?" That came as a surprise. A less athletic man than Donald would be hard to find.

"My father had hopes of me turning professional." He grimaced and studied the floor. "In that, as in so many other things, I was a disappointment to him."

I touched his arm. "Professional tennis is vastly overrated. You had a successful law practice and you're now a prominent Sherlockian, highly regarded by your peers."

He gave me a huge smile. "So right you are, Gemma. As for tennis, I had not the slightest modicum of talent or even the desire to play. My father refused to recognize that."

"I have the book you're after on order, but I can request a rush shipment, if you like."

"Thank you. I'm thinking of going to that conference on the West Coast, but . . ."

His voice trailed off, and I turned to see what had distracted him. Jayne stood at the closed sliding door between the shop and the Emporium. She knocked on the glass. Her hand shook, her face was excessively pale, and she didn't look too steady on her feet. I ran over and unlocked the door. She almost fell through it, and I grabbed her arm. "What's the matter? Are you okay, Jayne?"

"I don't feel too good."

"You need to sit down."

"I just need a minute. It's too hot in there."

Donald took her other arm, and we walked an unsteady Jayne across the floor to the chair in the reading nook.

Moriarty came out from his bed under the center table to see what was going on.

"Donald," I said, "run into the tearoom and get Jayne a glass of water."

He let go of her arm and stepped back. Beneath his thick glasses, his eyes were wide with concern.

"It's okay," she said. "I felt dizzy for a minute there. No need to fuss."

"Sit down," I said.

A Curious Incident

"I . . . I . . ." She groaned, leaned over, and in one great burst, threw up the entire contents of her stomach. Her legs crumpled. I grabbed her before she could hit the floor and guided her down as gently as I could.

She didn't move again.

Chapter Eighteen

M y own heart almost stopped.

"Jayne!" I dropped to my knees beside her. I lifted her head and cradled it in my lap, turning it to one side in case she was sick again. Her chest rose and fell, and I was so relieved to see it, I burst into tears. I checked her pulse. Weak, but present.

Behind me, I heard Donald shouting into his phone. "Ambulance. Two-twenty-two Baker Street. It's an emergency!"

Moriarty appeared next to Jayne. He reached out one paw and touched her arm. She didn't move, and he simply stood beside her, staring into her face. I didn't push him away.

"Ambulance is on its way," Donald said. "They'll be less than five minutes."

"Thank heavens."

"Is she . . .?" His voice shook.

"She's breathing." I touched Jayne's soft cheek. Her eyes were closed, but her chest continued to rise and fall and a pulse beat in her neck. "I'll go with them to the hospital. Can you mind the store until Ashleigh gets back?"

"Of course, Gemma."

"You'd better go into the tearoom and turn the oven or stove off. She might not have done that."

"Don't worry about the store," Donald said. "I'll clean up too."

The blessed sound of an ambulance getting closer and closer. Donald ran into the street to guide them to our door.

And then they were lifting me to my feet, asking me to step aside. Moriarty slipped back under the table. Quickly and efficiently, one of the medics checked Jayne's vital signs while the other spoke to me. "Do you know this woman?"

"Yes, I know her very well. We're business partners and friends. Best friends."

"Did she hit the floor hard or strike her head on anything?"

"No. I caught her."

"That's good. Does she have a history of fainting?"

"No, not at all. She came in here, said she wasn't feeling well, and . . . She didn't look well. She was pale and unsteady on her feet."

"Do you have any idea what might have happened? Something she ate maybe?"

I shook my head and wrapped my arms around myself. I was suddenly very cold.

They loaded Jayne onto a stretcher. She moaned but didn't regain consciousness.

I followed the stretcher into the street and hopped into the back of the ambulance. I sat on the hard bench as we sped through the streets, siren blaring, red lights flashing. My heart was in my mouth as I watched the paramedic tend to my best friend in all the world. I felt totally helpless. "Is she going to be okay?"

I didn't get an answer.

I called Jayne's mom first and then Andy. Leslie answered and I told her what had happened, trying hard not to sound as though I was panicking. I left a message for Andy to return my call as soon as possible.

Fortunately, West London's a small town, and it wasn't far to the hospital. The ambulance stopped, the doors flew open, and the stretcher was unloaded quickly and efficiently. I jumped out to see Jayne disappearing through the swinging doors. I followed her in, but I could go no further.

"If you can have a seat, please," a nurse said, politely but firmly. "We'll let you know when we have news."

I dropped into a chair.

My phone rang—Andy. I took a deep breath before answering and told him I was at the hospital because Jayne had taken ill. Nothing to worry about. When I finished, I realized I was speaking to dead air.

I waited. West London is a busy place in the summer months, and the hospital is no exception.

Andy arrived first, dressed in his chef's whites, his eyes wild and his hair standing on end. He dropped into a chair beside me. "What happened, Gemma?"

"I have absolutely no idea."

"Is she going to be okay?"

"I'm sure of it," I said, knowing no such thing. "Whatever it was, we got it in time."

Leslie arrived and took the chair on the other side of me. She gripped my hand.

Time passed slowly, but eventually the doctor came out. Leslie, Andy, and I rose to our feet as he approached. We put our arms around each other. I studied the doctor's face, searching for a sign—good or bad. But he was an older guy and had probably spent a lot of years giving the news to families, and he knew how to keep his face impassive.

"Ms. Wilson is resting comfortably," he said.

Leslie let out a low moan. Andy breathed.

"We'll be keeping her overnight for observation, but she should be able to go home tomorrow."

"Thank you, doctor," I said.

"Are you her mother?" he asked Leslie.

"Yes."

"A nurse will take you through to her."

"What happened?" Andy said. "I saw her last night and talked to her on the phone earlier today. She didn't say anything about being sick."

"I suspect food poisoning," the doctor said. "We'll run some tests."

"Food poisoning? That's not possible," I said.

"Are you the person who came in with her?"

"Yes."

"I'd like a word." He turned to the nurse standing behind him. "You can show Mrs. Wilson through now."

Leslie glanced at me.

"You go ahead. I'll follow."

No one invited Andy, but he went with them anyway.

"Were you with your friend the entire day?" the doctor asked me. "Did you see everything she ate?"

"Not the entire day, but she was with me when she wasn't working in her restaurant, and we didn't have anything to eat when we were together."

"She works in a restaurant? Doing what?"

"Are you new here?" I asked.

"I arrived two weeks ago, filling in for vacations. If it matters."

"I'm Gemma Doyle, and my friend is Jayne Wilson. We own Mrs. Hudson's Tea Room at two twenty Baker Street. Jayne's the head baker there."

"James Montgomery. Does Ms. Wilson . . . experiment with her baking?"

"Never. It's our busiest time of the year, and she doesn't have time for experiments. Besides, what would you serve in a tearoom that has the potential to be poisonous?"

"Food goes off."

I shook my head firmly. "Not in any kitchen Jayne runs. She's a professional baker. She's been doing this for years. We've never had the slightest complaint."

"If what you say is true, might she have picked up something somewhere else? Did she leave the premises for lunch or a snack?"

"Not today. We ate at a restaurant in town last night, but she didn't have anything that wasn't on the menu. Has anyone else shown up sick today?"

"No. If she'd eaten something that was off yesterday, it would have manifested before now."

"Are you sure it's food poisoning?"

"Something she consumed caused her to fall ill. We pumped her stomach, and the contents have been sent for analysis."

Too late, I realized that I should have told Donald not to clean up after Jayne's mishap.

"You say she was working all day, but you don't know that for sure. Maybe she went out for a sandwich or something?"

"She was working in the tearoom, and I was next door at the bookshop I own. If she'd gone out for any reason, she would have told me. We're business partners, and we keep an eye on each other's place. We took a break at quarter to three and went to the West London Country Club to watch a children's tennis tournament. I . . ."

"What?"

"I think I need to call the police." I pulled out my phone. "Fortunately, I happen to have the number at hand."

In the reception area, a woman began screaming. "Excuse me," the doctor said. He ran off, his white coat flapping behind him.

"Hey, Gemma." Ryan came on the line.

"I'm at West London General. Someone tried to kill me. They did almost succeed in killing Jayne."

Ryan never said "Are you sure?" to me, and he didn't now. "On my way. I'm about ten minutes out."

I returned to my seat. The screaming woman had come in with a child with what appeared to be a paper cut on his right thumb. The child, all curly red hair and freckles, looked around, wide eyed, while his mother wailed and moaned. He saw me watching and winked. I winked back.

Donald ran into the waiting room. "Gemma! What's happening? Is Jayne all right?"

"She's going to be fine. Her mom and Andy are with her now, and I'm waiting for Ryan."

Donald dropped into a chair. "Thank heavens."

"Everything okay at the store?"

"Ashleigh's there and she says to tell you she can close up if you don't get back in time. I turned the oven off in the tearoom and took out the cake that was in there. It looks to be done, but I don't know how to tell for sure. I mopped up the . . . uh . . . mess on the floor and ensured everything was spic and span once again. Is it the flu? It seemed to come on awfully fast."

"I don't know. They have tests to run."

"I sold a copy of *Dust and Shadow* by Lindsay Faye and two of *From Holmes to Sherlock*. I didn't know how to use the cash register, so I made change out of my own pocket. You owe me six dollars and twenty seven cents."

"Thank you, Donald."

"And one copy of *The Sign of Seven*. The customer had no cash and wanted to pay with a credit card, but I didn't know how to take that. I said he could take the book with him and come back tonight or tomorrow to pay. Was that okay, Gemma?"

"Yeah, fine. There's Ryan now. Oh dear, Louise has tagged along. Will you excuse me?" I stood up. "I'm going to suggest we find someplace private to talk. Can you call me if anything happens?"

Donald got to his feet. "Of course, Gemma."

I gave him a hug. "Thank you for being here for me."

"Where else would I be?" he said.

"At home with a glass of whiskey and a copy of *Villains, Victims, and Violets*?"

"Not when my friends need me."

I joined Ryan and Estrada at the doors leading to the main part of the hospital.

"What's going on, Gemma?" Ryan said in a low voice. "How's Jayne?"

"She's been admitted, but just for observation tonight. She's going to be okay." I glanced at Estrada and Ryan noticed.

"If this has something to do with the Wentworth case, Louise needs to hear it," he said.

"If it has something to do with any case, I need to hear it," Estrada said.

"Let's go to the cafeteria," Ryan said, "and try to find some privacy. Besides, I need a coffee."

The hospital's small cafeteria looked out over the nicely maintained gardens, but despite the pleasant setting and the big windows, it was a gloomy place. A handful of small groups of doctors and nurses in scrubs chatted in low voices, while visitors sat in silence, aimlessly stirring their coffee. A woman wept silently, and a man patted her arm. It was nearing the end of food service, and what little remained was dry and overcooked, left too long under heat lamps. The place smelled of over-brewed coffee, bacon grease, and despair.

I gave my head a good shake to dispel the feeling of gloom that had settled over me. Jayne was going to be all right. That was all that mattered.

"You okay, Gemma?" Ryan said.

I gave him a weak smile. "Just tired. It's been an emotional couple of hours."

"Anyone want anything?" he asked.

Estrada and I said no, and we found a table in a corner while he went for his coffee. We sat opposite each other. I smiled at Estrada. "Nice date last night?" I said in an attempt to make light, friendly banter.

Her eyes narrowed so much, I wondered if she could see me through them. "What do you know about that?"

"Me? I saw you in town. You went into the Blue Water Café at ten forty-five. Late for a dinner date, but you have a busy schedule at work. Or was it him who was running late? He looked like he might be a cop, but I haven't seen him around West London before. Maybe he's from a nearby town. I like your hair, by the way."

She shoved a length of caramel-highlighted hair behind her ear. "I'm not sharing details of my private life with you, Gemma Doyle."

I was momentarily set aback at the vehemence in her voice. I looked around to see Ryan approaching with his coffee.

"I only meant," I said, "that the highlights suit you. They bring out the depth of your natural color."

Ryan took the seat next to Estrada.

231

"Okay," she began. "Spit it out. What happened to Jayne, and why do you think an illness on her part was a deliberate attempt on you? You look, as you usually do, quite unscathed."

"I hope," I spoke slowly and clearly, "you are not implying that I have tried to make this about me. Believe me, I don't like the conclusions I've come to any more than you do. If you want to hear my reasoning, I'll tell you. If not—"

Ryan interrupted, "Tell us what happened to Jayne."

I did so, beginning with her knocking on the door of the Emporium. "The doctor suspects she's been poisoned, accidently or otherwise. Because the possibility of her accidently poisoning her own food and then eating it is nil—"

"Don't make assumptions," Estrada said.

"Assumptions? I am assuming nothing. I am taking into account what I know about the woman in question and her habits, and coming to the logical conclusion."

"Were you with her every minute of the day?"

"No," I admitted, "but—"

"But you don't know if maybe she went out for a sandwich and the cheese was bad, or if she ate lunch from a cheap buffet place and a tray of food wasn't kept hot enough."

"Aside from the fact that Jayne doesn't go out for lunch because she's busy providing other people with their lunches, how many other cases of food poisoning have arrived at this hospital this evening? According to the ER doctor, who might possibly know, none."

"This isn't—" Ryan began.

"Okay, Jayne didn't go out," Estrada said. "She was baking, you said. Maybe she used something that had gone bad, like the cream."

"Jayne would recognize cream that had spoiled."

"Enough!" Ryan slapped the edges of his hands together in what I've been told is a football signal for time-out. "All that is still to be determined. Did the doctor say anything about running tests?"

"Yes. He's sent the contents of her stomach for analysis. There's a job I wouldn't like. Makes me glad I'm a bookseller."

"And all-around snoop," Estrada muttered.

"What was that, Louise? I missed your insightful comment."

Ryan glared at me. "Detective Estrada, why don't you have a word with the doctor. If we're going to take this further, we need to hear from him firsthand, not from a secondary source. No matter how reliable that source might be. Tell him I want a rush on that tox report, and ask him to find out if any other hospitals in the area have had similar cases showing up today."

Estrada pushed herself to her feet. "Why don't I do that?" She walked away with quick, angry strides.

"Gemma," Ryan said once Estrada was out of earshot, "why do you antagonize her?"

"I didn't! I told her I liked her hair, and she got all offended. Okay, I don't really like it. It looked better before, but I didn't say that."

"You must have made more than a passing comment on her hair. I thought you two were getting on better. Never mind. Tell me why you think this was a deliberate attack, and if so, why it was aimed at you."

I settled into my chair, closed my eyes, stroked my cheek, and mentally called up memories of this afternoon. "Jayne and I went to the West London Country Club to watch Lauren Tierney play tennis. We arrived shortly before three and stayed for about an hour, maybe a bit less. Several people we know were there: Lauren's parents—both of them, Mrs. Ramsbatten from next door, Mike Nixon, Anna Wentworth's husband, and Manuel, whose last name I don't know, but he'd been Anna's gardener. He wasn't watching the game but came over to say hello. It's a ritzy club. Have you ever been there?"

"My dad plays there sometimes. He taught me to play when I was a kid, and I still like to get a round in with him when I can."

I opened my eyes. "You golf? Why did I not know this?"

"Probably because you never asked."

I like to think I don't have to *ask* people to know things about them, but this wasn't the time to consider what I might have failed to notice.

"I must say, I'm strangely pleased you didn't know that about me," he said.

One of the reasons our relationship has had such a rocky past is because Ryan doesn't like the idea that I appear to know what he's thinking or planning before he tells me. A totally disastrous—and abandoned—marriage proposal came to mind. I shoved it away.

"If it makes you feel any better that you didn't know," he said, "Dad hasn't played in more than a year because of his hip, and I don't have enough interest or the time to join a club on my own. Unless *you* want to. Do you play?"

"Heaven forbid."

"Back to the subject at hand. What happened at the club?"

"A few refreshments were laid out for the spectators. A plate of oatmeal cookies, which looked to have been made on the premises. A pitcher of lemonade and one of iced tea. I didn't have anything, but Jayne drank a glass of lemonade."

"You're reaching, Gemma. You say the drinks were in a pitcher. Unless Jayne was the only one who drank from it, then you have no reason to think it was tampered with. As you said yourself, no one else has shown up here today complaining of food poisoning. Which also doesn't explain why you think it was aimed at you."

"While I was waiting for the doctor to tell me what was happening with Jayne, I had some quiet time to think. Mrs. Ramsbatten had a glass of the lemonade, as did some of the others. Therefore, nothing was added to the lemonade."

"So how—"

I put up one hand. "Nothing was *originally* added to the lemonade. I asked for a glass, but I didn't take so much as a sip. It was handed to me, and at that moment the game broke at the end of a set. Sheila and Jayne went to talk to Lauren, and I followed. I put my glass under my chair. Untouched. When we got back, Jayne asked if she could have it, and I told her okay. She drank it all, and then we left."

"Who poured the drink for you?"

"Mike Nixon. Which means nothing, as it was unattended for about five minutes. When we returned to our seats, Mike and Manuel had disappeared, and David was talking to another group of people. Only Mrs. Ramsbatten remained in her seat, but she'd dozed off."

"Jayne didn't say anything about the lemonade tasting bad? It didn't look funny?"

"No. Many poisonous substances don't change the appearance, or even the taste, of what they've been added to, which is what's so dangerous about them. In this case, the pitcher and then the glass contained more than lemonade. There were slices of fresh lemon and a lot of mint leaves. At least, what looked to be mint leaves. Green stuff, anyway, chopped into fine pieces."

"And you think—"

"Everyone in this case is either a gardener or close to one. You and I both know the common garden is full of deadly substances, if one knows where to look."

Chapter Nineteen

Ryan sipped his coffee. "Not only gardens but the average kitchen cabinet's a virtual poison storehouse. Fortunately these days, unlike in your hero's time, it almost never goes undetected in an autopsy."

"Who's my hero?"

"Sherlock Holmes."

"I wouldn't say Holmes is my hero. I might admire his—"

"Let's not go there right now, Gemma. The tox reports will tell us what, if anything, Jayne digested." He glanced at his watch.

"Are you aware Mike Nixon has put his house up for sale?" I asked.

"Yes, I am. I didn't ask why because it's none of my business, although I'm aware he's been out of work for some time. I'm only telling you because it's public knowledge."

"He might need the money, but he's selling at far less than he'd get if he made a few improvements to the house itself."

"The man's money's his own business," Ryan said. "As long as it was not a motive for him to kill his wife, and nothing indicates that's what happened."

I opened my mouth to say something.

"Before you ask, they didn't have life insurance on either of them. Their policy was canceled about a year ago when Mike was laid off and they began cutting corners."

"They might have cut corners, but he still had time to visit Las Vegas."

"The extent of your knowledge amazes me sometimes. Yes, he goes to Vegas a couple of times a year. As it happens, he was in Vegas last week, and he got home the afternoon of the garden tour, only a few hours before Anna died. I asked him why he was away for the tour, and he said he never helped with the garden, he didn't care about it being on the tour, and Anna was happy not to have him under foot. In Vegas, he always stays at a cheap hotel off the strip, and he isn't a big player. He says Anna was fine with it. Her gardening and writing about gardening was her interest; visiting Vegas was his as long as he went on cheap package trips and his gambling came out more or less even."

"Which may or may not be true. You have only his say-so."

"He has no connections with organized crime that we can find, and judging by the state of his bank account, he's not in major debt. The house has a heavy mortgage on it, so he's not going to be too far ahead after selling it."

"Did you speak to Manuel, the gardener? About his relationship with Anna, I mean."

"We did. He says he worked for her on a casual basis, and that was the extent of their relationship. I told him garden club gossip says they were having an affair, and he said that bunch of old women are always gossiping about something. He was extremely nervous, and I'm not sure he was telling the truth. It's true that not many people like to be questioned by us. Some people lie because they're guilty, some lie because they're afraid of being accused, and some lie for the sake of it. We've not found anyone, I have to point out, who's prepared to say they have firsthand knowledge of this affair. They all say someone told them, and that someone says someone else told them. Even the person who the rumor appears to have originated with had to confess she might have jumped to conclusions."

"Which is how a gossip mill works."

"Precisely. He has no alibi for the time of Anna's death, but that also means nothing. He lives alone and says he was alone at home that night. He works hard and puts in long hours over the summer and goes to bed early. He has no police record and a solid job record. I asked him if he has any idea who might have killed Anna, and he said it must have been a random attack."

"I'm convinced he's the mysterious "M" who warned Sheila to stop bothering him."

"Perhaps, but I can't see what that has to do with the murder of Anna unless Sheila was jealous of Anna's rumored relationship with Manuel. That's nothing but conjecture: we've found no reason to charge Sheila with the murder."

"What about evidence at the scene?"

"Nothing at all that points to Sheila or anyone connected to Anna having been there that night, other than Anna's dog and Mike, who found her. Some cigarette butts, a couple of old beer bottles. The natural detritus that can be found in a public park. We've been running checks on all that and coming up empty." Ryan drained his coffee cup and stood up. "Let's get back and see how Jayne's doing."

Ryan conferred with Estrada and the doctor, and then they were allowed to talk to Jayne.

I didn't go in with them, but those hospital partitions have mighty thin walls and nothing but a curtain to act as a door.

Eavesdropping was scarcely worth the risk of incurring Estrada's wrath. Jayne was awake, but groggy and not able to talk much. She told them she felt sick, came to get me, and then passed out. Otherwise, she had no idea what had happened. She didn't remember drinking the lemonade, never mind noticing any distinctive flavor or smell.

The police left. Ryan said he'd go around to the country club to talk to the cooks, but he didn't expect to learn anything of importance. If someone had added poison to the guests' drinks, they'd not be likely to admit it. He also told me he was going to have forensic officers check out Mrs. Hudson's kitchen on the off-chance Jayne did eat something that had gone bad.

I didn't even bother to protest. The look on his face told me that would be a waste of time.

"Please don't have boxes marked 'poison investigation team,' with a skull and crossbones, being carried out of the tearoom."

"We can be discreet, you know," he said.

"If we want to be," Estrada added ominously.

I stayed at the hospital until Jayne was settled in her room. I gave her a kiss on the cheek, told her I'd contact Fiona and Jocelyn and tell them what was happening, and left her to the tender care of her mother and Andy. Donald gave me a lift back to town. I was so full of thought, I scarcely noticed the leaping pedestrians and blaring horns.

I called Fiona and Jocelyn and told them Jayne was ill and wouldn't be able to come to work for at least a day, so we'd close the tearoom. They both protested that they could run things—they'd done so when we were in London. I reminded them they were a heck of a lot busier in the summer than in January. I didn't want to say that I didn't know when the police would be finished poking their fingers into the flour or sniffing the raspberries. I promised to pay them for the day off, and they hung up happy.

"Donald told me what happened," Ashleigh said. "Is Jayne going to be okay?"

"Yes. Just something she ate."

"Hear that?" she said to Moriarty. "Jayne's going to be fine."

Moriarty washed his whiskers.

The store was particularly busy that evening, as though everyone in West London knew I had a lot of thinking to do and came in in a deliberate attempt to annoy me by patronizing my business.

Precisely at nine o'clock, Ashleigh bid Moriarty and me a good night and left. The cat crouched on top of the gaslight shelf and watched me go about my closing-up routine.

"She's going to be perfectly fine," I said to him.

He blinked.

"Someone doesn't want me investigating this case. I'd say that's a pretty good reason to get back at it, wouldn't you?"

Moriarty nodded.

* * *

I went straight home after closing the shop. I let Violet into the yard, put the kettle on, and made myself a cup of tea. I then decided tea wasn't up to the task and opened a bottle of wine. Once Violet was inside, I carried my wine into the den and settled into my favorite chair. The dog curled up at my feet.

I thought. I had absolutely no doubt someone had poisoned the lemonade, and they had done so because it was supposed to be my drink. Lemonade had been poured into other glasses and consumed by other people, but only Jayne fell ill. As far as I knew. Ryan had asked the doctor to call him directly if any other cases of possible poisoning showed up at the hospital. Theoretically someone could have added a few drops of an odorless, colorless liquid to the glass of lemonade when no one was looking, but until I found out for sure, my working hypnosis would be that all of the green leaves in the glass were not mint. The police had sent someone around to the golf club to collect the garbage from the kitchen and the bar, if it hadn't been picked up yet. As they were looking for a specific item—chopped and mushy green leaves—it shouldn't take them too long to find what they were looking for. If it was to be found.

A lot of "ifs."

Even if it could be proved that leaves disguised as mint were added to the glass, that still didn't identify who'd done it.

As for why, I could only assume this person wanted me to stop asking questions about the Anna Wentworth murder.

Had they intended to kill me or just warn me off asking questions?

They weren't aware that I had stopped asking questions and decided to leave the matter in the capable hands of the WLPD.

Once again, I called up a mental image of the scene at the tennis courts: the row of chairs, the groups of spectators. Sheila and David Tierney, Mike Nixon, Manuel, Mrs. Ramsbatten.

Mrs. Ramsbatten?

I thought about my neighbor. A quiet widowed lady who'd been a pioneer in computers a long time ago. One who had made friends with Uncle Arthur, let the dog out when I couldn't get home, and helped maintain our garden. One who walked with the aid of a cane, no longer had a driver's license, and kept every trinket that had ever crossed her path.

She'd been, by her own admission, at Sheila's house the night the garden had been vandalized, although she said the garden had been intact when she left.

There was much about Mrs. Ramsbatten's life I didn't know. I didn't really know Mrs. Ramsbatten at all. She was Uncle Arthur's friend, not mine. I waved at her over the garden gate occasionally, and until this week that had been the extent of our contact. She'd told me a few things about her early years, but they might not have been true.

Poison, they say, is a woman's weapon, but I've never accepted that. It's one of the few ways of dealing death without being too obvious about it, such as attacking a person on a darkened street late at night.

Which is what had happened to Anna Wentworth.

I had to believe I was not dealing with two separate cases here. The person who killed Anna had tried to kill me—and had almost killed Jayne.

Mrs. Ramsbatten had been in a position to add the deadly substance to the lemonade, but unless for some improbable reason she's been living undercover as a frail elderly lady for the past five years, she had not killed Anna.

I filed her under "unlikely" and went on to consider the others.

The only person I knew for sure who had not poisoned the lemonade was Sheila. I'd been with Sheila from the time I'd been handed the glass until Jayne drank from it.

I filed Sheila under "no."

Did that mean she hadn't killed Anna?

Not necessarily. It was possible Sheila had killed Anna and had put David up to killing me.

Why would he do that? To stop me asking questions. Sheila and David had been together today and seemed to be getting on slightly better. Had they decided to try to make a go at their marriage, but first I had to be disposed of?

I put Sheila back on the list.

I'd told Ryan I believed Manuel was "M." Garden club gossip said Manuel was having an affair with Anna. That might or might not be true. He'd denied it to the police, but it was possible he'd lied. He might have lied because he feared that admitting it would make him look suspicious in the eyes of the police. Which it would have.

If true, it could explain why Mike fired him as soon as Anna was dead, but from what I saw, there didn't seem to be any hard feelings between the two men. Sheila might conceivably have offed her rival to get Manuel for herself, but if that's what happened, her plan wasn't working. He wasn't interested in her, although judging by what I'd seen today, she hadn't given up hope.

David either hadn't noticed his wife's attitude toward the gardener or he hadn't cared.

Ryan had told me Mike and Anna didn't have any life insurance, and their house was heavily mortgaged. Meaning Mike wouldn't come into a lot of money because his wife had died.

Manuel? I simply didn't know enough about Manuel to make any educated guesses. I didn't know anything about him at all.

I reached for my phone. As I pressed the button to activate it, the time display caught my eye.

1:26 AM.

Perhaps my phone call could wait until tomorrow.

* * *

The moment I woke up the next morning, I fumbled for my phone and sent Jayne a text: *Still alive?*

When I came out of the shower, I read the reply: *I'll let you know later.*

Have they said when you can come home?
Waiting for doc's rounds
Call me when you know
Will do. Mrs. H?
Closed today
Mom's here

I signed off with a yellow smiley face. My own face was also smiling, and I felt a great weight lift from my heart. Jayne was going to be okay.

* * *

On Sundays, the shop doesn't open until noon, and if it's a nice day, I try to get to the beach for a good long swim. Today, I had something I needed to do before going into work, so I wanted to get to the beach early. I made my tea and poured it into a thermos and threw a couple of pieces of bread and some cheese together to make a sandwich. I made my apologies to Violet for not bringing her with me and headed out. First, I needed to speak to Mrs. Ramsbatten, and I hoped she was up.

I found my neighbor relaxing on her front porch, enjoying her coffee, reading the *Boston Globe*, and watching the small part of the world that is West London, Massachusetts, go by. Her car was still in the driveway, the "For Sale" sign in the window. "Good morning, Gemma. Another beautiful day."

"It is." I studied her face.

She touched her hair. "Is something the matter, dear?"

"No. I'm wondering how you're feeling."

"I'm feeling fine. Shouldn't I be?"

"No."

"It's nice of you to be concerned about an old woman who lives alone. People complain these days that they don't know their neighbors, and the elderly are often isolated, but I've never found that to be true with you and Arthur." She smiled at me.

I smiled back. If Mrs. Ramsbatten was a mob enforcer or Russian agent deep undercover in West London for the purpose of eventually murdering Anna Wentworth for reasons I couldn't even begin to fathom, she was mighty good at it.

"Jayne and I had to leave the tennis game early. How did Lauren do?"

"She and her partner won. They were so excited, it was a joy to see. It's a round robin tournament, so they'll go on to the next round next week." Mrs. Ramsbatten gave me a sheepish smile. "Although, I must confess, I dozed through most of it. Something about sitting in the hot sun. I didn't see you two leave."

"The lemonade they served was particularly good, I thought."

"The fresh slices of lemon and chopped mint was a nice touch," she said. Clearly Mrs. Ramsbatten had suffered no ill effects from the drink that had felled the much younger Jayne.

"I put my drink under my chair when we went to talk to Lauren between sets. Did you . . . uh . . . see anyone touch it?"

She blinked at me. "Why would someone do that? There was plenty for everyone."

"No reason."

She shrugged and I changed the subject. "The garden looks lovely. Manuel did a nice job."

"He did, didn't he? Such a nice young man. I'm glad I could help him out."

"I have a question for him. Do you have his phone number?"

She peered at me over the top of her reading glasses. "You have a question? You've never been involved in your garden before."

"Sure, I have. I'm keenly interested in gardening. I'm wondering how to best take care of . . . that plant there."

"Which one?"

"The . . . bushy one. I forget the name."

"That's a rose bush."

"Oh."

"Keep your secrets, Gemma Doyle." Mrs. Ramsbatten took her phone out of her purse. "I was young once, you know. Young and fancy-free. I had a life before I met Mr. Ramsbatten."

"I'm not—"

"Young women had more restrictions on their behavior in my day, so I'm quite jealous of your generation. Manuel is a charming man, although not what I'd call handsome, but good looks are so overvalued these days, don't you agree?"

"I'm not—"

She rattled off the number, and I entered it into my phone. "I'm not interested in Manuel. Not in *that* way."

She winked at me. "Whatever you say, dear."

I made my excuses and fled, my ears burning. I called Manuel from my car. Voicemail answered, and I left my name and asked him to call me when he had a chance.

I swam for half an hour and then enjoyed my picnic breakfast while sitting on my towel, watching the beach come to life. As I was getting into the car, my phone rang.

"Hi, Manuel. Thanks for returning my call."

"Not a problem," he said. "What can I do for you?"

"I'd like to talk, if you have time to meet me today."

His voice turned wary. "Talk about what?"

"Let's discuss that in person. I can come to where you are."

"I'm working all day."

"Where?"

"Here and there. Not at the golf club. What's this about? Is there a problem with the work I did in your yard the other day?"

"It's not about that. Everything looks nice. It's about Anna Wentworth."

"Anna?"

"I . . . help the police with their inquiries sometimes, and I have a few questions."

"I didn't know her very well," he said cautiously.

"Sure you did," I said. "Which is why I want to talk to you."

He paused for a long time, then sighed into the phone. "Okay, I guess. I can come to your house around four."

Maybe not a good idea to meet a murder suspect alone in my house. Normally, I'd ask Jayne to be my wingman. Not possible today.

"I'll be at my store all afternoon. Why don't you come there?"

"I suppose I can do that. The bookstore on Baker Street, right?"

"Yes."

"See you at four then." He hung up.

*   *   *

I was unlocking the front door of the Emporium and flipping the sign to "Open" when Jayne called to say she was home and her mother had put her to bed. She was, she said, feeling fine.

I didn't believe her, so I had her put Leslie on the line. "She's tired," Leslie said, "and slightly wobbly, but that's all. Nothing a day in bed and a nice bowl of homemade chicken soup won't fix."

"Call me if you need anything. Tell Jayne that too."

"I will," she said.

I made another call. "Donald, you did such a great job of minding the store yesterday in an emergency, I was hoping I could call on you again."

"Any time, Gemma. It would be my pleasure. Did the purchaser of *The Sign of Seven* stop by to pay?"

"Not yet. How about coming in at quarter to four for about an hour? I have something to attend to, but it's Ashleigh's day off, and Mrs. Hudson's is closed because of Jayne being sick."

"I'll be there," he said.

In between helping customers and calling to check on Jayne, I spent the rest of the day thinking. I didn't come up with any conclusions and was becoming increasingly frustrated.

Donald arrived five minutes early, dressed for the occasion (if not the weather) in his Inverness cape and deerstalker hat. I briefly considered hiring him to stand outside on the sidewalk and attract customers.

"I have a meeting at four," I said. "My guest and I will talk in the reading nook, but I'll need you to keep an eye on the store and help any customers."

"Happy to be of assistance." Donald made a deep bow, sweeping his arm before him.

What I was actually saying was, *I'll need you to keep an eye on me and call the police if Manuel tries to kill me.*

I instructed Donald on the basics of how to ring up a cash sale and told him to decline debit cards for the time being. I showed him how to record a credit payment, using the manual machine kept under the counter, in case the online system went down. He paid keen attention and even jotted down notes in a small notebook he pulled out of a pocket in his cape.

Manuel arrived right on time. He'd come from work in his gardening overalls and heavy boots, but his face and hands glowed pink from a recent scrubbing.

"Thanks for agreeing to meet me," I said.

He looked around the store. "Sherlock Holmes, eh?"

"Our specialty."

"Never saw the appeal myself."

Donald gasped in shock.

"Please, have a seat." I gestured to the wingback chair in the reading nook. Earlier, I'd taken a stool from behind the sales counter, put it next to the chair, and placed a pitcher of water and two glasses on the table on the other side of the chair. I'd nabbed some fresh raspberries from the tearoom kitchen and tossed them into the water.

Moriarty leapt onto a shelf to better listen in on the conversation.

"Nice cat," Manuel said.

Moriarty's whiskers twitched.

"Water?" I said.

"Sure."

I poured one glass, allowing a few raspberries to fall into the drink, and handed it to him. Manuel drank deeply, and he swallowed a berry, clearly not worried that I'd poisoned it.

He had not, I concluded, tampered with my lemonade. If he had, I would have expected him to be slightly, even if unconsciously, wary of anything I served him.

Last night, I'd realized I didn't have a good picture of Anna Wentworth. The only person I'd spoken to who knew her well, other than her husband, was Sheila. And Sheila wasn't exactly an unbiased observer.

"Tell me about Anna," I said. "You two were close."

The slightest smile touched the corners of his mouth, and some of the darkness behind his eyes lifted. "What makes you think that?"

When Donald and I had been at Anna's house on Tuesday, paying our respects to Anna's husband, Manuel had spent a lot of time trimming the flowers at the edge of the patio. Near enough to listen in on our conversation. I had to ask myself why he'd want to do that. *More than curiosity,* I thought.

"I observe things," I said. "You and Anna were close. Very close."

"The police asked me. I told them I wasn't having an affair with Anna. I don't see that it's any of your business anyway."

"I'm not with the police, but as I said, I observe things. And because I observe things, I sometimes see things the police do not. I want Anna's killer to be found and punished." I studied his face. "I think you do too, Manuel."

He turned his face away.

I gave him a minute, and then I said, "You and Anna were the object of garden club gossip."

His expression tightened. "That bunch. Half of them don't care about gardening; they're only wanting something to fill their time. That and have lunch and gossip."

"What about the other half? Are they more like Anna?"

"No one was truly like Anna. The soil was in her blood."

"Would you say that about yourself?"

"Not really. I like plants just fine. I like to make a garden look nice, and I'm proud when I do, but it's a job to me. I'm self-taught, and I've learned a lot over the years. My clients often ask my advice about the proper placement of plants and what sort of growing conditions they need. I'm happy to help, but personally I'd be okay living in an apartment in the city."

"Did you help Anna with her garden?"

"Didn't need to. She'd consult with me sometimes, but she knew far more than I did." He paused.

"And?" I prompted.

He said nothing for a long time. Moriarty perched on the shelf and watched, his tail flicking back and forth. In the background, Donald chatted to customers. A woman asked if she could buy the signed, life-sized cutout of Benedict Cumberbatch, and Donald told her it wasn't for sale.

"I suppose you'll tell the cops anything I tell you," Manuel said.

"I know you lied to them. They don't like that, but they're unlikely to do anything about it unless you deliberately withheld evidence. I won't tell them anything you tell me in confidence unless I think it pertinent to the investigation of her murder."

He sighed. Secrets are sometimes hard to hold. I'd told him I knew his secret, and he was relieved at the chance to let it out.

"It's not pertinent, but they'll think it is. Yes, Anna and I were close. More than close. We were planning to get married."

"Married? Wasn't she married already?"

"Haven't you heard of divorce?"

"Yes, but—"

"So, for once, the garden club gossip was right. This spring was all about getting ready for the garden tour. As soon as that was over, she was going to kick her good-for-nothing husband to the curb and file for divorce."

I wondered if that truly was Anna's intention. She wouldn't have been the first woman to string a lover along with no intention of ever leaving the wronged husband.

Whether it was true or not didn't matter. All that mattered was that Manuel believed it was.

"Won't happen now, will it?" His dark eyes filled with tears. He poured himself another glass of water as an excuse to look away from me. "I loved her a great deal."

"Did Mike Nixon know this?"

"Spouses often know without being told, don't they? I overheard them arguing a week or so before she died. Something about going to court. He said he couldn't afford a court case. That's what I think he said anyway. I was outside and they were in the kitchen, so I didn't get all of the conversation. Even after that, he was never anything but formally polite toward me. Maybe he genuinely didn't care what she got up to, like she said."

"He sacked you mighty fast as soon as Anna died."

"I wasn't surprised at that. He never had the slightest interest in Anna's garden, other than as a source of income, so he didn't want the expense anymore."

"Source of income?"

"Her garden was an advertisement for her books, blog, and the consultancy business."

While we talked, I'd kept one ear open as to what was going on in the shop. Customers came and went, and Donald chatted to them. He needed to do some work on his sales pitch. A twelve-year-old boy looking for beach reading wouldn't be interested in a biography of Sir Arthur Conan Doyle, no matter how fascinating that book might be to Donald.

"I loved Anna," Manuel said. "I wanted us to be together. Always."

I studied his face. He'd loved Anna and he was grieving her—that I believed—but it didn't mean he didn't kill her. People who kill in a burst of anger often come to deeply regret it.

"If you go to the police on your own initiative, I won't tell them what you told me," I said. "Tell them you didn't think your relationship was relevant to her murder and you didn't want to confuse matters."

"Which is true."

"In particular, they need to know because of your situation regarding Sheila Tierney."

His eyes widened. "Her! What do you know about that? I can't believe she told you she's been making a thorough nuisance of herself."

"She didn't need to. Sheila has, for lack of a better word, a crush on you. She and Anna were friends once, but they'd fallen out recently. If Sheila knew you and Anna were lovers and planning to get married and she wanted you for herself, she'd have a reason to get rid of Anna."

"You can't possibly believe Sheila killed Anna. Not over me! She was becoming a pest, always asking me to come and work for her, saying she wouldn't take no for an answer, or suggesting we go out for a drink so she could get some ideas for her garden. She told me her husband traveled a lot of the time and she was alone at home. Poor, lonely Sheila. I told her I wasn't interested. I tried to be polite about it, but eventually I stopped being polite and warned her off."

"You put a note in her postbox on the weekend. She didn't get it because of subsequent events."

"How do you know that?"

"As I said, I know a lot of things."

"The night Anna died, the police took Sheila down to the station for questioning, but they let her go. People were saying she'd done it. I didn't know what to think, but I never believed that. Are you saying Sheila killed Anna because of me?"

"No, I'm not."

Sheila hadn't tried to poison me. I rarely make assumptions, but in this case, I decided to assume that if Sheila killed Anna in an attempt to hook up with Manuel, her husband David would be unlikely to support her by trying to bump me off.

Then again, such a situation wasn't impossible, and therefore not an idea I could afford to eliminate.

"The police," I continued, "have far more information than I do. What you have to tell them about Sheila's state of mind might be important."

"Sorry to bother you, Gemma." Donald poked his head into the reading nook. "That lady's asking if you'll be getting any more copies of *City of Scoundrels* by Victoria Thompson."

I glanced across the room to see Mrs. Fallingham, one of my best customers, smiling and wiggling her fingers at me.

"For her, I'll put in a special order," I said. "Tell her I'll give her a call when it comes in."

He tiptoed away.

By the time I turned back to Manuel, he'd stood up. "I'll talk to the cops. I'll see you next Wednesday."

"What's happening on Wednesday?"

"That's the day I work at your house."

"Oh, right."

Manuel left and I joined Donald at the sales counter. It was almost five o'clock; the store was empty of customers, and Donald was looking highly pleased with himself.

"How'd it go?" I asked.

"Extremely well."

"How much did you sell?"

"I didn't actually *sell* anything, Gemma, but plenty of people said they'd come back. A woman was interested in a romance novel, and I showed her Volume I of the Canon, the one that contains "A Scandal in Bohemia," but that wasn't quite what she had in mind."

"We stock gaslight mysteries, Donald. Plenty of them have a strong romance angle. Did you tell her that?"

He blinked rapidly. "Why would I do that? She's going to think about coming back to get Volume I. Once she's started the Canon, she'll be hooked for life. The mother of a young boy who was looking for a book said if he ever had a school project on Sir Arthur, they'd know where to come."

"Thank you anyway, Donald."

"Always happy to be of help, my dear. During the times my expertise wasn't required, I had a chance to study the layout of the store. You don't have a lot of space, but I'm thinking if you get rid of those books over there"—he indicated the gaslight shelf—"which don't have anything to do with Holmes or Sir Arthur, you'd have more room for additional volumes of the Canon or books on Conan Doyle himself. Really, my dear, do you need to stock so many mugs and puzzles and other foofaraw?"

"I'll keep that in mind. Will you look at the time? Almost five. No need for you to stay any longer." I edged toward the door.

He followed me. "Did you learn anything useful?"

"Nothing I didn't know already. But it can be helpful to have my impressions confirmed."

Chapter Twenty

The shop closes early on Sunday; after bidding Donald adieu and locking up, I went over to Jayne's. Andy opened the door to my knock and let me in.

I found Jayne sitting in her living room, her feet on a stool, mug of tea in hand, looking totally adorable in a pink dressing gown. Her face was scrubbed clean and her hair piled loosely at the back of her head.

I gave her a kiss on the cheek. "You look good."

"I feel perfectly fine, Gemma." She gave Andy an affectionate smile. "Everyone needs to stop fussing over me. Neither Mom nor Andy will let me do so much as make myself a piece of toast."

"You had a scare," he said.

"And now I'm recovered. Gemma's here, so you can go to work."

"I'm not sure . . ." he said.

"But I am. Off you go." She made shooing gestures.

"You'll call me if you need anything, Gemma," Andy said, "or if there are any . . . developments."

"Sure," I said.

"You mean if I feel sick again," Jayne said. "Which, I can assure you, I won't."

Andy gave her a chaste little kiss on the top of her head, and I walked him to the door.

"Now you'll call if—"

"'Bye." I slammed the door.

"Enough of this tea," Jayne called. "There's a bottle of wine in the fridge. Help yourself and bring me one."

I carried two glasses into the living room. "I wasn't planning on staying long. Do you need me to?" I handed her a glass.

"No. But don't tell Mom or Andy you've left me alone."

"Shall I order something in for dinner?"

"No need. Mom stocked the fridge with more than I'll eat all month."

"You're lucky to have people around you who care so much."

Jayne gave me a radiant smile and lifted her glass. "I am lucky. And I know it. Cheers."

"Cheers." We clinked glasses.

Jayne took a sip and then said, "So, who tried to kill me?"

"What makes you think anyone did?"

"A year ago, the very idea wouldn't have crossed my mind. I guess I've been spending way too much time around you. The doctor was full of questions about where and what I'd eaten, and he was specifically interested in the lemonade I had at the tennis game. Then Ryan and Louise came in and asked the same thing, so I'm assuming the lemonade was poisoned somehow. It was full of stuff—slices of lemon and some herbs or leaves."

"How did it taste?"

"It tasted like lemonade. Lemony. The leaves were mint, I think. Obviously, you think there was more in there than lemonade."

"I do."

"So who tried to kill me? Or at least make me sick?"

"No one. It had to have been aimed at me. The glass had been poured for me, if you remember."

"I don't remember, but that doesn't matter. Who gave it to you?"

"Mike. Which doesn't mean he added the . . . whatever it was. I put the glass down and left it unattended for several minutes. Mrs. Ramsbatten was there the whole time, but she fell asleep. As for who it might have been, I don't know, Jayne. Any one of the people who were at Lauren's tennis match might have put something in the drink when no one was looking. Except for Sheila, who was with us when the . . . whatever was added."

Jayne sipped her wine in silence. I studied her face. She looked fine, as she kept saying she was, but someone had tried to kill her. Even if they intended to get someone else—that is, me—it had still been a traumatic event. "Why don't you take a few days off? Maybe go up the coast with Andy, stay in a nice B&B, walk on the beach, eat at nice restaurants."

I should have known better than to even make the suggestion. Jayne's eyes widened in horror. "It's the middle of the season, Gemma. Andy has a restaurant to run. I have Mrs. Hudson's. Even if I wanted to, which I don't, it's too late now. I called Fiona and Jocelyn earlier and told them we'd be opening tomorrow, regular hours. Enough of me. How was your day?"

I filled her in on Donald's attempts to be a salesclerk. "I suspect he has plans to eliminate everything he doesn't think relevant to or respectful of the Great Detective and his creator."

We drank our wine and then moved to the kitchen, where Jayne popped a chicken casserole into the microwave and pulled a premixed salad and bottle of homemade dressing out of the fridge. Over the meal, we talked about everything but the Anna Wentworth killing.

By the time I was scraping my plate clean, Jayne was smothering a yawn.

"Bed for you, ducks." I got to my feet and gathered the dirty dishes.

"It's barely past seven o'clock, Gemma."

"Your body has had a shock. If you're planning to be at work at the usual time tomorrow, you need a lot of sleep tonight." I put the dishes in the dishwasher and the remains of the casserole into a plastic container. "Promise me if you don't feel well or start getting tired tomorrow, you'll go home. Even if you have to close the tearoom early."

"I promise," she said.

"Liar," I said.

* * *

Violet greeted me in her usual exuberant fashion. I greeted her in return, although perhaps not quite so exuberantly. Greetings over, I served her dinner and settled down to read for a while. Unless and until there were more developments in the murder investigation, I didn't know what I could do. It was probably too early for Ryan to have the results of the tests on Jayne's stomach contents, but that didn't matter. I knew she'd been poisoned and was almost certain the poison had been meant for me; what had been used didn't matter all that much, although it would be worth knowing if the intent had been to kill me or only to make me sick for a few hours.

I didn't think I could ask Ryan outright if he'd heard from Manuel. If he hadn't, he'd demand to know what I was talking about. I'd promised Manuel I wouldn't reveal what he told me if he went to the police himself. I had to give him some time.

So I curled up in my favorite chair and fell into my book. Violet wandered into the den to keep me company. When I next looked up, it was dark outside and Violet was snuffling in her sleep. I checked my phone. Ten o'clock. Time to take the dog for a quick walk and then myself to bed.

"Walk," I said.

Violet scrambled to her feet and ran for the mudroom door. I didn't plan to go far, so I slipped on a pair of thin ballet flats rather than the trainers or sports sandals I usually wear for our walks.

We stood outside under the light over the mudroom door for a few minutes, taking in the surroundings. The scent of basil and the other herbs Mrs. Ramsbatten had planted filled the air. Cars went by, not stopping nor slowing. Violet nosed around the ground at my feet, but nothing attracted her attention.

I kept my senses alert and my attention on Violet as we walked through the dark streets. I couldn't forget that someone had tried to kill me—or warn me off—yesterday. They'd failed, and that might have frightened them from trying again. Or not.

Violet sniffed at every lamppost and bush while I enjoyed the peace of the night. A strong wind was blowing inland, ruffling my curls and the fur on Violet's back and bringing the delicious scent of the sea with it. Lamps burned in a few windows, and the blue glow of a TV shone behind curtains.

It was, I realized, exactly a week, almost to the minute, since Anna Wentworth had died. I turned at the next corner.

We walked past the empty park. The children's swing set squeaked in the wind as we approached the small wooded area. It was late, and not many people or cars were out. Gradually, I became aware of footsteps behind me, keeping pace with mine. I slowed, turned slightly, and peered into the darkness, but I could see nothing and no one. The footsteps stopped. I looked down at Violet, sniffing at a patch of grass that looked no different from any other patch of grass.

"Violet?" I said softly.

The dog didn't look up. Her nose twitched and her tail moved. She appeared to be sensing nothing out of the ordinary. I increased my pace and she abandoned whatever scent had proved to be so interesting to trot beside me.

Footsteps again. Getting closer. Firm and strong and purposeful. Not a dog walker or a wanderer. I was nearing the darkest spot on the street, and that burnt-out streetlamp had not been replaced. I took a deep breath and slipped my free hand into my pocket and grabbed my phone. I stopped, muttering a curse, and leaned over as though to tie my shoe. I took a deep breath, summoned all the energy I could; then, in one swift movement, I stood upright and whirled around, the hand gripping my phone held out in front of me, the other holding the leash loose.

"Nice night, isn't it?" The woman behind me was dressed in jogging clothes and bright pink and yellow trainers, earbuds in her ears and a white wire trailing into the phone strapped to her upper arm. She pushed a button on her phone as she passed me and, with a burst of speed, disappeared around a corner. I let out all the breath I'd been holding.

Violet, who'd sensed no danger, looked up at me, her head cocked to one side in a question.

"Sorry. Looks like I'm somewhat jumpy tonight." I let go of my phone and the dog and I stood in the gap between the streetlights, listening to the sounds of the town of West London at night. The sky was clear, with no moon, and even in the reflected glow of the city, a scattering of the brightest stars shone in the sky.

A Curious Incident

I stepped off the sidewalk and entered the darkness of the woods. Violet ran ahead of me as far as the leash would allow her, sniffing the ground. The lights and intermittent noises of the street fell behind us. A small animal scurried through the undergrowth and dead leaves, and small branches crunched under my feet. Violet woofed softly. I didn't switch on the flashlight app on my phone. I wanted to experience the dark. I wanted to feel what Anna Wentworth had felt in the moments before she died.

I was concentrating so hard on my feelings of darkness and solitude I didn't watch where I was putting my feet. I stepped on the edge of a small rock and it slid out from under my foot, throwing me off balance. I grabbed at a branch, missed and, getting no traction from my shoes, fell backward. The back of my head met the hard ground, and the world went dark.

Chapter Twenty-One

Something warm and wet rubbed my cheek, and a high-pitched whine came from my right, close by my ear.

Confused, unsure where I was, I opened my eyes. I was lying on rough ground. Leafy branches swayed overhead in the gentle breeze, and I could see a few pinpricks of light shining through them. It was very quiet. My head swam, and then the whine came again. I recognized Violet's long nose and liquid brown eyes and I remembered stepping into the copse, slipping, and falling. I remembered the footsteps I'd thought had been following me, and listened for the sound of breathing or the crunch of dead leaves: for an indication that someone was close by, watching me. But other than Violet, I sensed nothing. I lifted one hand and rubbed her ear.

"I'm okay," I said. "I think."

The dog yelped in relief and began licking my face with a vengeance.

I mentally checked myself out. The back of my head hurt, but nothing else seemed to be damaged. I wiggled my feet and flexed my wrists, and to my infinite relief my fingers and toes moved as commanded. I groaned and slowly sat up. Violet danced backward and yipped at me. I gave the back of my head a tentative touch and felt a lump already forming. The patch of hair over it was wet and sticky. I pulled my phone out of my pocket and checked the time: 10:35. I'd been unconscious for maybe five or ten minutes.

A car drove past on the road, but the woods were all-concealing, and no one stopped to see if I needed help.

Violet whined again, and I gave her a thorough rub. "You must have been scared. Aren't you a good girl to stay with me."

She barked in agreement. I struggled to my feet. I wasn't too sure if my head was going to remain steady, so I didn't lean over to pick up the end of the leash. "Let's go home," I said. "If I pass out again, you need to go for help."

She ran on ahead, her leash dragging behind her. When she reached the sidewalk, she stopped and looked behind her to check I was following.

Go for help.

I made a phone call. "Sorry to bother you so late, Manuel, but it is important. Do you have Anna's dog?"

"Anna's dog? You mean Peony? No, why would you think that?"

"I'm wondering where he is."

"Peony was Anna's dog, and she loved him a great deal. I would have taken him if I could, but I live in an apartment building with a no-dog rule. When I was at the house for the last time and Mike told me I was fired, I asked about Peony. Mike said he was moving so he'd given the dog away. I don't know where he went. Is something the matter?"

"Nope. Nothing at all. Good night."

I hung up and called Sheila Tierney. I asked her about the people who'd come to watch Lauren's tennis game.

"It's late for a call," she said rather rudely, I thought. "Why do you want to know anyway?"

I wasn't in the mood to make polite small talk. "Because I do. I'll come over there and knock you up, if I have to."

"You'll do what?"

"Get you out of bed."

"Whatever." She told me what I wanted to know, and I hung up as she yelled, "Wait! What—"

The next number I needed wasn't in my phone. That call would have to wait until I got home.

I then called Ryan, who answered on the first ring. "Good evening, Gemma."

"Where are you?"

"I'm at home. About to go to bed. Why do you ask?"

"I know who killed Anna Wentworth. I'm out walking Violet. We'll be home in about ten minutes. Meet us there."

"Are you going to give me a hint?"

"No."

Violet and I made it home in eight minutes, but Ryan's car was already parked in front of the house. He'd dressed in a hurry, probably pulled clothes out of the laundry hamper or off the floor.

"What's going on?" he asked as we walked up the driveway.

"Let's go inside."

The motion sensor lights had come on, and Ryan stood behind me as I unlocked the mudroom door.

"Hold on." He touched the back of my head. "There's blood in your hair. Gemma, what's going on? Did someone attack you?"

"I tripped over a rock, slipped, and fell. It was a total accident caused by nothing but my own carelessness. I passed out for a few minutes. No damage was done other than a sore noggin and a big lump, but the blow knocked some sense into me."

"It doesn't look that way to me. You're making absolutely no sense."

Now that I'd arrived home, delayed shock hit me. I dropped into a kitchen chair and put my head in my hands. Violet headed for her water bowl and drank deeply.

Ryan crouched in front of me and folded my hands in his. He looked into my eyes. "You okay, Gemma? If you hit your head, you need to go to the hospital."

"I'm fine. A bit unsteady. I just need a minute."

"Tea?"

I gave him a heartfelt smile. "I'm turning you into a worthy partner for an Englishwoman. Yes, please. Tea would be perfect."

He filled the kettle and plugged it in.

"Don't forget to add the tea bags to the pot," I said. "In trying to make sense of this case, we neglected to take into account the curious incident of the dog in the nighttime."

Ryan whirled around. Worry filled his lovely blue eyes. "I'd better get you to the hospital."

"I'm not reciting lines from "Silver Blaze" in some sort of Sherlock-inspired delirium. I'm telling you what happened not far from here last Sunday."

"As I recall from the story, the curious incident of the dog in the nighttime is that the dog did nothing in the nighttime. But Anna Wentworth's dog did do something. It went home."

"Exactly. And I realized a few minutes ago when Violet stayed by my side when I was unconscious, that her behavior was the norm for a loyal dog. Leaving their owner lying on the ground and trotting off happily home would have been a curious thing for a dog to do. I was out cold for maybe five or ten minutes."

He sucked in a breath. "That's a long time to be unconscious, Gemma."

"Never mind that now," I said.

"Okay. I'll worry that you need urgent medical attention later."

"Sarcasm does not become you. I suspect if I'd been unconscious all night, Violet would not have left my side." She put her chin on my lap, and I rubbed her ears.

"That's entirely possible but not necessarily applicable to Anna's dog, which is what I assume you're trying to get at. Your dog didn't have anyone to go to for help. Arthur's away. Violet's never been to my place. She might not know how to get to Jayne's or Irene's on foot. Anna's dog went home to her other owner."

"Anna's dog. That's the entire point, Ryan. The dog was not Mike's dog. Mike didn't like the dog. The first thing he did after Anna died was get rid of it."

I glanced at Violet, her huge brown eyes so full of loyalty and, dare I say it, love. Poor Peony. His owner dead, and him abruptly sent to an uncertain fate. I shoved aside a thought of the dog wondering what was happening to him and why Anna hadn't come to get him. "No, that dog would not have left Anna's side after she fell. Which means he didn't go home, alert Mike that something was wrong, and lead him to his wife's body. Mike didn't need the dog to take him to Anna because he knew exactly where she was. He killed her. He would have realized that no matter how careful he was, he would leave some DNA or other evidence in the woods along with his wife's body. I'm assuming you found such?"

Ryan nodded.

"What better way of accounting for his presence than pretending to find her? He would have told you he'd dropped to his knees beside her, wept and wailed and cradled her lifeless body in his arms as he vainly attempted to perform some sort of resuscitation. He couldn't say he'd gone looking for her when she didn't come home, as the body was out of sight of the road and she hadn't been gone all that long anyway. He couldn't leave her there for an appropriate length of time, as someone might come across her and call nine-one-one, and after the police and ambulance arrived, he wouldn't have been allowed anywhere near."

Ryan put a cup of tea on the table in front of me. I picked it up and cradled the warmth in my hands.

"Hold still. Let me have a look at this." He separated the strands of wet hair and touched the lump with gentle fingers. It didn't hurt too much. He dabbed at it with a warm cloth as he spoke. "Suppose I buy that. And I am buying it because you're saying it, but not everyone will. Why? Why did Mike Nixon kill his wife?"

"Anna was going to leave him for Manuel. Did Manuel call you earlier?"

"He came down to the station, and we had a nice long chat. That you know about it means you put him up to it."

"I made a friendly suggestion. Did he tell you why he'd lied?"

"He'd been in some trouble with the police when he was in high school. He hadn't, according to him, done anything, but the cops focused on him rather than the kids from the better side of town who'd been responsible. He doesn't trust the cops. I checked into that case, and it seems he was right. He and his friends were eventually cleared."

"I confess that I might have been off-guard because I liked Mike. I felt sorry for him. He put on a good act when Donald and I called on him."

"It happens. Some people know what behavior's expected, and they do it."

"As for his reasons, threat of divorce is no reason for murder in this day and age, but financial ruin is. Mike's only source of income was Anna's gardening books. That was threatened by Sheila's proposed suit against her. Manuel overheard Mike and Anna arguing about a court case. He thought they meant the impending divorce, but I don't think that was it. Mike knew Sheila was planning to sue Anna. Anna probably would have settled before it went to court. Sheila's case is pretty solid because she still has the manuscript pages she wrote."

"She can sue Anna's estate even if the woman herself is dead." Ryan gave my head a final pat. "I'm no doctor, but my diagnosis is that you're going to live." He took a seat opposite me.

"Glad to hear it," I said. "Sheila can sue, but the complications around that will be substantial. The community won't like it if Sheila sues the poor grieving widower. If she wants to keep writing and publishing gardening books, she needs the goodwill of gardeners. Whether she goes ahead with the suit or not is irrelevant, not if Mike thinks she'll drop it now that Anna's dead. Anna was not only about to be sued, meaning if she lost and she would have, she'd lose a substantial part of the revenue from her books, which was Mike's primary source of income, but on top of that she was about to divorce him. She would have taken her income with her, along with her share of their assets, whatever remained after Sheila's suit, leaving Mike with just about nothing and a gambling habit to support. You told me he doesn't have big losses in Vegas and travels on cheap package deals. But minor losses soon become large ones, and those casinos have a way of luring regular package travelers into spending more than they can afford."

"How am I going to prove this? Your guesses—"

"I never guess."

"Your conclusions then. They won't stand up in a court of law."

I smiled at him. "I have absolutely no idea. I'll remind you that you're always telling me to do the thinking and to leave you to do the proving. You'll have to build a case, one small incident at a time. I phoned Sheila before calling you and asked her why Mike had come to Lauren's tennis game. She called him Saturday morning, hoping they could forget about all the recent unpleasantness—her words, not mine—now that Anna was dead. She wanted to make a little party out of attending the tennis game, and she told him I'd said I'd drop in. He knew I'd be there, and he brought something along in case he had the chance to poison me."

"Why would he want to do that?"

"I believe the realtor told him I'd been in his house. I wanted to call her and ask, but I didn't have her number available. Her card's around here somewhere."

"I'll take care of that."

"People know I've been asking questions, and Mike thought I was focusing on him, although I was no more curious about him than I was about anyone else in this case. A guilty conscience makes people see shadows where none exist."

"Did Sherlock Holmes say that?"

"If not, he should have. One other thing's still bothering me, though. The vandalism to Sheila's garden. I can see no reason Mike would have done that unless he wanted to warn Sheila off from continuing with the lawsuit, and that would have been a pretty dumb thing to do. First, it would have had her running straight to the police, and second it would have provided her with more ammunition for her complaint. She wouldn't have welcomed him to her little group at her daughter's tennis match if she thought he'd done it. Besides, didn't Mike say he was in Vegas that night?"

"He was."

Violet put her head on my knee, and I stroked her soft ears. I thought of Peony, Anna's dog. Peony . . . "It was Anna. Wasn't it?"

Ryan nodded. "Tell me how you know. You figured it out right there, didn't you? I could see it in your face."

"I'd better work at getting more control over my emotions."

"Not from me, I hope."

I said nothing in answer to that. "Anna's dog's named Peony after her favorite flower. A few days ago I wouldn't have known a peony from a pumpkin, but I saw a picture of one in Anna's book and I admired it. Large, attractive flowers on a big bush."

"And . . ."

"I didn't realize the significance at the time, but Sheila's peonies were untouched." I closed my eyes and thought back to the state of Sheila Tierney's garden when I'd seen it. I'd been a fool for not noticing the pattern to the destruction. Now that I was thinking about it, the significance was obvious. "A peony flowers in early spring, so the blooms are past now. The bushes weren't harmed, yet they're next to a bed of flowers that was excessively damaged. The destruction to Sheila's garden looks far worse than it is, Ryan."

"It looked pretty bad to me."

"On the surface, yes, but no permanent damage was done. Branches were cut, but branches can grow back if the trunk or base of the tree or bush isn't destroyed. The flowers on the rose bushes were cut off, but the plant itself was not harmed. Roses can grow back. The annuals were dug up and thrown around, and big holes left where they'd been planted, but annuals can be replanted. The perennials, which cannot be so easily replaced, were largely untouched. If they had been cut, it was only the foliage. No damage was done to the roots. Considering the way the garden is laid out, annuals mixed with perennials, rose and peony bushes in adjacent sections, it's obvious the vandal knew something about gardens. They knew what would cause genuine damage to the plants, might even kill them, and what would not. And they avoided that." I opened my eyes and smiled at Ryan. "Anna was, everyone except Sheila tells me—and I think we can disregard Sheila's opinion—a passionate gardener. She would never have destroyed a garden. Any garden, but particularly not one as fine as Sheila's. No, the damage was all cosmetic. Shocking, yes, and ruination to Sheila's hopes for the garden tour trophy, but not permanent."

"You're right, as you usually are. Anna destroyed Sheila's garden."

"How do you know?"

"We found her prints on some rocks that had been artfully arranged to make a sculpture. The sculpture was broken, the stones scattered. Sheila told us she got those particular rocks and stacked them to resemble what the Inuit call an *inukshuk* after she and Anna argued. Anna had no reason, no legitimate reason, to have ever touched them.

"As for why Anna would do such a thing, we'll never know for sure, but I suspect it had to do with Sheila's chances at winning the trophy. The women at the garden club said Sheila was the one to beat this year. It's possible Anna, like Mrs. Ramsbatten, went around to Sheila's house the night before the tour for a look and realized that Sheila's garden was better than hers. Anna would have been humiliated if Sheila won, and Sheila would not have accepted the trophy graciously. She would have rubbed it in Anna's face and would have kept on rubbing. It might even have provided more ammunition for her intended lawsuit."

"What does all that have to do with the murder of Anna?"

"It can't be a coincidence Anna died the night after she wrecked Sheila's garden. Mike must have been wanting to get rid of her for some time, but he didn't know how to accomplish that. The husband's always the first suspect, as everyone knows. When Mike heard about the very public fight between Sheila and Anna, he grabbed the opportunity to frame Sheila. Sending an innocent person up the river didn't seem to bother him too much. He told me he didn't like her. He called her a user."

"It might have worked if he'd been a bit smarter. Planted something of Sheila's at the scene, for example."

"But he wasn't a bit smarter, and he didn't have time to think it all through. If I may make a suggestion, you need to find someone who originally told you they saw Mike hurrying through the streets in search of Anna. It's entirely possible they got the time wrong. It's also possible your well-meaning officers asked the neighbors if they saw a man with a dog. I suspect that if the dog hadn't been mentioned, the potential witnesses wouldn't have brought it up."

"We try very hard not to put ideas in people's minds, but somehow, things slip through." Ryan stood up. "Looks like I have a long night ahead of me. I don't want you on your own tonight, Gemma; you did have a blow to your head. I don't think Jayne's up to looking after you, and her mother's busy fussing over her. There's Irene, but she'll be wanting to make a story out of it. Who can I call at this time of night?"

* * *

I knocked lightly on the guest room door. The sound of a passing freight train came from within. I knocked again, this time with enough force to rattle the wood.

"Donald! Donald! Time to get up. Breakfast is ready."

The train snuffled and snorted, and then came a mumble that I took to be a vague understanding.

Violet trotted after me into the kitchen. Sausages were sizzling in the frying pan; bacon cooking in the oven; eggs scrambled in a bowl, waiting to be added to the frying pan; and bread was in the toaster. The table was set for two, with butter, jam, marmalade, tomato salsa, and pickles in place.

While I waited for Donald to make an appearance, I sipped my tea and checked the online news. Nothing from the police about an arrest in the Wentworth murder. Ryan and his team would be combing through every detail of Mike Nixon's life and asking him a lot of hard questions. If there was something to be found, they'd find it, and if he was crackable, they'd crack him.

If not . . . They couldn't take a case to court based on the curious incident of the dog in the nighttime. More than one killer had gotten away because the police couldn't prove their case.

"Good morning, Gemma." Donald came into the kitchen, showered and shaved and dressed. "You shouldn't have made breakfast. That's what I'm here for. To help. How's the head this morning?"

"Perfectly fine, thank you." I didn't have a headache, and while the lump on the back of my head was about the size of one of the eggs I'd recently cracked, it wasn't painful unless I touched it.

Ryan had called Donald last night and told him I'd had a fall and needed to be watched in case of a concussion. Donald immediately hurried over, full of concern. He'd fussed over me and— blushing furiously all the while and trying not to peek at me in my nightwear—ensured I was settled into bed with a book and a glass of water close at hand. Whereupon he'd gone to the guest room and slept the entire night through.

If Ryan asked, I'd lie and say Donald had woken me every two hours as instructed.

Now he took a seat at the kitchen table, and I stood up. "Coffee?"

"That would be nice, thank you."

I served his coffee and then added chopped red peppers along with fresh chives and basil, picked from the bed next to the mud-room door, to the bowl of eggs. I cooked them lightly and served up two plates.

Donald unfurled his napkin. "This looks delightful. I didn't know you could cook, Gemma."

"I can do breakfast, but that's about all. Arthur's the cook in our house."

"The eggs look nice with that touch of color. What's the green stuff?"

"Chives and basil. Mrs. Ramsbatten planted a herb container by the kitchen door."

"As long as you know what they are," he said, digging in. "I don't know much about plants myself. I trained as a chemist, not a botanist."

I froze, my fork halfway to my mouth. I don't know anything about plants either, but I knew these were chives and basil because my neighbor told me they were chives and basil. I knew chives and basil weren't poisonous because people ate them all the time.

I leapt to my feet. "I've just remembered an appointment. Gotta run. Thanks for coming over."

I grabbed my keys from the hook by the door and then turned to face a startled Donald. "Finish your breakfast and you can let yourself out. Would you mind giving Violet a short walk before you leave? Thanks."

"Oh no. Ryan told me I was to escort you to the store." Donald grabbed a slice of toast and followed me. I didn't bother to argue.

"Perhaps we should take my car," he said.

I didn't bother to argue with that either. I got into my own car, and he did too.

I used Bluetooth to call Ryan. "Oleander," I said when he answered.

"What?"

"Do you have the toxicology report on the contents of Jayne's stomach yet?"

"No. I'm expecting the preliminary this afternoon."

"Tell them to check for oleander."

"Okay. Where are you now? You're supposed to be resting. Are you with Donald?"

"I'm here," Donald called out. "Although I have no idea where we're going in such a rush."

"Have you spoken to Mike Nixon this morning?" I asked.

"Not yet," Ryan said. "Before I do that, we're reinterviewing people on that street about last Sunday night."

"One more question," I said. "Did you call the realtor who's selling Mike's house?"

"It's on my list."

"Do that now and ask her what time she told him I'd been in his house. Donald and I are heading for the library. Meet us there."

"Are you going to tell me why?"

"No. You might want to tell the computer boffins to be on the alert."

"What?"

I hung up. Realizing that I'd be late to the store, I called Ashleigh to ask if she could come in early, and she agreed.

We arrived at the library minutes before opening. The moment Teresa unlocked the doors, Donald and I rushed in.

"Good morning," the librarian said.

"'Morning."

"Can I help you with anything?"

"Nope," I said. "We're waiting for the police."

"The police? Is something wrong?"

"Nope."

She glanced at Donald.

He shrugged.

While we waited, I used my phone to check garden plants. I zoomed in to get a close look at a photo of beautiful pink flowers and nodded to myself in satisfaction.

Ryan and Louise Estrada arrived. Ryan looked baffled, Louise annoyed. Then again, Louise always looks annoyed when I call them out.

"What's this about, Gemma?" she snapped. "I hope you don't think we're at your beck and call all the time."

I didn't bother to mention that they *had* come when I called. "Did you find out the answer to my question, Ryan?"

"If you mean the realtor, I did. Mike came home only minutes after you left, and she told him she had a prospective buyer who toured the house and seemed very interested. When she told him that person was the woman who owns the bookstore in West London, he got agitated and said she wasn't to waste any more of her time talking to you."

"Which," Estrada said, "is what I assume you expected her to say."

"I did, but I needed the timing to be confirmed. Now that you're here as witnesses, I have a question for Teresa."

"You do?" The librarian said. "What?"

It was early enough that no patrons had arrived yet. The other librarian was watching us with much interest.

"Were you working on Saturday afternoon between eleven and three?" I asked.

The two women exchanged glances. "Yes, we both were."

"Do you know Mike Nixon?"

They nodded. "He's a regular patron. Terrible thing about what happened with his wife."

"Did he, by any chance, come in on Saturday and use one of the computers?"

"I can't say for sure," Teresa said. "Saturday afternoon's our busiest time of the week. I know he's been in since Anna died, because I offered my condolences, but I can't be sure of the day or time."

"The computer logs will have a record," the other librarian said. "Patrons sign in with their library card number."

"Can you check that now?" I asked.

She glanced at Ryan.

"Please," he said.

She went behind the desk and activated the computer. "Mike Nixon's number was used at twelve forty-five on Saturday. He was on for twenty minutes. Computer number two."

"You'll want to confiscate computer number two, Detectives," I said.

"Why do I want to do that?" Estrada said.

I smiled at the librarians. They smiled at me.

"If you'll excuse us a minute." Ryan led the way to a corner next to the history shelf. Estrada and I followed, and Donald, uninvited, tagged along behind.

"I believe," I said as the scowling visage of Winston Churchill chomping on his cigar peered over my shoulder, "Mike Nixon searched for information about poisonous plants on that computer. Remember, he isn't a gardener. He had no interest at all in gardening—that was his wife's passion—so he wouldn't have known a poisonous plant from any other. I have to admit that's a gap in my own knowledge. I must rectify it when I have the time."

"Spare us," Estrada said.

"That he added oleander leaves to the lemonade is a guess on my part, although as I might have pointed out at other times, I never guess. I noticed mention of using oleander as a backdrop plant or to line a fence when I was leafing through Anna's book, along with a warning that it's highly toxic. It's common in these parts because it's hardy, attractive, and easy to grow."

"I thought you didn't know anything about gardening," Donald said.

"I pick up the odd bit of knowledge now and again. Anyway, back to the subject at hand. Almost certainly at one time or another, Anna would have regaled her husband with talk of poisonous plants, including oleander, or he might have overheard her and Sheila planning their books. But having no interest in gardens, he wouldn't know what it looks like or how much is needed to make a person sick. That information is freely available to anyone who wants to look it up, courtesy of Google. Mike's not a total idiot, and he had to be aware the police would search his computers and phone if they began to suspect him in his wife's death. Or mine, if it came to that. So he came to the library."

"Why the West London Library, where he's known?" Estrada asked.

"A matter of timing. He found out in the late morning that I'd been inside his house. There could only be one reason for me to do that, and it isn't because I'm interested in buying it." I turned to Donald. "He's a friend of yours, right?"

"I wouldn't say a friend. More of an acquaintance."

"But a Sherlockian. You talked about me with him."

Donald threw Ryan an apologetic look. "I might have mentioned that you and I are great friends and that you've occasionally been of help to the police when they were stumped."

Estrada snorted. "You mean you told him Gemma's a snoop and all-around busybody."

"I didn't—"

"If you want to put it like that," I said. "Mike knew, because Sheila Tierney told him, that I was going to be at the tennis game yesterday afternoon. He didn't have time to go to another town to use the library and wouldn't have wanted to draw attention to himself by taking out a library card in order to use their computers. He came here, found out what he needed to know, hurried home, picked a handful of oleander leaves, chopped them up, and put them in his pocket." I held up my phone. "This picture is of an oleander bush. Anna had a particularly attractive specimen at her house, next to the patio. I saw it myself, the day Donald and I visited.

"If Mike has ever been to the country club, and he told me he's an occasional tennis player, he would know they add mint to their lemonade. He didn't know whether he'd get the opportunity to poison my drink, but he took the chance."

Ryan let out a low whistle.

"If," I said, "you can find evidence that someone searched for information about poisonous plants on computer number two at the time Mike Nixon was logged on, and if whatever substance he read about matches what Jayne consumed, you can charge him with attempting to kill her."

"But not with the murder of his wife," Donald said.

"One thing at a time," Ryan said. "Once we have him locked up on one charge, we'll have time to investigate the other."

"And," Estrada said, "one thing usually leads to another. When he realizes we know all about the poisoning, including the visit to the library, he'll assume we know more than we do. He'll talk."

Donald threw me a huge smile. "Once again, Gemma's cracked the case for you."

"We would have gotten to it eventually," Estrada said.

Chapter
Twenty-Two

As Louise Estrada predicted, Mike Nixon eventually broke down and confessed to the murder of his wife, Anna Wentworth. Further digging on the part of the police showed that not only was he gambling increasingly heavier amounts in Vegas—and subsequently losing more—only days before his wife died, he had become engaged to a nineteen-year-old diner waitress while there. He hadn't told her he was married, but he'd said that once he cleared up some unspecified financial problems back home, he'd move permanently to Las Vegas. She proudly showed the Las Vegas police a diamond engagement ring, which turned out to be as fake as my copy of the cover of *Beeton's Christmas Annual* of 1887.

* * *

The morning after the news of Mike Nixon's arrest hit the media, Irene Talbot came into the shop.

"So," she said, waving the *West London Star* in my face, "it was Mike after all."

"Looks like it."

"Your intrepid reporter has been up all night writing the Pulitzer-winning report."

I grabbed the paper. A picture of Mike and Anna in her garden in happier times, arms around each other, smiling broadly, occupied most of the front page. The large-print headline was what I would categorize as overly sensational.

"Have you heard from Sheila recently?" Irene asked.

"No, I haven't. Should I have?"

"Yes, you should have. She should be thanking you for clearing her name. Without you, she would have been facing life behind bars."

"It wouldn't have come to that," I said modestly.

"Sure, it would," Ashleigh said. Moriarty's entire body was stretched across the sales counter to allow Ashleigh to rub his tummy. His eyes were closed, the end of his tail twitched, and he purred happily. A handful of customers browsed the shelves.

"Can I see?" Ashleigh held out her free hand, and I put the paper in it.

"You don't have to tell Sheila that," Irene said. "In the end, it was the same old story. A man wanting out of his marriage, but too greedy to get a divorce like any sensible person would."

"That's about it," I said.

"I've decided never to get married," Ashleigh said. "The chance of being murdered is too high." She'd dressed today as though repelling men was her intention. Hair pulled tightly back into a sturdy bun, thick glasses (with clear lenses as her vision was perfectly fine), a long-sleeved, high-necked, ill-fitting brown dress that fell past her knees and had a tear in the hem, flat brown shoes. "I don't see mention of Gemma's name anywhere here."

"And thank heavens for that," I said.

"Virtue is its own reward," Irene said. "Speaking of marriages, Sheila and David are going to work on repairing theirs."

"That's good to hear."

"Starting with a romantic weekend in Provincetown. Sheila would have preferred to go to Paris or Barbados, but part of the repairing the relationship deal is that they're going to take a good long look at their finances. They have a friend with a house in Provincetown, so they'll be house-sitting for their second honeymoon, not shopping at Dolce and Gabbana on the Champs-Elysées or basking in the hot Caribbean sun."

A customer tentatively approached the counter. "Excuse me . . ." she said to Ashleigh. Ashleigh put down the paper and reluctantly went to assist her.

"Is Lauren going with them?" I asked.

Irene checked her watch. "What sort of a second honeymoon would that be? No, she's going to stay with me. In fact, I'm meeting them here around about now. Lauren will be starting at the public school in the fall, and I'm hoping the change won't be too hard on her. I'm going to be doing my aunt gig full out, if she needs me."

"I'm glad to hear it," I said.

The bells over the door tinkled, and Sheila and Lauren came in. Sheila was dragging the pink suitcase, and Lauren had the cat carrier in one hand and a tote bag of feline supplies tossed over the other shoulder.

Lauren put down the carrier and charged at me, arms outstretched. She wrapped her arms around me and I hugged her back. "Thank you so much, Gemma," she said when we'd separated. "You saved my mom."

"I'm glad I could do my small part." I looked at Sheila. "I hear you're going on holiday. Have fun."

"It's been years since I've been to Provincetown. I'm so looking forward to it." Sheila wasn't a very good liar, but she was making the effort. Maybe she'd be able to convince herself that the love of her husband and daughter was worth the reduction in circumstances.

Moriarty stood up. He stretched every inch of his body before leaping off the counter. He walked up to the cat carrier and put his nose to it. Snowball's tiny pink nose peeked out.

"Don't you have something to say to Gemma, Sheila?" Irene said.

"What?"

Irene jerked her head. "You know."

"Oh yes! I'm so excited. I have a new book coming out. Anna did a small amount of work on it already, so it's going to be published under both our names. A sort of tribute to her. Isn't that exciting?" The smile cracked. "I'm going to be so busy, but it's going to be great fun to be out in the world again. I'm going back to school in the fall. I'll be teaching tenth-grade history at West London High. I'm so excited about that!"

"Congratulations," I said.

"I mean about the other thing," Irene said.

"It's okay, Irene," I said.

Sheila flashed her perfect white teeth at me in what she intended to be a smile. I smiled back. "If I could have a quiet word?" she said.

"Sure." I led the way to the reading nook. I didn't sit and neither did she.

Sheila rubbed her hands together and avoided my eyes. "I need to thank you for all you did. You helped me, and I appreciate it."

"I didn't do it for you, you know. If you'd been guilty, I would have told the police so."

She glanced over her shoulder to where Lauren was telling Irene that Snowball needed to meet other cats, and Irene was apologizing for not having a pet. "I know," Sheila said, "but it doesn't mean I'm not grateful." She took a deep breath. "Hearing that Mike killed Anna has come as quite a shock. How two people who married because they loved each other can drift so far apart . . ." Her voice trailed off. I said nothing and let her gather her thoughts. "I knew their marriage wasn't exactly a close one, but I never thought . . . Anyway, David and I are rethinking a great many things, and we'll be doing a lot of talking in Provincetown. About our marriage, our financial situation. Our daughter, most of all. He's going to consolidate his business, spend more time closer to home, and help me with the business part of releasing the new book."

"When it comes out, let me know. You can do a signing here, if you'd like."

"Thank you." She looked directly at me for the first time. "Thank you."

"You're welcome." I moved to join the others, but I was a moment too late. Before I could stop her, Lauren opened the door of the cat carrier. Images of flying, spitting cats, collapsing bookcases, traumatized little girls, terrified customers, and my own shredded arms ran through my mind. "No!" I took a step toward them.

I stopped.

Snowball came out of the carrier. She nuzzled her head and shoulders into Moriarty's chest. Moriarty rubbed his chin against the top of her head. Both cats lay down, and Moriarty wrapped his body around the smaller cat. Snowball purred. Moriarty closed his eyes.

"Look, Gemma," Lauren said. "They're best friends."

"Will wonders never cease. I hope, Lauren, you and I can continue to be friends." I glanced at Sheila, who gave me a genuine smile. "Any time you need a break, either of you, you're always welcome in the Sherlock Holmes Bookshop and Emporium. It would appear that Snowball is welcome here also."

Moriarty meowed.

* * *

At twenty-two minutes to four, I opened my mouth.

"Partners' meeting," Ashleigh said. "Back in twenty. Got it."

"You could pretend to be surprised at my activities."

"Gemma, I am constantly surprised at the things you get up to. So surprised, in fact, that when you do the expected, I have to comment on it."

"Oh," I said.

"Excuse me," an elderly man said, "but I believe I owe you twenty-four dollars?"

"You do?" Ashleigh said.

"I was in here on Saturday, and the other clerk, a gentleman, couldn't process my credit card payment, so he let me take the book on a promise."

"Thanks for coming back," Ashleigh said.

I left her to take care of the transaction and stepped through the adjoining door into the tearoom. I stopped dead in my tracks. Andy and Jayne were sitting together on the bench seat in the window alcove. A plate of desserts, including red macarons, and a selection of tea sandwiches were in front of them. Instead of a teapot and matching cups, a gold foil-topped bottle was in an ice bucket next to six crystal flutes. Andy said something, and Jayne laughed and laid her hand on his arm.

Jayne is a beautiful woman, but at that moment, she was almost ethereal. Andy beamed at her, his smile full of such joy that if he were a woman, I'd have said he looked radiant.

No customers were in the restaurant, and although it was still twenty minutes to closing, the sign in the window had been flipped over and the door to the street locked.

I swallowed heavily and struggled to control the tears threatening to form.

Jayne's my best friend. I'm closer to her than I've ever been to anyone. Everything was about to change.

I didn't know if I was ready for that.

Actually, I did know. I wasn't ready. But I would have to be, for Jayne.

Fiona and Jocelyn came out of the kitchen, and Ashleigh stepped into the tearoom, pulling the door closed behind her. "What's up?" she said.

Fiona giggled. "Wait and see."

I took a seat and Ashleigh, Fiona, and Jocelyn squeezed around the table. I smiled at Jayne. I smiled at Andy.

They looked at each other, and Jayne took a breath. Her eyes shone with love and joy. "We have news!" she announced.

"You do?" I said. "Whatever could that be?"

Chapter
Twenty-Three

I let myself into the house through the mudroom.
Jayne and Andy were engaged and planning a wedding next spring. I was going to be a bridesmaid.

I was happy for her. I was happy for him. Their engagement happened very quickly, but they'd been good friends for a long time, and I suppose when like turns to love, you know it's right.

Things in our lives would change, but they wouldn't change too much—not at first anyway. Jayne assured me she had no intention of leaving Mrs. Hudson's.

We'd toasted the happy couple with excellent champagne and talked about wedding plans. Ashleigh and I had then gone back to the Emporium, and Fiona and Jocelyn began cleaning up the restaurant. Andy headed to his own job, and Jayne announced that she planned to get a couple of hours of baking done for tomorrow.

I'd had one last piece of investigating to do in the Anna Wentworth case, and earlier I'd made a phone call and arranged an appointment for six o'clock. I was getting home from that appointment now. I dropped my purchases on the kitchen table.

A Curious Incident

Violet sniffed at my legs. Something was up—she could smell it on me, and it wasn't news of Jayne and Andy's engagement that had caught her attention.

"You might as well come with me," I said. "I've something to show you. Lives are changing, and yours is about to also."

I opened the passenger door of the Miata.

Violet's ears rose in shock.

I reached in and picked up the white bundle of fur. A rough pink tongue licked at my face.

Violet barked.

"Violet," I said, "meet your new brother. This is Peony. He was abandoned at the Humane Society, and he needs a new home. We're it."

Acknowledgments

A book is never the work of one person, and I have two people in particular to thank for helping me make the world of Gemma and Jayne and the gang the best I can achieve. Cheryl Freedman, my good friend, turns her professional editor's eye on the manuscript and makes many helpful suggestions and offers encouragement. Sandy Harding works hard to fix my mistakes and oversights and provides even more encouragement. Thanks very much to them both.

Thanks also to Kim Lionetti, my agent at Bookends, and to the crew at Crooked Lane Books for their support of this series and all my writing efforts.

And to Sherlockians everywhere. Keep on believing.

Read an excerpt from

A Three Book Problem

the next

SHERLOCK HOLMES BOOKSHOP MYSTERY

by VICKI DELANY

available soon in hardcover from
Crooked Lane Books

CROOKED
LANE

NEW YORK

Chapter One

"You're sure we didn't go through a warp in the space-time continuum and end up in Jolly Old England?"

"Not according to the GPS." Jayne Wilson peered at her phone. "Still Cape Cod. Still West London, Massachusetts."

"Still the twenty-first century?" I asked.

"So this says."

I steered the Miata down the long driveway, passing rows of towering oak trees, their leaves turning yellow with the season. Between the flash of tree trunks I could see green lawns stretching into the distance, hedges and low stone walls, curving flower-beds, a line of oaks and maples, bursting with autumn color, and the azure sea sparkling on the far horizon. "You must be right," I said. "Too sunny to be England."

The driveway took a wide turn, the house came into view, and Jayne sucked in a breath. I might have gasped myself. The house was three stories tall, made of weathered golden stone, with tall curtained windows, numerous brick chimneys, and a grand portico waiting to greet guests. The driveway opened into a spacious courtyard and then it narrowed again to curve around the house, slipping between it and the detached four-door garage with dormer windows above which had probably once been staff accommodation. Those doors were closed now and two cars stood in the courtyard: a gleaming, recently washed and polished silver Lexus and a Honda Civic that seemed to be primarily constructed out of mud and rust.

A man stood to attention under the portico, next to one of giant iron urns on either side of the great oak door. The urns were empty, and the man wore a black suit, stiffly ironed white shirt, black waistcoat, and black bow tie. His shoes were so highly polished the sunlight bounced off them. His black hair was slicked to one side with hair oil, but he'd missed a bit and a curl escaped from behind his right ear.

"Is that Mr. Masterson, do you suppose? Jayne said.

"Oh no. The gentleman of the house would never greet the paid workers. That, my dear, can only be the butler."

Jayne giggled.

I pulled the Miata to a halt next to the front steps. The butler rounded the car and dipped his head, just a fraction. He was considerably younger than the norm for a properly trained and experienced butler, being in his early twenties. The escaped curl indicated this wasn't his regular role in life. "Good afternoon, Ms. Doyle," he said in a deep, sonorous voice. "Precisely on time. Mr. Masterson appreciates punctuality." Something approaching an embarrassed smile touched the edges of his mouth and he shifted his shoulders and stretched his neck slightly, trying to loosen contact with the tight collar.

"So I've been told," I said.

He glanced at Jayne. "Ms. Wilson?"

"Hi," she said.

The van that had followed us out of town lumbered down the driveway and pulled in behind us.

"I am Smithers," the butler said.

"You're kidding?" Jayne said. "Oh, sorry."

A flash of humor touched his eyes, and he said, "This weekend anyway. I will instruct your staff to carry on around the house to the kitchen entrance at the back. You may park over there."

"That's okay," I said, matching his tone. "My staff need supervision."

"Very well. I'll give you time to unload and have Mrs. Higgins meet you in the kitchen to show you to your rooms in half an hour."

He dipped his head and stepped back. I waved to the driver of the van to tell him to follow and we drove slowly around the house. At the rear, the façade of a nineteenth-century stately home nestled deep in the Home Counties fell away, and the house became just a big mid-twentieth-century American house on a huge lot.

"This is so exciting." Jayne clapped her hands. "I've lived in West London most of my life and always wondered what this place is like. People talk about it, but no one's ever been invited inside. No one I know, anyway. Not even my mom. She's insanely jealous that we're spending the whole weekend here and she has to miss it."

I parked close to what I took to be the kitchen door and the van pulled in beside me.

The weekend catering staff, otherwise known as Detective Ryan Ashburton, jumped down from the van. "Impressive place," he said.

"I've seen better," I said.

Jayne and Ryan both laughed. "Gemma Doyle, you can be such an English snob sometimes," Jayne said, and I grinned at her.

"We have half an hour to take the food in and get it put away," I said to Ryan, "before the housekeeper shows us to our rooms."

"The housekeeper? Was that guy who spoke to you out front the organizer of this shindig?"

"Of course not," Jayne said. "That was the butler."

"A housekeeper and a butler," Ryan said. "Fancy."

"Fancy," Jayne said, "is the word for this gig."

I opened the unlocked kitchen door while Ryan and Jayne started unloading the van. We (meaning Jayne) were here to cook and serve six meals, plus drinks, snacks, and nibbles, and so we'd brought a lot of stuff. In addition to what we'd need to feed the weekend house guests, the van was packed with assorted paraphernalia I'd grabbed off the shelves at my store, the Sherlock Holmes Bookshop and Emporium.

Jayne didn't run a catering business; she was busy enough as the head baker, part owner, and manager of Mrs. Hudson's Tea Room. Ryan Ashburton didn't normally work as sous-chef and dishwasher, and I didn't make a habit of combining my own meager cooking skills with the role of Sherlockian expert. Because I'm neither a cook nor a Sherlock expert.

But Donald Morris, who is a Sherlock expert, a regular patron of my shop, and a good and loyal friend, had sung Jayne's and my praises to the organizer of this weekend. We were being paid for our troubles, and paid very well indeed.

Well enough for us to leave our businesses in the hands of our assistants for the weekend after Columbus Day, when most of the tourist hordes had left the Cape and the slow season began. Jayne's mother, Leslie, was looking after my dogs, Violet and Peony, as my great-uncle Arthur (also a Sherlock expert) would be joining the house party as a guest. This house is no more than a ten-minute drive from my place, but we'd been offered overnight accommodation, so why not take it? Particularly as we were expected to be on hand to serve late-night drinks and hearty hot breakfasts.

This weekend would be all Sherlock Holmes, all the time. Our host David Masterson was a prominent, not to mention rich, Sherlockian. He'd been wanting to organize a special weekend for his fellow followers of the Great Detective for a long time, but a suitable venue hadn't presented itself. Last year the owner of Suffolk Gardens House, a twentieth-century replica of an English stately home, died, and his heirs immediately put the house up for sale. They weren't getting a lot of offers, if any, so in order to bring in some income the house was rented out for special occasions. Donald told David about it, David realized the property was perfect for what he had in mind, and here we were today.

The English stately country home feeling fell away when we walked into the kitchen. Instead of a warm Aga, heavily trod and creaking floorboards, scrubbed pine workbenches, brick walls, elderly wet dog snoozing under the rocking chair next to an open fireplace, there were two top-of-the line ovens, a huge gas range, stainless steel freezer and fridge, a white marble-topped island about the size of a small Caribbean country, rows of bright orange cabinets, and a glass and chrome table surrounded by six orange leather stools. Everything was clean and tidy except for two widebowled glasses containing the residue of red wine in the sink, and the trash bin by the kitchen door. It was missing its lid, and I peeked in to see a handful of crumpled white napkins, an empty pizza box, and two empty bottles of a good Oregon pinot noir.

Ryan and I carried in boxes while Jayne started poking in cupboards, getting the lay of the land, so to speak, and issuing orders. "Gemma, you can start stacking the nonperishables in the pantry. Ryan, get all that cold stuff out of the coolers into the fridge. Anything that's frozen needs to go into the freezer."

"Yes, ma'am." He gave her a salute and me a wink.

"I love this kitchen." Jayne sighed happily. "It's my dream to have a kitchen as big and as well-equipped as this one someday."

"The house is for sale," I said. "Contents included. Maybe you and Andy can buy it."

She smiled at the thought and absentmindedly twisted the engagement ring on her finger, but she said, "Fat chance." Jayne had recently become engaged to our friend Andy Whitehall. Summer and early fall had been so busy for the both of them, they hadn't had the chance to set the date, make any plans for the ceremony and celebration, or even talk about where they were going to live. I was starting to fear I'd have to lure them to my house one day and lock them in the basement until they got on with it. "It would be nice, though," she said dreamily. "Imagine having all this cupboard space." The kitchen at Mrs. Hudson's Tea Room was about a quarter the size of this one.

A floorboard creaked in the hallway and a young woman came into the kitchen. "Hi. I'm Annie, aka Mrs. Higgins. You must be Gemma and Jayne."

In another break from English stereotypes, the housekeeper wasn't a stern-faced woman with a pronounced accent and a stiff bun, but a tall woman in her early twenties with short blond hair, rows of piercings through both ears, a tattoo of a dragon curling up her right arm, and a welcoming smile. She wore white shorts and a red shirt under a denim jacket. Sturdy Doc Martens were on her feet.

"We are," I said. "Nice to meet you." We all shook hands, and I introduced Ryan. I couldn't help but notice her checking him out. Ryan is always worth checking out, but particularly so today in casual jeans and a loose T-shirt, with his black hair uncombed and the dark stubble coming in on his strong jaw and beneath his high, sharp cheekbones.

Annie tore herself away from admiring Ryan and turned to Jayne. "You finding everything okay?"

"Pretty much. We brought most of what we'll need, as per the instructions Mr. Masterson sent me."

"Good, because I'll try to help you if I can, but I only got here this morning myself, and I've been busy getting the bedrooms ready."

"Shall I assume you aren't a professional housekeeper?" I said.

She grimaced. "Got it in one. My name's Annie Masterson, but for this weekend, I'm not supposed to be related to David so I'm to be called Mrs. Higgins. David insists on having his pretentions and we all find it easier just to go along with him. In real life I'm in show business, but I'm temporarily between gigs."

She didn't, I thought, look entirely happy about playing the servant role, but she'd decided to make the best of it. "It's a hard time, I've heard, on Broadway these days."

She looked at me quickly, and then she grinned. "I'm not on Broadway, but you recognized me! What did you see me in?"

"Gemma notices things," Jayne said before I admitted I'd never seen this woman before, on stage or off. She was young, tall, and pretty, and not at all overweight by normal standards, but her body was softer and plumper than was acceptable for American actresses, so she was unlikely to be in film or TV. I also guessed (although I always insist I never guess) she appeared on stage rather than film, as she had a deep voice and a certain presence, a way of walking and holding herself that indicated she'd been trained to be observed. Mr. Masterson, the organizer of this weekend, lives in Manhattan. Therefore, Annie most likely lives in New York City also. Meaning she either works in commercials, soap operas, or the stage, and I settled on the latter.

"I've never quite made it to the big time," she admitted. "Not yet anyway, but I've been in some off-Broadway shows and I recently toured in the Midwest. Unfortunately, that ended not long after it began, because it turns out that people in Kansas farming communities are too busy in the summer months to come out for a live show in the high school gym. But," she held up her right hand, showing me crossed fingers, "I'm eternally optimistic, and I'm young enough to still have time to get that big break. As for this weekend: I'm your housekeeper, David's not my uncle, and I'll show you to your rooms. David and the first of the guests are here already, and the rest are due to arrive at five."

"Cocktails and canapés at six in the drawing room," Jayne said. "Dinner at eight. Is that still the plan?"

"Right." Annie pulled a slip of paper out of the pocket of her short white shorts. Definitely not an outfit you'd ever find an English housekeeper wearing. "I see you have two rooms. Oh, you're together." She glanced between Ryan and me, trying to hide her disappointment.

Ryan put his arm around my shoulders. "Yup."

* * *

We followed Annie out of the kitchen and up the rear stairs. The servants' stairs: narrow, curving, ill-lit. As we were here to work, our rooms were on the third floor and at the back of the house. They were, Annie told us, originally staff quarters, but over the years, as the need for rooms for live-in maids and kitchen workers declined, the rooms were upgraded and turned into additional guest accommodations. Ryan immediately hit his head on the sloping ceiling; he cursed and I smothered a laugh. Our room wasn't large, and it was plainly and practically furnished, but it had a fabulous view over the pool, closed for the winter, and the now-empty patio, across the lawn and ornamental gardens to the woods lining the back of the property. It was mid-October and the trees were a riot of color.

"Nice digs," Ryan said after Annie had left, testing out the bed by bouncing on it. "Long as I don't stand straight."

I turned away from the window. "It's nice of you to do this for us."

"You don't have to thank me for spending a weekend at Suffolk Gardens House. This place has always been the talk of the town, and so far I'm not disappointed."

"This isn't a holiday. You're supposed to be working, remember."

"I'll look at it as though I'm on one of those cooking vacations in Tuscany. I don't mind helping Jayne in the kitchen, and I don't mind spending time with you. Speaking of which . . ." He patted the bed.

"We should unpack."

"There'll be plenty of time to unpack later." He gave me a wicked and totally irresistible grin, and patted the bed again.

I stepped away from the window.

A knock sounded at the door. "Come on, you two," Jayne called. "No time for lollygagging around. I have to finish putting all my food away and check what's available in the way of linens and dishes. Ryan, I need you to prepare the vegetable tray while I arrange the cheeses."

"No one ever eats those vegetable tray things," he called.

"Perhaps not at police functions," she called back. "Maybe not Sherlockians either, but it's expected."

"A man's work," Ryan said, pushing himself reluctantly off the bed, "is never done."

Chapter Two

"Splendid, Gemma, absolutely splendid." Donald Morris beamed at me. Barely able to contain his excitement, Donald had arrived at Suffolk Gardens House half an hour early and joined me in the drawing room as I was putting the finishing touches on the display.

I straightened a life-sized cardboard cutout of Benedict Cumberbatch and Martin Freeman as Holmes and Watson. I had another one of those back at the store, signed by Benedict himself when he'd visited the Emporium over the summer as a favor to his parents' friend, my great-uncle Arthur.

"I don't think Holmes's head should be at that angle, Gemma," Donald said, not at all helpfully. He tilted his own head and peered at the images.

"Ryan had trouble fitting this into the van with all Jayne's supplies and so poor Benedict has a droopy neck. Pass me that tape will you, please?" I did my best to straighten the offending piece.

As the part owner and manager of the Sherlock Holmes Bookshop and Emporium, I would never say so out loud, but I tend to fall on the side of those who think you can have too much tacky Sherlock stuff. David and his friends, I had been assured, did not.

I arranged pipes and deerstalker hats and magnifying glasses, maps of London as it would have been in Holmes's day, and copies of nineteenth-century railway timetables around the room. I picked up the box at my feet. "One more room to do. You can help me." Annie had shown me around earlier so I knew my way to the library.

It was a lovely library, as befitted a pretend grand old house. Two walls were lined with built-in, floor to ceiling bookcases, stuffed with books with brown, black, or red binding, most of them old, dusty, and slightly tattered. A huge plastic, and very dusty, philodendron loomed next to a small alcove tucked into the far wall containing a large wooden desk, the surface bare now but showing signs of use and considerable age, and a standard office chair. A sliding door opened onto the patio and swimming pool. The fourth wall contained an enormous fireplace. Crumpled newspapers and kindling had been laid in the hearth and a stack of logs rested in a U-shaped iron container next to it. I studied the wallpaper above the mantle. "I can't shoot holes into the wall, unfortunately, so I brought something to fake it. Hold that chair."

Donald obediently held the chair while I climbed onto it and arranged decals resembling bullet holes into the shape of a "patriotic VR." The wallpaper was beige and gold, not red, but not much I could do about that.

I placed three hardcover books on the desk: later-edition copies of *The Hound of the Baskervilles*, *The Sign of Four*, and *Valley of Fear*. I arranged them as though the occupant of the chair would soon need to consult them.

I then scattered more props as well as reproductions of the *Times* and other London newspapers of the era around the room along with some biographies of Sir Arthur Conan Doyle I'd brought from the bookshop. I piled a stack of Holmes-related puzzles and brain teaser games onto the side tables and laid out a Sherlock Holmes jigsaw puzzle on the round table in the center of the room for the amusement of guests. Earlier, Ryan had brought in the DVD player and portable screen onto which we'd project the movies I'd brought and tucked them into a corner.

I stepped back to admire my handiwork.

"Perfect," Donald said. "I might almost believe I'm in the sitting room at 221B."

"As are you," I said, referring to his outfit.

He smiled shyly. Donald was dressed in a brown tweed suit with a bright red waistcoat and a stiffly starched white shirt. A red cravat was tied at his throat and a gold watch dangled from his waistcoat by a thick gold chain. The gold itself was fake; Donald doesn't have the money for such frivolities. A deerstalker hat was on his head.

"You look as though you're about to bound across the moors in pursuit of the great spectral hound," I said.

"Precisely the mood I'm hoping to achieve at cocktails. I have a dinner suit ready for tonight, and formal wear for tomorrow evening." His eyes narrowed as he studied me. "I, uh . . . trust you're going to change, Gemma."

I looked down at my T-shirt, jeans, and scruffy trainers. "This won't do?" I said seriously, before laughing at his expression. "Don't worry, Donald. We're here at your recommendation, and I won't embarrass you."

"You could never do that, my dear," he said. "You should have brought a violin and some sheet music with the sort of tunes Holmes would have played."

"I don't sell violins or music. Everything I brought, I pulled off the shelves of the Emporium." I glanced around the room. "Don't you think it's enough?"

"Sufficient for the library and the drawing room. I was thinking of appropriate items for the music room."

"This house has a music room? Annie didn't show me that."

"David's invitation letter said some of the weekend participants had musical talents. I popped my head in earlier and saw a grand piano."

Even though the library door was closed, we clearly heard the sound of Smithers's voice, and a man answering.

Donald clapped his hands. "The guests will soon be arriving! Talk to you later, Gemma." He bustled out.

I smiled after him, gave the room one more look over, and then went upstairs to change. Nice to have a house with a back staircase, so I didn't have to run into anyone before I was ready.

I stopped at the kitchen on my way. The delivery from the liquor store had arrived and been unpacked, and the empty cardboard boxes were stacked by the door. Jayne was taking a tray of pastries out of the oven as I came in. "Those smell good," I said. Ryan was chopping a mountain of vegetables.

"There is nothing," I said, "sexier than a man in an apron."

He growled at me. The apron was pink and frilly. Jayne wore a matching apron over a loose-fitting black skirt and crisp white blouse. Her shoes were black flats and her only jewelry a pair of small hoop earrings. She always took off her engagement ring when she baked. By rights Jayne, as the head cook, should stay in the kitchen and Ryan, as the assistant, should be the one circulating with drinks and serving the food. But, as he was the lead detective in our town's police department, he put his foot down at being seen in public acting as a waiter.

A Three Book Problem

I was here to provide the Sherlockian touches, but I'd also be helping Jayne in the kitchen and acting as a waitress when needed.

We should have had more staff, but my shop assistant Ashleigh was needed to keep the store open, and Jayne's two helpers would be working at the tea room. Jayne had been putting in overtime for weeks (meaning even longer hours than usual) to get food in the freezer for them to serve when she was away. Jayne's mother, who was originally supposed to help out, had come down with a cold at the last minute. In one way, that wasn't entirely a bad thing as now she could take care of Violet and Peony, whereas the original plan was for my neighbor Mrs. Ramsbatten to pop in and refresh the dogs' dishes and let them into the yard. Mrs. Ramsbatten loves the dogs and is happy to look after them, but she's too elderly to take two lively animals out for a walk.

If worst came to worst, I'd corral Donald and even Great-Uncle Arthur into washing dishes, chopping vegetables, or serving cocktails.

"Everything under control?" I said.

"What would you do if it wasn't?" Ryan asked.

"Tell you two to get it under control while I carry on with what I planned to do," I replied.

"Under control." Jayne arranged the fragrant, piping-hot pastries on a platter. It took a lot of willpower, but I managed to resist snatching one up.

I passed Annie in the third-floor hallway. She'd changed out of her shorts and Doc Martens into a calf-length black dress with a white collar and white cuffs. A black cap with lacy white trim covered her short blond hair and the long sleeves of the dress hid her tattoos. She'd removed all her earrings and slipped her feet into sturdy, lace-up black shoes.

"Goodness," I said, "you do look the part."

She glared at me and tugged at the collar. "This thing itches and my feet hurt already, but I'll do what I have to do. I'll consider it a performance and this getup my costume. It's almost five and the guests will be arriving in a few minutes. I'm to meet them at the door with Billy . . . I mean Mr. Smithers, and show them to their rooms." She continued down the hall, muttering darkly.

I smiled to myself as I went into my room. Annie might not know it, but the dour, sharp-faced housekeeper was a staple of historical fiction and she was playing the part perfectly.

I don't normally wear any sort of costume to Sherlock events, but I'd been asked to "fit in" this weekend, and so I would. For tonight, I'd found a dress in a vintage clothing store. Not quite of Holmes's era, it was peach satin, very 1920s, coming to just below the knee, with straight lines, a dropped waist, and a tasseled hem. I paired the dress with a long double strand of fake pearls, my own pearl earrings, and above-the-elbow white gloves. I studied myself in the mirror, and decided I'd do. At five foot eight, I'm tall enough to wear this style of dress, but not thin enough to do justice to the sleek lines, and my mop of dark curls is nothing at all like a smooth '20s bob, but it was a costume, not an attempt at an imitation. Satisfied, I returned to the kitchen.

I wheeled the bar cart—already loaded with a bucket full of ice, glasses, bottles of wine, gin, vodka, whiskey, mixes, and little plates of olives and slices of lemon and lime—to the drawing room, while Jayne carried in a tray of cocktail nibbles. Mr. Smithers, we'd been informed, would act as bartender.

I doubted Smithers was his real name as much as I doubted he was a real butler. Judging by his age, he was probably also an out-of-work relative of our host, same as Annie.

Of our host, there had been no further sign. So far, other than the brief encounters with the butler and the housekeeper, we hadn't met anyone, but it was obvious that people were in the house. Voices came from behind bedroom doors, leaked through walls, drifted down the stairs, a phone rang and was answered, floorboards creaked overhead. The walls and doors of this house were surprisingly thin and sound carried. Everything looked authentic and impressive, but, I'd soon realized, beneath the surface this house had been built quickly and on the cheap.

That didn't matter. It was all a pretext: it wasn't two hundred years old and nestled deep in the rolling green hills of the Home Counties either.

In addition to my great-uncle Arthur and Donald Morris, five guests were expected, plus the host David Masterson, here to re-create the atmosphere of an English country house weekend in the era of Sherlock Holmes. Rather than riding to the hounds or venturing out on shooting parties, the group would discuss the minutiae of the Canon, toss around outlandish theories, and play Holmes-related games and puzzles. They'd do all that between lavish meals and plenty of cocktails. It was to contribute to the atmosphere that I'd been invited, and to provide the food that Jayne had.

"I hope we get a chance to have a look around the house," Jayne said. "What I've seen of it so far is marvelous, but I'm not surprised this place hasn't sold. It must be worth a heck of a lot, never mind the upkeep on the grounds and the inside."

"A rich man's folly," I said. "And now his heirs can't get rid of it. They can't stop maintaining it either, or it'll never sell."

"Do you suppose it has any secret rooms, priest bolt holes, or the like?"

I smiled at my friend. "Your imagination's running away with you. This house was built in 1965, not the seventeenth century. No need to hide priests."

"It might be a modern house," Jayne said. "But they've gone all out decorating it as though it isn't." Paintings of English pastoral scenes hung on the pale green walls of the drawing room, the sofa was covered in pink flowered damask, the armchairs in cream touched with pink. The heavy drapes matched the sofa and a dark wood coffee table was centered on the thick green and pink rug.

At first glance the room was lovely, but when I looked closer, I could see that the carpet had a stain in the center and the edges were fraying. Dirt was ground into the arms of the armchairs, the tops of the drapes and picture frames were thick with dust, and the paintings were tourist-shop prints.

This room, this house, this setting, was a fantasy. No matter: the guests would enjoy it and that was what this weekend was all about.

I glanced at my watch. Five minutes to six. Almost show time. At that moment, the door opened and a man came in. Like Donald, he was dressed for the occasion.

"Mrs. Wilson and Miss Doyle, I presume. Pleased to meet you. I'm David Masterson." He was quite short at five foot five and almost as round as he was tall. His brown hair was thin on the top and he blinked rapidly at me from behind Coke-bottle bottom lenses. I estimated his age as early fifties, slightly younger than I'd expected. The small amount of information I'd found on the internet concerning our host hadn't mentioned his age.

We shook hands. His grip was limp, his hands soft and moist with lotion. He glanced around the room and gave a brief nod of approval. Jayne slipped out, back to the kitchen to get started on dinner prep. Smithers arrived, suitably dressed all in black, and took his place behind the bar, back straight, hands folded behind him, feet slightly apart, eyes straight ahead.

"May I offer you a drink, Gemma?" David asked. "If I may call you Gemma?"

"You may, and a glass of white wine would be nice."

"I am paying you to be here this weekend, but I want you to consider yourself one of my guests. Please feel free to take advantage of all the amenities this house has to offer. When your attendance is not required, of course."

His accent was upper-class New York City, and he spoke formally, far more formally than any middle-aged American should. I wondered if that was put on for the weekend or if it was the way he always spoke. He was obviously to the manor born, what Americans would call a trust fund baby. His soft pale hands were recently manicured, he was close-shaven, his cheeks slightly rosy, his small teeth blindingly white. He smelled of expensive aftershave and hand lotion. His face was lightly tanned, not a deep summer or Caribbean-vacation tan but the coloration a resident of the Northeastern United States would get by walking from the house to the car, maybe sitting outside at a restaurant patio in the summer.

I never go into a new situation blind, and I'd done my research into David Masterson. Outside of the world of the devotees of Sherlock Holmes, where he was very well known, there wasn't much to find, and I hadn't seen a picture of him other than standing at the back of a group. David's maternal grandfather had made a fortune in New York City development and real estate, and his son, David's uncle, had piled an additional fortune on top. The uncle had given up control of the company a number of years ago, and it was now publicly traded and managed by a board of directors. David himself didn't, according to what I could find, seem to do much at all except study Sherlock Holmes. He'd self-published a handful of scholarly works on the subject. When I heard about this weekend, I'd ordered copies for the store and read one of them, as much as I could get through before falling asleep. His writing was pedestrian, his topics unoriginal and uninspired.

David's mother had been well known as a supporter of classical music. She made hefty donations to, and often served on the board of, the Metropolitan Opera and the New York Philharmonic, as well as smaller and lesser-known classical music companies. My research showed that following his mother's death, David had maintained her monetary contributions to her favorite organizations, but he himself played no active part in the arts community. Those hefty donations had abruptly stopped about a year ago, with no explanation given. To the public at any rate.

David gave Smithers a short, sharp nod, and the butler took a bottle of mid-priced New Zealand sauvignon blanc out of the ice bucket and poured my drink. Jayne had been given a free hand with the food for the weekend, but David had taken care of ordering the booze. Unasked, Smithers then prepared a whiskey with a splash of soda and one ice cube for his employer.

Precisely at six o'clock the guests began filing into the drawing room. The men were in suits and ties, the women in cocktail dresses, one historic and one modern.

I put a smile on my face and circulated. The guests were a mixed bunch indeed. Two women, both in their fifties, one as tall and slim and sharp-boned as a former fashion model, one round of body, frizzy of hair, heavy of bosom, and pudgy of cheeks. The three men varied from a handsome chap in his mid-thirties, to a man in his forties with a heavy unkempt black beard and round belly, to a buzz cut–bearing gentlemen in his sixties with the tone and bearing of a former military man. I wouldn't have been surprised if his pajamas were stamped "Semper Fi." They were all Americans and all from the East Coast. The younger man gave me a long look followed by what he might have intended to be a wink, as he accepted a beer from Smithers. Beer in hand, he took a step toward me, but David stopped him and asked him if his accommodations were satisfactory.

At six fifteen, I slipped up to Donald. He and the frizzy-haired woman, stuffed into a gorgeous floor-sweeping blue and silver dress dotted with black beads, were examining the railway timetables and discussing what route Holmes and Watson would have taken to get from Charing Cross Station to Devonshire, the location of the fictional Great Grimpen Mire.

"Sorry to interrupt," I said. "Can I have a moment, Donald?"

"Oh, Gemma." He blinked at me, coming back to the twenty-first century. "Have you met Jennifer Griffith?"

"Not yet. Pleased to meet you." Jennifer briefly came out of the nineteenth century to greet me, and then immediately returned to her study of the railway schedule.

"Have you heard from Arthur?" I asked Donald when we'd stepped away. "It's not like him to be late, not for something like this."

"Not today. I spoke to him earlier in the week. I asked if he wanted a lift this afternoon, but he declined."

"I'd better give him a call." I'd left my phone upstairs and prepared to run up and get it. My uncle was fit and hearty and more than capable of looking after himself, but he was approaching ninety and it was natural for me to worry.

I hesitated when the drawing room door opened, and Annie ushered in my friend Irene Talbot. It was immediately obvious

Irene hadn't come to give me any bad news. Not only was she smiling and looking around her with shining eyes, but she was dressed in a stunning one-piece evening jumpsuit of wide-legged black trousers, three-quarter-length sleeves, deep neckline trimmed in black satin, and a matching black satin belt. A tiny black bag on a metal chain hung from her shoulder. Her hair was piled high on her head, and her mouth was a slash of deep red. She saw me watching and gave me a wiggle of her fingers. Annie pointed toward the bar, where David Masterson was chatting to the former fashion model, and Irene thanked her and came into the room, almost floating in her uncharacteristically elegant clothes and stiletto heels.

I hurried to join her. "Irene, what are you doing here? Do you know where Arthur is?"

"Just a minute, Gemma. Let me introduce myself to my host first."

"Your host?"

"Mr. Masterson, sorry I'm late. I'm Irene Talbot." David turned to her with a smile and extended his hand. "Delighted to make your acquaintance, Ms. Talbot. May I call you Irene? I'm David. We don't stand on formalities here."

I glanced around the room. I'd seldom been to a more formal gathering. Then again, this might have passed for informal in Holmes's day.

"No apologizes necessary," David continued. "Please, make yourself at home. Can I offer you a drink?"

"Do you have a gin and tonic?"

"Of course. What country house party would be complete without a properly made G&T?" He half-turned and snapped his fingers at Smithers. Smithers rolled his eyes, but he prepared the drink without a word.

Irene accepted her drink, full of ice and a slice of lemon, and took a sip. She sighed with pleasure, thanked David, and joined Donald and me. "Arthur called me this morning. You'd already left for the store, and he didn't want to bother you."

I shook my head. "Instead he's given me a heck of a fright. What's happened?"

"He's gone to Spain. The Costa del Sol."

"You can't be serious. Today?"

"Yup. An old navy pal of his had a heart attack. He lives in Spain and he's summoned Arthur to his side for one last hurrah."

"Oh, dear. That's terrible."

"Not according to Arthur. The friend had the heart attack a week ago. It was mild, but it made him realize that time's running out, so when he rose from his sickbed he decided to throw a big party and summoned the old crowd."

"But . . . but what about this weekend? It's been planned for ages."

"I guess Arthur decided Spain would be better." Irene took another sip of her drink. "As nice as this place is, I would have too. He called David to say he wasn't coming, and asked if I could take his place. David said sure." She spread her arms. "And here I am. I tell you, Gemma, I've had quite the day trying to pull together formal clothes at the last minute. I found this little number at the secondhand shop."

"But . . . but. Irene, why would Uncle Arthur ask you to take his place? You have absolutely no interest in Sherlock Holmes."

She put her index finger to her lips. "Keep your voice down. I've been thinking maybe I'd like to learn, and I told Arthur that when I was at your place for dinner last week."

"I don't remember you saying anything of the sort."

"You were in the kitchen, trying to save the chicken. It wasn't too bad either, Gemma. Not once you'd scraped the burnt parts off."

"Thanks. I think."

"The potatoes were lumpy, though. I'll get you a proper potato masher for Christmas."

"Let's return to the original subject, shall we? This weekend David Masterson has invited a circle of Sherlock experts to exchange knowledge and participate in informed debate. You, Irene, don't have any knowledge to exchange."

"I'll listen intently and agree with everyone." She grinned at me. "Come on, Gemma. Do you think I was going to pass up the opportunity to spend a weekend at Suffolk Gardens House? Everyone in West London is dying to see this place. The owners almost never invited anyone here, and now that it's for sale you have to prove to the realtors you can afford it before you get a showing."

"You checked on that?"

"Sure I did. Tell me you didn't?"

I didn't answer. Of course I had. "Try the mushroom tarts. They're fabulous."

"Don't mind if I do," Irene said. "Another reason I came is because Arthur said Jayne's doing the catering." She helped herself to a cocktail napkin and one of the flaky pastries.

"Did Arthur tell you that because Jayne doesn't have any helpers with her, the plan is he and Donald will work in the kitchen when required. Doing the dishes and the like."

"No, he didn't mention that."

I smiled at her. "You'll like the kitchen. All the modern conveniences."

*   *   *

The cocktail party passed uneventfully. I amused myself, between telling the guests what my role here was, by studying their interactions. It soon became obvious they didn't have much in common. Not even an interest in Sherlock Holmes, which was ostensibly the reason for this gathering.

The frizzy-haired woman, Jennifer, the bearded man, and the older man, who went by the names Cliff and Steve, chatted comfortably with Donald about the Great Detective and discussed the props I'd brought. The former fashion model, Miranda, drank steadily and sat by herself most of the time, a carefully arranged look of total boredom on her face. Eventually, she left the room, drink still in hand, without a word to anyone. The young man, Kyle, gave up on me and tried to charm Irene. Irene didn't seem entirely averse to his attentions. "I'm from New York City," I heard him say to her. "A musician."

David didn't interact with his guests very much. I noticed the occasional little smile Jennifer threw in his direction, and the way he stiffly pretended not to notice. Kyle, Steve, and Cliff avoided speaking to David or even looking at him. In turn, he stood by himself, sipped his whiskey, and watched everyone with a sly smile on his face.

Was he, I thought, pretending to be the Great Detective? Observing everything and everyone while not getting involved? If so it was an odd approach to hosting a weekend.

"Nice party." The bearded man came up to me and offered me a huge smile. "I'm Cliff. Cliff Mann. How do you know David?"

Our host's head turned at the sound of his name, but he made no move to come and join us.

"I don't," I said. "I haven't had the pleasure until today. I'm one of the hired help. I brought all the props you see around you."

Cliff looked confused. "You mean the hat and pipe and stuff?"

"Yes. I own a shop in West London. The Sherlock Holmes Bookshop and Emporium. If you're a Sherlockian you might have heard of it."

"I . . . uh . . . yes, yes, I think I have. You sell books, do you?"

"Anything and everything to do with the Great Detective. Do you collect yourself?"

David took a step toward us. "I . . ." Cliff said. "No. No, I don't. Excuse me." He scurried away.

That was odd, I thought, but I put it out of my mind. I was supposed to be working. The platter of mushroom tarts hadn't lasted long, and I whisked it off the table and took it into kitchen. We'd be serving dinner at eight, so the canapés wouldn't be refreshed.

The morning room, where breakfast would be served, was next to the kitchen. As I passed I heard the squeak of a drawer. I peeked into the room to see Miranda closing one drawer and opening another. She put a hand in and rifled through the contents. She didn't hear me, and I slipped away. This wasn't my house, and it wasn't any of my business if Miranda was admiring the furniture.

In the kitchen, Jayne was seasoning the soup and Ryan chopping tomatoes and cucumber for the salad. I took a moment to admire him. Nothing more attractive than a man preparing food.

Ryan heard the creak of the floorboards and looked up. He gave me a grin. "How's it going out there?"

"Well enough. The guests have all arrived, with one exception. Uncle Arthur isn't coming. He's gone to the Costa del Sol instead."

"Sounds like Arthur," Jayne said. "My goal in life, should I be fortunate enough to live so long, is to be an Uncle Arthur. Old and fancy free. Taste this and tell me if it has enough salt." She scooped a spoonful of thick orange liquid out of the pot and held it out to me. I tasted. I sighed with pleasure. "Yummy. What is it?"

"Carrot and ginger."

"Where's the Costa del Sol?" Ryan asked.

"Spain."

"Arthur went to Spain with a day's notice?"

"You know Arthur," I said. "He comes. He goes. The food's almost finished, so I'll start clearing up. Oh, Irene's here in Arthur's place."

"Irene Talbot?" Ryan asked.

"Yup."

"I've never known her to be interested in Sherlock Holmes. Is she planning to do a piece for the paper?"

Irene was a reporter—the only full-time reporter left in these days of dwindling newspaper revenue—at the *West London Star.*

"If she is, she's undercover and I don't think that would be such a good idea," I said. "No, she's here to see the house and eat Jayne's food and wear fancy clothes."

I picked up a tray and headed back down the long dark hall-way, past the rows of stern-faced gentleman with enormous whis-kers and pale ladies with feathers and lots of jewelry glaring at me from their dusty gilt frames.

". . . most preposterous theory I've ever heard," the bearded man was saying as I came into the drawing room. His face was turning red and his eyes bulging. "A disgrace to the memory of Sir Arthur."

The former soldier faced him, braced for combat. "I'll have you know, Cliff, that respectable scholars—"

"Respectable! Ha. You mean people like you, Steve Patterson. Pack of dilettantes, the lot of them."

David wasn't in the room, but Miranda had returned. The others clutched their drinks and the last of the canapés, awkwardly watching the exchange. Smithers passed Irene a fresh drink.

Donald approached the arguing men, trying to smile, wringing his hands in front of him. "Now, now, gentlemen. Let's remember that we're all friends here."

Steve turned on Donald. Spittle flew. His small eyes were dark in a dark face. "What makes you think that?"

"I . . . I . . ." Donald floundered. "Aren't we?" he finished weakly.

I stepped forward and spoke loudly, trying to sound as though I was in command. Someone had to be in the absence of the host. "It's time to freshen up before dinner. Drinks will be served in the library at seven forty-five, and dinner promptly at eight. Please don't be late. At eleven we'll be showing *The Scarlet Claw* starring Basil Rathbone in the library."

"Excellent!" Donald exclaimed. "One of my absolute favorites."

"Rathbone is *so* overrated." Miranda suppressed a yawn. "People only like him because they're expected to. Don't you agree, Jennifer?"

"What? Uh . . . Don't be ridiculous," the frizzy-haired woman stammered. She took a long glug of her drink.

"You don't know what you're talking about," Cliff said.

Miranda turned on the bearded man. "And I suppose you think your taste is so much better, Cliff? As if."

The others began chiming in and soon the argument had moved on to a discussion of who was the best of the old-time Holmeses on film.

I put my tray on the table and piled it with used dishes, dirty glasses, and crumpled cocktail napkins. Smithers began closing the various bottles and placing them under the cart in an unmistakable signal that the bar was closing. Kyle snatched the wine bottle out of the cooler before Smithers could put the top back on it.

The guests filed out of the drawing room. A sub-argument had broken out over the virtues (or lack thereof) of the various Watsons.

The young man approached me and held up the wine bottle. "We weren't properly introduced. Kyle Fraser."

"Gemma Doyle."

"I'm not entirely sure what your role here is this weekend, Gemma. Why don't we find a quiet spot where we can finish off this bottle and you can tell me?"

"Sorry. One of my roles is to help the cook. Right now, I suspect I'm needed in the kitchen."

"You're English!" His eyes twinkled. He was a good-looking man. And didn't he know it. "I love English people. Come on, sneak away with me. Let's have some fun. Let those old fogies argue about Sherlock this and Holmes that."

"I have enough fun in my life, thank you." I picked up my tray, turned, and walked away.

"Hey!" I heard him say. "Irene, what's your hurry? Let's find a quiet corner and finish this bottle."

I headed toward the kitchen, feeling that I was again being watched over by someone's disapproving ancestors. As I passed the library, low and angry voices came out of the not-quite-closed door. I slowed. What can I say? I'm naturally curious.

"You should have told me," a voice said. I couldn't make out who it was. "I never would have come, not if I'd known he'd be here."

"You can always leave," David replied.

". . . pest . . . I don't know why you aren't . . ."

"Because I don't want to."

The voices trailed off as they walked away from the door.